PURRFECT GEMS

THE MYSTERIES OF MAX 64

NIC SAINT

PURRFECT GEMS

The Mysteries of Max 64

Copyright © 2023 by Nic Saint

All rights reserved. No part of this book may be reproduced in any form by any electronic or mechanical means including photocopying, recording, or information storage and retrieval without permission in writing from the author.

This is a work of fiction. Names, characters, places, brands, media, and incidents are either the product of the author's imagination or are used fictitiously. The author acknowledges the trademarked status and trademark owners of various products referenced in this work of fiction, which have been used without permission. The publication/use of these trademarks is not authorized, associated with, or sponsored by the trademark owners.

Edited by Chereese Graves

www.nicsaint.com

Give feedback on the book at: info@nicsaint.com

facebook.com/nicsaintauthor
@nicsaintauthor

First Edition

Printed in the U.S.A

PURRFECT GEMS

Ezra finds himself in the impossible situation that he must be married with kids within a year. So when his roommate suggests he rent a wife and borrow a baby the plan doesn't seem as crazy to him as it sounds. But what woman in her right mind is going to marry a guy like him?

Sylvie hates her boss, which is funny, since her boss hates her too. And then there's Julie, the fortunate result of an unfortunate marriage. Sylvie wants to turn her life around, but doesn't even know where to begin. Until she gets an unusual offer.

Sarah's kleptomania lands her in hot water when she is caught stealing an expensive diamond ring. Within a week she loses her job, her apartment and her boyfriend. With nowhere else to turn, she asks Odelia Kingsley to help her get her life back on track.

Barnaby runs a successful flower shop in the heart of Hampton Cove. His only regret is that he never found love. What he does have is a belligerent mother who likes to run his life. Barnaby knows he should probably make some changes, but how?

Before long the paths of these four people will cross, leading to some unexpected situations. But one thing is for sure: their lives will never be the same again.

CHAPTER 1

*E*zra Burns had always found it hard to deal with the curveballs life threw at him, but as he got older it was getting worse. So when he stepped out of the elevator and found himself face to face with a young woman he had never seen before, it took him a little while to realize that instead of staring at the woman, what he should be doing was nod a friendly greeting and go on his merry way.

More than him, the girl was distinctly aware of the social niceties required in this type of situation and so she produced a polite smile and waited for him to move so she could proceed. When he simply stood there like an idiot, the smile slowly morphed into an expression of confusion, which finally gave way to her first utterance.

"Can I..." She gestured to the elevator, and a wave of mortification washed over him when understanding penetrated the inertia that had momentarily taken possession of both his brain and his limbs.

"Oh, of course!" he said, stepping aside.

He watched as she sailed past him, flicking a confused glance at him as she did—a glance that gave him the impression she was trying to decide whether he was mentally challenged or simply the usual stalker type.

It took a moment for the elevator doors to close, and in that brief moment their eyes met and they shared another awkward exchange. He, transfixed as before. She, seriously considering calling the police and having him escorted from the premises and shipped off to prison post-haste.

Finally the doors closed and the spell was broken. Ezra shook himself, blinked a few times, and wondered what was wrong with him. He normally wasn't in the habit of cornering young persons of the opposite sex in elevators and staring at them like some aspiring sex offender. And as he replayed the cringeworthy scene in his mind, he groaned.

But since life in the big city never stops, not even to give a young man who's come under the spell of a young woman he just met a moment's respite to reflect, a throng of people displaced him, eager to ride the next elevator car up to their respective floors.

It was a sad-looking Ezra who could be seen five minutes later exiting the office building, reminiscing about the conversation that had just taken place and that had decided his future—such as it was.

His aunt Emily, who had the forethought of writing up a will before she passed away a week ago, had also instructed her lawyer to invite the respective parties involved to the reading of that last will and testament in his office located in the heart of New York City. Ezra, who lived on the other side of town in a modest walkup in the Bronx, had wondered if he should wear black at the meeting, or his usual outfit. Not being intimately familiar with the protocol when attending a post-funeral meeting in a lawyer's office, he had decided to opt for the happy medium: he'd worn his trusty black jeans, a black button-down shirt and had even managed to dig out a pair of black trainers from the back of his roommate's closet, who just happened to share his shoe size. The only thing he hadn't changed was his wild mop of blue-colored hair, though he had managed to tame it down with a substantial amount of hair gel, making him look like a junior executive of a Silicon Valley tech startup. In actual fact he was a waiter by profession—not by design but by happenstance, since his best friend since high school was the nephew of a diner owner who had been so kind to take a young Ezra under his wing and teach him the ropes of the business. Not that it mattered all that much, since Ezra was still being paid minimum wage for a job he didn't even like.

As it was, Ezra didn't even remember his aunt Emily, and he certainly couldn't remember ever having met the woman. So when the letter came announcing her departure from this mortal coil, it took him a while to figure out how she fit into the grand scheme of things. It took a call to his mom to stir the recollection of a rich aunt who'd severed all ties with the less well-off side of the family a long time ago. He had mourned the death of his aged relative for all of five seconds before wondering how much she had left him and what he was going to do with all of that money.

He would quit his job, of course, since being a waiter never held all that much appeal to him. And then he could finally make his dreams come true: buy as many comics as he had space to store. Apart from that he might also buy his own NFL team and spend the rest of his life enjoying the highs and lows of life as a team owner and rubbing shoulders with the sports greats of this world.

Unfortunately his aunt Emily, even though she probably was as rich as Croesus, had other plans for her distant nephew. What plans, Ezra did not know. What he did know was that he wasn't going to buy any NFL teams in the near future. And he wasn't going to quit his job any time soon either. Not if he wanted to keep making rent on his miserable little apartment at the end of the next month.

All in all there had been no less than four nephews in that meeting with the high-powered lawyer, all of them around Ezra's age, and all of them complete unknowns to him. As it turned out, none of them left the office with their bank balance having received a welcome injection of dough. Instead, they all looked as punch-drunk as Ezra had been feeling after the lawyer's announcement that there were certain stipulations in Aunt Emily's will they would have to adhere to if they wished to see one damn cent of the woman's money. The main stipulation was that they had to be legally married with kids before the year was out. And if that wasn't bad enough, they also had to lead the clean and wholesome life of the upstanding citizen, a fact that would be scrupulously checked by the private detectives the lawyer had hired in accordance with his late client's wishes. When Ezra had cleared his throat and asked what Aunt Emily meant with clean and wholesome, the profusely whiskered specimen behind the mahogany desk had cut him a look from under a pair of bushy brows of such vehemence and disapproval Ezra had immediately retreated back into his shell like a particularly timid turtle.

"The third stipulation," the lawyer had thundered to his browbeaten audience, "is also the easiest one." He forced himself to smile—which on his weather-beaten face looked more like a rictus grin. "You must hold down a job and prove yourselves worthy members of society. So no slackers!" he had growled, the sunny smile vanishing behind a dark cloud as he slammed the desk with his fist.

On the whole, Ezra thought as he staggered down the stairs that marked the entrance to the subway, for his peace of mind he should probably write the meeting off as largely a waste of time, except perhaps as a study of human character, and forget all about it. He might currently hold down a job, though he had the impression waiting tables wasn't on Aunt Emily's list of respectable professions, but since he didn't even have a girlfriend, and probably wasn't ever going to find one even if he tried, he didn't see how he would ever qualify for the pot of gold that awaited the recipients of Aunt Emily's largesse at the end of the rainbow. And then of course there was the clean and wholesome aspect of the whole affair. The lawyer had been a little vague on what exactly constituted this coveted state, but Ezra couldn't escape the notion it involved a marked lack of the type of daily stimulants in which he enjoyed partaking, such as weed, cigarettes and lots of booze.

A remark one of his cousins had made upon leaving the lawyer's office confirmed this point of view. The fellow, who was both pale and extremely skinny, had told the others in a sort of strangled voice that he had once read an article about Aunt Emily that stated she was one of the main benefactors of the Anti-Alcohol League and the temperance movement in general, which told the nephews of the dearly departed all they needed to know.

If they were ever going to see any money from that inheritance, not only would they have to get married, have kids and hold down a regular job in a respectable profession, but they would have to become teetotalers!

It wasn't too much to say that it was a downcast and despondent Ezra Burns who took his seat on the subway. Any fellow subway rider would have agreed that he looked more like a dead man walking than the upstanding citizen Aunt Emily was looking for when she drew up that will.

CHAPTER 2

I'm particularly proud to state that my sense of vigilance was at an all-time high as I staked out the molehill located on my property. Okay, so technically the backyard belongs to Odelia and Chase, but as I like to embrace the notion of ownership, as celebrated in the corporate world, in a not-so-strict sense of the word it also belongs to me. Or I should probably say to us, since our little band of felines comprises four: Myself, Dooley, Harriet and Brutus. And when you tell me that four cats is far too much to be owned by a single family, let me remind you that Odelia's parents live right next door, and also her grandmother. So as cuddles go, and flicks of the tail against unsuspecting legs, there's plenty of humans to go around for the four of us. And as a pleasant side effect, plenty of kibble being distributed.

The molehill had suddenly and quite unexpectedly returned to these shores, after having gone out of style for a little while. You see, the original owner of that molehill had become a dear friend of ours, assisting us in one of our inquiries. Since then she and her family had migrated to the field behind the house, but now it looked as if they had decided to take up residence in our backyard once more.

"What are you doing, Max?" asked Dooley as he came ambling up to me. He had used this lull in the proceedings to pay a visit to his litter box and had only now returned.

"I think Jackie and Dave are back," I said, gesturing to the sizable molehill. "So I'm waiting for Jackie to pop her head out so I can say hi."

"Oh, that's so great! I love Jackie and Dave! They're so nice."

"They are nice," I concurred. Now if only they wouldn't act so much like moles and decide to show their faces…

"I just saw Harriet," Dooley confided, stretching himself out on the lawn and making himself comfortable.

"Yes?" I said, not seeing much that was newsworthy in this particular statement since we saw Harriet all the time.

He leaned in and lowered his voice in a conspiratorial manner. "She told me she's thinking about changing her appearance."

"Is that a fact?" I said, not all that interested in the vagaries of Harriet's life. Our white Persian friend is particularly prone to mood swings, you see, and tends to think that whatever mood has presently gripped her is so important the whole world should sit up and take notice.

"She says she wants to have an operation to change her appearance," Dooley continued as he sniffed at a blade of grass. When said blade of grass proved to have been selected by a ladybug to carry the burden of its existence, he studied the ladybug with distinct interest.

"An operation?" I asked, never allowing my eye to leave that molehill lest Jackie or her husband Dave put in an appearance. As everyone knows it's hard to catch a mole unawares. Blink and you miss them.

"Yeah, a big operation by a big surgeon," Dooley

continued his selection of the highlights from Harriet's mental regurgitations. "A surgeon who knows what they're doing is how she explained it to me," he said, quite unhelpfully, I might add.

"So what does this operation entail?" I asked, interested in spite of myself.

Dooley shrugged. "Something about wanting to become a male," he said, which had me look up in surprise.

"Harriet wants to become a male?"

"That's what she said. She says males get all the opportunities in the world of show business, and females get ignored, especially when they're not as young as they used to be. So she figures she's tried to make a career as an international diva as a girl, now she's going to try the same as a boy."

I goggled at my friend, and it wasn't too much to say I was startled, and even flabbergasted and dumbfounded. "You're kidding," was all I managed to say in response.

Dooley thought about this for a moment, then shook his head. "I don't think so. Harriet said she's going to have the operation soon, at least if Odelia is prepared to pay for it, and she wasn't laughing when she said it." A sort of vacant look crossed his face, and I could tell that he was throwing his mind back to the moment Harriet had shared this momentous news. "And neither, for that matter, was Brutus," he finally revealed. "Laughing, I mean."

"No, I can imagine Brutus wouldn't find it particularly funny that his partner has decided to change her gender."

"But why, Max?" asked Dooley. "What does it matter to Brutus if his girlfriend is suddenly his boyfriend now?"

I stared at my friend for a moment, then shook my head. It's at moments like these that I admit to feeling unequal to the task of mentoring my mentee, as Dooley sometimes likes to describe our relationship. "Um," I said therefore, very eloquently, too, I might add. "Well..." I cleared my throat once or twice. "The thing is..."

All the while Dooley's gaze was steadily and unwaveringly fixed on me. It was a mellow gaze, with a certain measure of expectation, as if I was going to say something truly intelligent and momentous. It added to my not-inconsiderable level of anxiety of not knowing exactly how to respond to his question. Why does it matter that one's girlfriend suddenly decides to become a boyfriend? I guess it's one of those aspects of life that's hard to fathom if you haven't experienced it for yourself.

"The thing is, Dooley," I said, after having given the matter some more thought, "that it all comes down to something that is known as buyer's remorse. Imagine for a moment that Odelia decides to buy a new type of litter."

"Why?"

"Because it's on sale."

"Okay. Proceed, please."

"Let's say she buys lavender-scented litter but when you arrive home and you proceed into your litter box you find you thoroughly dislike the scent. In fact it totally puts you off."

"Puts you off?"

"From doing your business."

"Doing a poo or doing a pee?" asked Dooley. He had closed his eyes and screwed up his face and was trying to imagine this particular scenario I was outlining for him.

"Doesn't matter," I said.

"Well, it does matter," said my friend. "Think about it, Max. When you take a poo you spend a lot more time inside your litter box, so you'll be exposed to the scene and the scent for a much longer time. Whereas if you take a pee—"

"Yes, all right," I interrupted him before his musings led us astray. "Let's suppose it's a poo," I said.

"Okay, so a poo on lavender-scented litter," he said, nodding seriously. "What happens next, Max?"

"So you dislike the litter to such an extent that it puts you off your poo."

"That's not good," he said. "That can lead to constipation, Max, and we all know what constipation does to your insides. It blows them up and that can lead to some serious damage to your gut."

"Exactly!" I said. "So you tell Odelia that you don't like the lavender litter, and ask her why she didn't get you the usual stuff, which you've used and enjoyed for many years."

He opened his eyes. "I hope she doesn't buy us the lavender litter, Max. I don't want to get constipated, you know. Before you know it, Odelia will take us to the vet and that's never a fun prospect."

"It's just a hypothetical situation, Dooley," I assured him. "Nobody is buying us lavender-scented litter."

"Oh, phew!" he said, looking much relieved.

"But you see what I mean? You go and buy what you think is a fine type of litter, a type of litter you will enjoy, but instead what you get is something completely different. Something that makes it almost impossible to do your business. And the same thing goes for Brutus and Harriet."

He nodded pensively. "Okay, so in this scenario, who's the poo and who's the pee? Or better yet, who's the lavender and who's the litter?" But then his face cleared. "Oh, I know. Harriet is the lavender and Brutus is the litter, right?"

"What's all this about litter?" asked a familiar voice. It belonged to Brutus, and as usual the butch black cat had stealthily snuck up on us like a panther.

"Oh, Brutus," said Dooley, well pleased. "We were just talking about you. You're the litter and Harriet is the lavender, and if you don't like it, you have to tell Odelia and she will return it to the store and get you the regular kind." He leaned in. "I don't like lavender either," he confessed. "Though I know some cats swear by it."

Brutus looked confused, and I didn't blame him. I would have been confused if I was being compared to a bag of litter. "What are you talking about?" he demanded.

"We were discussing Harriet's operation," I told him.

Immediately his face sagged, and so did the rest of him. It was interesting to watch: almost as if his spine suddenly turned to jelly and so did the rest of his bones. He dropped to the ground and just lay there, looking quite forlorn. "It's terrible," he lamented. "Of all the horrible tricks life has ever pulled, this one takes the cake. Can you imagine me dating a guy? Me?!"

"But you're not dating a guy," Dooley pointed out. "You're dating Harriet."

"Who is soon going to turn herself into a guy!" Brutus cried in dismay. Big tears were now rolling down his cheeks. "I've been trying to talk her out of it, but she says it has to be done. In fact it's the only way to make a career."

Dooley patted him on the back. "It's all right, Brutus. I don't like lavender, either. Not for a poo and not for a pee."

This only served to make him cry even harder. Finally, when his grief was spent, he turned a teary face to me. "Max," he said in a croaky voice. "Max, my dear, dear friend. Can't you talk sense into her? Tell her she can't just go and change…" He quickly glanced at Dooley. "Well, it?"

Dooley smiled. "What's 'it,' Brutus?"

Brutus swallowed. "Well, the operation, of course."

Dooley must have sensed there were deeper mysteries that needed to be plumbed, for he followed up with, "What exactly is going to happen when Harriet has the operation?"

Brutus and I shared a look of concern. "Um…" I said, returning to my favorite old standby. Then I thought I saw movement at the molehill and said, "Oh, look! It's Jackie!"

Dooley's attention immediately turned to the object under observation, and when he failed to locate Jackie, he approached the molehill in question to study it from up close. It was then that a creature did burst out of the ground, almost hitting Dooley on the nose and causing the three of us to scream out in surprise.

It wasn't a mole, though, and it definitely wasn't Jackie. It was a rat. And a very large, hairy rat at that!

CHAPTER 3

The rat stared at me and I stared right back, even though every instinct I had told me to run to the hills! Unfortunately there aren't any hills in the immediate vicinity of our home, so that wasn't the solution I was looking for either. So instead I just sat there, and wondered if this was one of those life-defining moments you always hear so much about. You know, when the rubber meets the road, and a tectonic shift takes place in one's life. Would I be able to define a 'before the rat' and an 'after the rat' moment in my life? As all these thoughts and a lot more flashed through my mind, I didn't think I had any hope left, and that in fact my last moment had come. In other words, it was one of those 'see your life flash before you eyes' type of situations. At least until the rat finally opened its mouth and spoke.

"Hey there, fellas," he said, and I could see that his nostrils quivered a little. Whether in happy anticipation of having a little chat with us or from an urgent desire to gobble us up whole I did not know. "My name is Footsie. What's yours?"

"Max," I said after swallowing once or twice. Could it be? Could it be that this rat—this massive rodent—didn't have as its primary desire to hunt us down and slay us and have us for lunch? It was hard to believe.

"Dooley," said Dooley with a noticeable quiver in his voice. "My name is Dooley and I hope you're not going to eat me, Mr. Rat. I'm not very tasty, you see. And I have a lot of hair. And we all know that hair is very hard to digest."

The rat merely grinned at this, showing two sets of razor-sharp teeth that didn't give me any faith in the happy ending.

"And who might you be?" asked the rat, addressing Brutus.

"B-b-brutus," said Brutus, and he looked as pale and drawn as any black cat can look. "My name is B-b-brutus."

"So nice to finally make your acquaintance," said Footsie. "I've been meaning to talk to you guys, you see. Ever since I arrived here in this very nice backyard of yours, I've been wondering what makes you people tick, you know. I mean, what's the situation? There's this woman, and then there's a guy, but there's also all of these other people. And even an infant. And so when I saw you guys parading past on a regular basis, I told myself: Footsie, I said, you really have to work up the courage to address these nice folks. And so when I heard you talking just now, I knew the time had to come to put my money where my mouth was and just venture out and do it!" He swung a tiny fist as he spoke these words, and I have to say I was quite surprised by this do-or-die speech.

"You were… nervous about meeting us?" I asked.

"Oh, sure. You may not know this, but rats are a very timid species. And since I never knew my father, I'm even more timid than most. It's a Freudian thing. And then there's the fact that my mom was very protective, you know. She always kept me close and never let me go off on my own. And that kind of stuff has an impact on a young rat." He shrugged. "I can tell I'm boring you with my life story. So what's your story? Have you lived here long? Are you three brothers? And what's with all the humans that keep coming and going all the time? The old lady—"

"That's Gran," said Dooley. "She's Odelia's grandmother." And so in short order he gave the rat a brief overview of the family we lived with. But even as he rattled off the family connections, Brutus kept giving him nonverbal hints, which Dooley blithely ignored.

I guess Brutus had a point. There was no sense in giving this rat the ins and outs of the family we lived with, the lay of the land, so to speak. After all, maybe his good-natured bonhomie was simply a ruse, and Footsie was the mere vanguard of a veritable rat army, waiting to strike.

I hoped that wasn't the case, of course, but sometimes you have to be careful. And as Odelia's cats, we do have an obligation toward our family. We may not be guard dogs, per se, but in a sense they do rely on us to act as their protectors.

"Okay, I think that's enough, Dooley," I said therefore, when our friend had been going on for a while and was getting into the nitty gritty of what made our family tick. "I'm sure Footsie isn't interested in all of that stuff."

"Oh, but I most certainly am," said Footsie. "In fact I absolutely love it. You see, I never had a human family of my own to take care of me, so in a way I'm a little envious of the bonds you have obviously managed to create here."

"They are a nice bunch," Brutus admitted, though he continued to look skeptical, I have to say.

"They are great people," said Dooley, enthusiastically endorsing our humans. "The absolute best, in fact."

Suddenly a sort of wistful look came over the big rat. "Oh, I wish I could move in with you. Wouldn't that be nice? To wake up every morning at the foot of your very own human's bed, seeing your little bowl of food ready and filled to the brim with the good stuff? Getting cuddles and caresses at all hours of the day and night. Someone to take care of you and love you and treat you like one of their own…"

Dooley smiled. And before we could stop him, he said, "So why don't you move in with us, Footsie? There's plenty of room for you in the house. And plenty of love in Odelia's heart to accommodate a nice upstanding rat like you."

"Dooley!" Brutus hissed, looking quite shocked now.

"What?" said Dooley innocently. "It's true, though, isn't it? Odelia has plenty of space in her heart since she has a very big heart. And the house is big enough to accommodate another pet. And Footsie is such a nice, well-behaved rat I think he will be a great addition to the family. So what do you say, Footsie? Do you want to join us?"

Footsie was positively beaming at us now. "Are you kidding me? I would love to join your family. Absolutely."

"Consider it done," said Dooley. He held out his paw. "Welcome to the family, Footsie!"

Oh, boy.

CHAPTER 4

Dooley felt very happy with himself. His role in the family structure was usually the meek and mild one, with the others taking the lead—alternatively this could be Max, or Brutus, or Harriet, but hardly ever Dooley. And now he had taken a leading role and he had to admit he liked the feeling it had given him. He felt powerful—strong. Like a real leader! And so as Footsie retreated back into the hole that had once been the entrance to the lair built by Jackie and Dave, to gather his stuff, as he explained it, and would return in due course to take up his newfound position in the family, Dooley turned to his friends with a big triumphant smile on this face.

"Our family of four has just turned into a family of five!" he said almost jubilantly.

But the expressions he met weren't as jubilant as he was feeling. On the contrary, both Max and Brutus looked upset for some reason. Brutus was the first to speak.

"How could you?" he said in a low voice.

"How could I what?" asked Dooley, thoroughly mystified.

"How could you invite a rat to live with us! A rat, Dooley!"

"He's a very nice rat," said Dooley defensively. "In fact you hardly notice he's a rat at all. He could be a cat, only his nose is probably a little pointier. And I'm sure he's as fond of kibble as we are." He turned to his best friend. "Max? Why are you looking at me like that?"

"Because I'm a little upset, Dooley" said Max, quite surprisingly.

"Upset? But why?"

"Because you just invited a rat to live with us," said Max with a shrug, repeating almost the same thing Brutus had said. "Maybe you should at least have consulted with Odelia before you invited Footsie into our home. I mean, it is her house, and she'll be the one who has to feed Footsie, and give him his own space in the form of a spot on the couch."

"I wonder what rats eat," said Brutus with a frown. "Mice, probably. Or bugs, maybe? They certainly don't eat kibble, like we do."

"I think Footsie is a very nice rat," Dooley repeated stubbornly. "And he's very well-behaved. And I think he'll make for a great addition to the family." Though Max did have a point that he probably should have consulted with Odelia first. She was, after all, the owner of the house, and so technically she would have to approve any additions made to the roster of pets allowed to live with them.

"I think we should put this to a vote," said Max now. "All in favor of allowing Footsie to live with us, raise your paw."

Dutifully, Dooley held up his paw. Unfortunately Max and Brutus didn't, which made this a painful process.

"You gotta love democracy," said Brutus with a grin. "Looks like you lost, Dooley. Better tell Footsie when he comes back that your invitation has been rescinded after a majority vote."

"But I don't want to tell Footsie that he can't come and live with us," said Dooley. "Oh, look, you guys, can't you just give him a chance? You'll see, he'll fit right in. I just know he will. I have a hunch about Footsie."

"And I have a hunch that he won't fit in at all," said Brutus. "And my hunches are usually correct. Wouldn't you agree, Max?"

But Max wasn't committing himself to any endorsement of Brutus's powerful powers of hunchdom. Instead, he said, "We could always accept him for a two-week trial period. See how it goes. Then if things don't work out, we can have another vote, and this time include Odelia and Chase in the process, as we should have done now."

It was a decent compromise, and one Dooley could definitely live with. Brutus didn't seem convinced. "Let's simply deny him now," he suggested. "And make sure he never sets paw inside our home. Rats are harbingers of all kinds of bacteria and lethal diseases. So the further we keep him away from us and our family, the better off we are."

"We could wash him," said Dooley. "Make him take a bath before he sets foot inside the house? Or we could take him to Vena and make sure he gets a full check-up before he comes and lives with us. Wouldn't that be a better idea than simply to deny him access to our lovely home? After all, we should share what we have, Brutus. Not hog all the good stuff and leave the rest of the animal kingdom to languish in darkness and despair." Both Max and Brutus stared at him. He frowned. "Did I say something funny?"

"No, quite the contrary," said Max with a smile." You said something very wise and very important, Dooley."

"Very deep," Brutus admitted. "Very deep indeed."

Dooley smiled a little self-consciously. He wasn't aware that his statement had been any deeper than anything else he'd said. But he would take the compliment, as he rarely received them, and Brutus was stingy with them anyway.

A soft mewling sound came from nearby, and soon they were joined by Harriet, who looked a little perturbed. "Hey, you guys," she said. "Now look what she did."

They all looked, and when Dooley didn't see anything out of the ordinary, he asked, "Who did what, Harriet?"

"Marge, of course," said Harriet. "Who else?" Her eyes turned upward, and when Dooley followed the movement, he finally saw. Harriet had a big pink bow on top of her head for some reason.

Dooley laughed. "Oh, you look funny, Harriet. You look like an Easter egg."

"I'll bet that's where she got the idea," Harriet grumbled. "She must have been looking at sites for Easter decorations and liked the bow so she decided to try it out on poor old me."

"I think it looks… interesting," said Brutus, who could barely contain his glee.

"Oh, don't you start," said Harriet. "It looks horrible, doesn't it? And I look horrible."

"No, you look fine," Brutus assured her. "Very, um… feminine."

Harriet cut him a look that could kill, and Brutus wiped the smile from his face.

"Don't you understand? I don't want to look feminine," Harriet lamented. "I want to look butch. I want to look like you, Brutus. Very manly and very butch. It's the only way to get ahead in this world, after all. Nobody pays any mind to girls like me. But if I were a man, now that would be a different story."

"I thought you wanted to be a diva?" said Max.

"I do want to be a diva," Harriet agreed. "But nowadays all the best divas are men, aren't they? Like that kid with the tattoos. What's his name? Harry Styles. And all of those rappers. They're all men, and they're very successful, too."

"There are a lot of female divas," Max pointed out. "Like Celine and Mariah and Barbra and Adele. I thought you wanted to be like them, Harriet?"

That's what Dooley also thought. But apparently not, since Harriet shook her head decidedly.

"It's no use. The people you're referring to are the exception to the rule. Most successful people in the world are men, and women have a hard time getting ahead. So from now on I'm going to be a male, and I hope you respect that."

Brutus looked decidedly unhappy, Dooley saw, and now he finally understood why. They had talked about this, and it was exactly as Max had said: when you're used to having your litter smell like one thing, and suddenly it smells like something else entirely, it's not a lot of fun. So he patted their good friend on the back. "You'll just have to learn to like lavender, Brutus. There's no other way."

For his intervention he got giggles from both Max and Brutus, and a blank look from Harriet. So he told her, "You're the lavender-scented litter, Harriet, when you turn into a male. And Brutus isn't used to lavender-scented litter, so it's going to take a little getting used to, you see."

But obviously Harriet didn't see, for she continued to stare at him. Then finally she decided simply to ignore him, as she often did. With a sweep of her tail, she said, "So please do me a favor, sugar cakes, and remove this dreadful bow from my head."

It was with some reluctance that Brutus complied with her urgent request, and when finally the bow was lying on the lawn, they all stared at it. For some reason Dooley had the impression its removal marked the advent of some new adventure, though he couldn't quite see what form it would take. And, perhaps more importantly, what smell.

CHAPTER 5

*E*zra arrived at the apartment he shared with his good friend Jake Barker feeling a little under the weather. He'd set out to the meeting with the lawyer with hope filling his heart. But that hope had been well and truly squashed. No way was he ever going to be able to adhere to the stipulations his aunt Emily had made. He didn't even have a girlfriend, much less a wife—not to mention kids!

He entered the apartment and made a beeline for the fridge to grab a cold can of beer. Yanking one from a six-pack he popped the top and settled down on the couch, but not before removing some of the debris from last night: a large pizza box and a couple of empty bags of chips. He then plunked down onto the couch and proceeded to stare blankly before himself.

It was only when the door opened and closed again that he was pulled from his reverie. By then the can of beer was empty and he was feeling a little less as if the world was out to get him. So he wasn't going to inherit. Big deal. He'd managed without Aunt Emily's money before, he would manage now.

Jake walked in looking like the gentle giant that he was, the eternal smile that seemed fixed on his moon-faced features firmly in place. "Ho ho ho," he said by way of greeting. "So who's the millionaire in our midst, huh? How much did you get? A million? Ten million? A hundred?"

"Zero," said Ezra sadly. He might have steadily been coming to terms with the fact that he was never going to be rich, but the injustice of it all still stung.

Jake blinked. "Zero? But I thought you said your aunt was loaded?"

"She was, and now someone else will be rich, but it isn't going to be me." And so he explained in a few brief words what had transpired. He conveniently left out the auspicious meeting with the most beautiful girl in the world, since according to his friends he met the most beautiful girl in the world a couple of times a day—every hour, on the hour—so this wouldn't impress Jake in the least.

Jake removed some more debris from the couch and sank down next to his bud. "Huh," he said as he let it all sink in. "So I probably shouldn't have bought this." He took out an expensive-looking phone from his jacket pocket.

"You didn't," said Ezra in a low voice.

Jake's grin said it all. "I did!"

It was the new phone that folded in ten different places that Ezra and Jake had both been craving ever since the announcement of its imminent launch had been made.

"How much?" said Ezra.

"Too much, now that you're not going to be the next Rockefeller," said Jake ruefully. He hesitated. "I can always give it back. I got it from Ahmad." Ahmad was their local pirate king, who sold his illegal wares on a nearby street corner.

"Keep it," said Ezra. It was a crazy expense, and one they couldn't afford, but sometimes you have to make these big gestures, especially when life has kicked you in the teeth—or in this particular case the late Aunt Emily.

"So a real job," said Jake, holding up his index finger. "And a wife and family," he added, holding up his middle finger. "And last but not least, no more booze."

"Or any other intoxicating substance," Ezra supplied.

"So no weed, huh?" said Jake. "That's criminal, bud."

"I know, right?"

It was criminal. And would involve a major lifestyle shift that he simply didn't think he was capable of.

"Look, the job part is easy. I'll talk to my uncle and tell him to give you a fixed contract. I'm sure he won't mind."

"Are you kidding?" Ezra scoffed. "Your uncle is an even bigger tightwad than Aunt Emily. And the lawyer told us that being a waiter doesn't count as a job."

"Okay, but so you can probably find some job somewhere, right? I mean, anything will do, correct?"

The lawyer hadn't made any further specifications about the type of job he was supposed to hold down, so that part was probably the most feasible. "No, I think any job will do," he said therefore. "But that still leaves the wife, and the kids—and the temperance part." He shivered at the thought of never being able to touch a drink ever again. Or a cigarette. Or a bong! He glanced at the very sizable bong that stood right in front of the two friends on the coffee table. The thought of never being able to take a whiff made him sad.

"So the job is a cinch," said Jake, still working through the evidence of his late aunt's perfidy and trying to counter it with good old-fashioned logic and an abundant dose of positive thinking. Not that it would do a lot of good, but at least it took Ezra's mind off the sobering thought that he would always be a waiter at a lowly diner and would always share an apartment with his slacker buddy Jake. "And so is the temperance part."

"Oh, you think so, do you?" he said, and if he sounded bitter it was because he was.

"Sure! You simply drink at home, and the same goes for the illegal substances you're not supposed to indulge in."

"You're forgetting one thing."

"What's that?

"The detectives."

"Oh, twaddle," scoffed Jake. "You don't expect them to suddenly show up on our doorstep and raid the place, do you? And besides, if they do, you simply tell them the booze in the fridge and the bong and the weed is mine."

Ezra felt touched by this display of friendship and solidarity. He teared up. "You would do that for me?"

"Of course! You're my best bud, bud. So let's just say that they do manage to gain access to the apartment, maybe using a common ruse like checking the electric meter or something. So we'll simply put Post-its on those cans of beer in the fridge and on the bong, and everything else you're not supposed to indulge in, and put my name on it. Easy-peasy. Now the next part is the girl, right?"

"Not the girl, the wife," he said morosely, and wondered if he should get another drink. But since he felt entirely too demoralized to get up, he decided to try on this quaint notion of temperance for a moment. Take it for a spin.

"Okay, so you do know that there are solutions for that kind of stuff, right?"

"What do you mean, solutions?"

"You hire a wife! Bam—done! I'll bet there are plenty of girls who would be more than willing to get married to you and go through the motions while you prove yourself the perfect heir. All we have to do is find one and bingo!" He clapped his hands. "We're back in business, bud!"

The small flame of hope that had briefly surged in his

bosom flickered and died. "And how many girls would want to have my babies? Not a lot, I would guess."

Jake eyed him closely, then relented. "No, I guess you've got me there. No matter how much money you pay them, not a lot of women would actually go that far. And besides, there's probably laws against that kind of stuff."

They both sank down on the couch, locked in a state of deep despair as they contemplated what could have been. Then Jake reared up again. "I've got it!"

"You have?" Ezra said, thoroughly surprised. He'd never known Jake to be an intellectual giant, but his friend was really on fire today. The prospect of all of that money, probably. Or the idea that he could buy himself a dozen new foldable phones if the inheritance went Ezra's way.

"You just borrow a baby!"

Ezra closed his eyes and performed a mental head thunk. "Jake," he said quietly. "Get real, bro."

"What are you talking about? It's the perfect solution! You rent a wife and you borrow a baby and call this lawyer fellow and show him both, and tell him to write you a check and boom! Here comes Mr. Moneybags!"

"There's no such thing as borrowing a baby," said Ezra gently, reluctant to rain on his friend's parade when he was so obviously having a ball spinning these unrealistic scenarios and relishing in them. "A baby is not like a car, buddy. You can't go out and rent one for the weekend."

"I know a baby is not like a car, but I'm sure you can borrow one from someone. And you don't even have to tell the person you're borrowing it from that you've got some ulterior motive. All you have to do is sign up as a babysitter, and pretty soon you'll be drowning in babies!"

"Don't you think this lawyer is going to check if the baby is actually mine? I'll probably have to show him a birth certificate, and all of that stuff."

"Birth certificates can be forged."

"Marriage certificate, wedding pictures…"

"Photoshop. Done and done!"

Somehow he didn't think it was quite as easy as that, but clearly Jake had gone off the deep end and was living in cloud cuckoo land. And since he didn't feel like wallowing in misery for the rest of the afternoon—and he had a job to get ready for—he got up from the couch and stretched. "Maybe it's better this way," he said. "This whole being rich business sounds like a big pain in the ass anyway."

"So you're giving up?" said Jake, sounding wounded. "Just like that?"

"I was never in the race to begin with, buddy," he said, and headed for his room to get ready for work. For a while he'd been rich—at least in his head. And now that it was all over, and his hopes and dreams had come crashing down with the little speech this lawyer had given, he just had to accept what was and move on. It wasn't hard, for like he had told Jake, you can't really give up on something you never had in the first place.

As he slipped into his work outfit—a crisp white shirt and dark slacks—he briefly flashed back to the girl he had met in the elevator outside the lawyer's office, and enjoyed the memory of that lovely face and that trim figure. But knowing he would never see her again, he soon put her out of his mind as firmly as the inheritance. Five minutes later, as he left the apartment, he saw that Jake was still on the couch, deep in thought.

CHAPTER 6

*D*ooley may have enjoyed doling out invitations to perfectly strange rats, but that didn't mean we had to accept this as a *fait accompli*. Then again, maybe he had a point. There was no reason to suspect that Footsie was a bad sort. On the contrary, maybe he was a great fella and we would all get along together like gangbusters. So when Footsie finally emerged from his underground lair, where presumably he had been packing his meager belongings into an overnight bag, his welcome committee consisted of four cats—two of whom were highly skeptical, one who was willing to give him a shot (moi) and one who was dancing with joy at the fun that we would have on those late nights when the home was quiet and not a soul stirred. It was at times like these that Dooley often remarked how nice it would be to have another little friend to play with, since my idea of fun mainly consisted of lying on the couch and nodding off.

"Let's go, Footsie," said Dooley. "I'll show you the house."

"Nice," said Footsie, who looked both relieved and eager to join our family.

Dooley led the rat, who was just about his size, through the pet flap and into the house, while the rest of us hung back. No way was I going to break the news to Odelia that from now on her pet household consisted not of four but five members. If Dooley was so adamant about adding a fifth member to the team, he could do the honors of telling Odelia.

"Correct me if I'm wrong, Max," said Brutus. "But there were four Beatles, right?"

"As far as I know," I said.

"And four Rolling Stones?"

"Give or take," I agreed.

"And four members of ABBA?"

"Uh-huh."

"So why add a fifth member? Things are going great, aren't they?"

"They most certainly are," I said.

Brutus shook his head. "I really hope Odelia puts her foot down, cause I don't agree with this decision at all."

"Oh, I don't know," said Harriet. "From time to time it's good to shake things up, you know. Make some noise."

We both stared at her. She'd been in a strange mood, and judging from this remark her mood was getting stranger still.

"You do realize that in order to be a male you have to go through a long and complicated process, don't you?" I said, and I couldn't hide the tinge of concern I was feeling for her wellbeing. Declaring you're a male from now on is all well and good, but there are certain aspects of life as a male that aren't a given but have to be grafted on through surgery, so to speak. Like certain appendages where no appendages were before, for instance.

"Like I told you guys, Harriet is fully prepared to have the surgery," Brutus said, eyeing his partner with concern. "She even found the surgeon, haven't you, snuggle pooh?"

But Harriet waved our remarks away with an airy move of her tail. "Let's not make this more difficult than it needs to be," she said. "I did some more research on the internet and it turns out that these days you don't even need any operation. It suffices to simply declare your intention of being a male and that's it. You don't have to go through all of that complicated surgical stuff anymore."

"You don't?" I said, much surprised. "But I thought—"

"There's no need! We have come a long way as a society, you see, and so if you simply state that from now on you're a male, that's all it takes. You're a male!"

"So what about your name?" asked Brutus. "Are you still going to go by the name Harriet?"

"I hadn't thought about that, but why not?" said Harriet. "There's nothing to indicate that Harriet can't also be a male name, is there?"

"I've never known a male cat named Harriet," I said musingly, "but I guess you're right," I hastened to add when she cut me a scathing look.

"If I say that Harriet is a male name, it's a male name," she snapped. "So from now on I'm Mr. Harriet, is that clear? And you'll do well to treat me like one of the boys."

Brutus and I shared a look of concern. How were we going to treat Harriet like one of the boys? Now that was an interesting question. I had absolutely no idea!

We entered the house through the pet flap, and saw that of Dooley and Footsie there was no trace. "Where are they?" asked Harriet, a very apt question, for the big confrontation with Odelia had apparently not taken place yet. And frankly I wasn't looking forward to it either.

And then we heard it: loud voices coming from upstairs. And when I say loud voices, I actually mean loud screams of terror and certain dread.

"Sounds like Odelia met Footsie," said Brutus with a grin of delight.

We didn't make any haste walking up the stairs. Best to let these scenes of domestic drama play themselves out without your presence being required. And true enough, by the time we arrived in the bedroom, where apparently the big showdown had proceeded, Odelia was on top of the bed, a pillow in her hands and staring down at Footsie and Dooley, who were on the floor looking up at her. Dooley was trying to make the necessary introductions but Odelia wasn't having it.

"Get that filthy monster out of here right now!" she said, making her meaning very clear indeed.

"He's not a monster," Dooley insisted. "He's our friend. His name is Footsie and he's going to live with us from now on."

"Over my dead body!" Odelia screamed.

"That can be arranged," said Footsie in a low voice. But when he saw that I was looking at him intently, his expression morphed into one of regret. "She's not taking me seriously, Max. The moment she laid eyes on me she started screaming. Now how can I prove myself if she won't even give me a chance, huh? It's not fair!"

"Max, get this creature out of here!" Odelia demanded.

Seeing as the situation didn't leave me any choice, I decided to intervene. So I stepped to the fore, cleared my throat, and said, "Odelia, this is Footsie. Footsie, meet Odelia, our human. Odelia, Footsie is a very nice, well-behaved and hygienic pet who has been looking for a home to call his own for a very long time. So after long deliberation the four of us have decided to take him into our hearts and into our home, and we hope you approve."

"For a two-week trial run," Brutus added.

"For a two-week trial period," I agreed. "So what do you say?"

"He looks vicious," said Odelia, eyeing the creature with suspicion. "Just look at those teeth. I'll bet he'll bite us the moment our backs are turned."

"Now how is that logical?" asked Footsie. "How does that make sense? How can I bite you if your back is turned?"

"You could bite Odelia's tushy," Dooley suggested.

"That is an option," Footsie agreed. "But I can assure you, lady of the house," he said, raising his voice and addressing Odelia, "that I have absolutely no intention whatsoever to bite your tushy, or anybody else's tushy for that matter. At least if you feed me enough. If you don't feed me… Well, I guess in that case all bets are off." He grinned as he said this, then added in an undertone, "Just kidding. Jeez. You people got no sense of humor."

"He's not going to bite you," I translated the big rat's thoughts on the matter. "Not even when your back is turned."

"Rats are filthy," Odelia said, listing another one of her objections, of which I had the impression she had many, many more. "They spread all kinds of diseases. I'll bet they even spread the plague. Didn't they spread the plague in Europe?"

"That was a long time ago, lady," said Footsie. "You can't really hold me responsible for something some distant ancestor did, can you? Or do you want me to point out to you what you did when you first landed on these shores?"

"Let's not go there," I suggested, starting to feel more and more uneasy in my mind about my self-appointed role of peacekeeper. "Okay, so he says he's a healthy rat," I said instead. "And he promises not to spread any diseases."

"And to prove it he's willing to go to Vena and get a clean

bill of health," Brutus added, cutting a sly look at the rat, who gave Brutus a decidedly nasty look in return.

"I don't mind going to the vet," said Footsie with a shrug. "Whatever it takes, right?"

"Okay, if he's willing to go to the vet," said Odelia, "and he promises to behave…" She thought for a moment. "So here's the deal," she finally stated. "If you, Max, are prepared to vouch for Footsie, I'm willing to take him into the house for the next two weeks. How about it?"

I gulped. "Vouch for Footsie?"

"Take it or leave it," she said, and held the pillow aloft, prepared to slam it down on the large hairy rat if need be.

"Okay, fine," I said. "I'll vouch for Footsie."

"Thanks, Max," said Footsie. "I appreciate it."

"I also vouch for Footsie," Dooley piped up. Even though he was Footsie's biggest proponent and champion, he hadn't contributed a lot to the negotiations. But now that the hard part was over, he sprang back to life. "So is he getting his own litter box? And his own food bowl?"

"I guess," said Odelia, without much enthusiasm. She cautiously stepped down from the bed, never taking her eyes off Footsie, who was rubbing his front paws with marked glee. He looked like the rat that got the cream.

"You made a great decision," I whispered to Odelia.

"He's not sleeping on the bed," she whispered back.

"I heard that!" said Footsie. "And for your information, I have no intention of sleeping on the bed. I'm fine wherever."

"He's fine wherever," I translated the rat's words, earning myself a stern nod from my human.

I couldn't help but suspect she wasn't happy about this situation we had thrust upon her. Not very happy at all!

CHAPTER 7

Sylvie Mitchell wasn't having a great day. First she had forgotten to charge her phone, which had died overnight, resulting in the alarm not going off, and by the time she had woken up it was already half past seven. Then for some reason the boiler had gone on the fritz which had resulted in a cold shower—a very short cold shower! And then of course she hadn't been able to squeeze into the first subway car and had to wait for the next one. By the time she did actually get to work her boss was already pacing her office and darting very angry looks at her when she arrived. Instead of calling her into her office, she had called her on her phone, which had led to an awkward scene where she could see her boss in her office calling her and telling her to get into her office ASAP.

She would have preferred it if her boss treated her like a normal human being, but even on regular days when she arrived on time and had been able to take a hot shower and make sure she was feeling up to facing a new day, Mrs. Woods didn't treat any of her staff like regular human beings. So today was even worse than usual.

"Can I just remind you that we're in the middle of the biggest deal this company has ever seen?" asked Mrs. Woods once Sylvie was standing in front of her. The woman wasn't even looking at her. Instead she was looking out of the window of her corner office at the scenery outside. The streets of New York stretched out below them, with so many people looking like ants it must have fulfilled some kind of deep-seated sense of superiority that was presumably very pleasing to a woman who led her department with an iron fist. "So your arriving late is not on, Sylvie. Is that clear?"

"Yes, Mrs. Woods," she said quietly. She could have told her boss about her phone battery that had died overnight. Or about the lack of hot water or the subway. But there was no point. Mrs. Woods saw her underlings like so much biomatter designed to fulfill a certain function. When it didn't, its contract was terminated. And she had already terminated so many contracts this past month that Sylvie counted herself lucky that she hadn't been among them.

"This is the first and the last time we're having this conversation," said Mrs. Woods, and now she did turn around to face her underling. Her cold gray eyes were blazing and she looked more formidable than ever, Sylvie thought. She had often wondered if this woman was married, and if so, how her husband managed. Then again, maybe it was not a good idea to consider these questions, since obviously there was such a giant chasm between the kind of life her boss lived and her own life it was simply better not to even go there. Almost as if a mere mortal would dare to fantasize about the life the gods led on Mount Olympus.

"Dismissed," said Mrs. Woods curtly, and Sylvie hurried from the office. Once she was back at her own desk, she noticed she had actually stopped breathing for the past ten minutes, which was physically impossible, but still felt as if it might be true.

Her colleague, the indomitable Frankie Parker, turned and lowered her voice. "What did she say?"

"That if I'm late again I'm done," Sylvie said, also keeping her voice down, even though the door to their boss's office was closed and there was simply no way she could overhear their conversation. Then again, maybe she could, since the woman seemed to have developed some kind of supernatural senses and always seemed to know exactly what was going on, even though she rarely set foot outside her office or—God forbid—mingle with the rest of them.

"Better watch out," said Frankie. "I heard she fired another two copy editors."

"Two?" said Sylvie. "But she just fired David last week."

David was their good friend, a very sweet and kind—and extremely talented—copy editor. When he was fired it sent a shockwave through the entire department, and made them all feel ill at ease, figuring that if David was fired, any one of them could be next.

"I liked David," said Frankie wistfully, for she had always had a thing for that young man. "I miss him."

"He's fine," Sylvie reminded her friend and colleague. "In fact he's better off now than he was when he was still with us."

Which was what David had told them when they met him for a drink last night. Which was the reason Sylvie was so late arriving home, forgot to charge her phone and overslept. Maybe she should keep the late-night shenanigans for Friday night and the weekend from now on. David might have immediately found another job, but then he was universally admired and very talented, whereas Sylvie was simply a personal assistant and so was Frankie. If they lost their jobs, no one would be clamoring to hire them as competition was stiff in the job market.

Mrs. Woods looked up from her computer, and Sylvie

stiffened. But then relaxed again when their boss got up, grabbed her phone and took a personal call while pacing her office.

"I don't think I'm going to last much longer anyway," she told Frankie.

Her friend looked appalled. "What? Why?"

"Do you really have to ask?" she said, gesturing in the direction of their boss's office. "The woman is crazy!"

"But what are you going to do?"

"I don't know, but at this point I'm starting to think that any job is better than this one."

"No, it's not," said Frankie decidedly. When Sylvie stared at her, she repeated, with more emphasis this time, "It is not!" She shrugged. "For one thing, it won't have me." She gave her a sheepish grin, and Sylvie softened.

"You're right," she said. Then she got an idea. "So why don't we both leave, and both start a new job—together?"

"Oh, honey, you know that the chance of us finding a new job is slim—non-existent, even."

Sylvie deflated somewhat at this notion. "Yeah, I guess you're right." The problem was that neither of them had any discernible talent, apart from having mastered the job they were currently in, which wasn't that big a deal. So likely this was as far as they would get in life: working for some psycho boss who never gave them the time of day, and treated them like chattel, if she could be bothered to remember their names.

But then the phone started ringing and before long both Sylvie and Frankie were engrossed in their work. It was a busy day, and by the time their lunch break rolled around, Sylvie was exhausted. She would have taken lunch with Frankie, as she did on most days, but she had some shopping to do. By the time she got back, with only minutes to spare, some big guy with slicked-back blue hair had blocked the elevator, and after they had danced around each other for a while, him staring at her as if she had a zit on her nose, she finally managed to get into the elevator. As it closed, she saw that he was still staring. Which is why she turned to the mirror and checked her face. What she saw were the usual heart-shaped features she had lived with all her life, framed by the same curtain of glossy blond hair. But no zits that she could see, and no remnants of the short night she'd had and which she hadn't been able to thoroughly rinse off in the shower. Phew. Then again, if she had looked weird, Frankie would have said something. No, the guy was probably just another random weirdo, of the type that was prevalent in the city. The moment she stepped out of the elevator, she had already forgotten all about their brief encounter.

CHAPTER 8

*D*ooley had finished showing Footsie the house and we returned to the living room.

"Nice place," said Footsie appreciatively. "I think I'll feel right at home here." He glanced up at the couch. "So is this where you like to spend time?"

"It is," I confirmed. "Dooley and I like to sleep here during the day, when we're not spending time in Odelia's office, that is. And then in the evenings we like to watch television here as a family."

"And what about you guys?" asked Footsie, addressing Harriet and Brutus.

"You *guys* is correct," said Harriet. She turned to Brutus. "See? It's not so difficult, sparky star. Even Footsie can see that I'm one of the guys. So no more moping, all right? I'm a guy, you're a guy—we're a family of guys." Then she turned to Footsie. "To answer your question, Footsie," she said, adopting a kind and polite tone, "Brutus and I mostly spend our time next door, in the house that belongs to Odelia's parents Marge and Tex."

"I wouldn't mind taking a peek," said Footsie. "If it's not too much to ask?"

"Oh, no, of course not," said Harriet, who seemed to have made a 180-degree about-face in her opinion of our new rodent friend. "I'll do the honors, shall I?" And without awaiting our approval, she led Footsie through the pet flap and was gone, leaving the three of us behind.

Brutus, who had been staring at the pet flap, now shook his head. "I don't know," he said. "It's going to take some getting used to."

"I think he's a very well-behaved rat," said Dooley. "So I don't think it will take us long to get used to having him around."

"I wasn't talking about the rat," said Brutus. "I was talking about me dating a guy, all of a sudden."

"Oh, that," said Dooley, as if it was a minor thing.

"Yeah, that," said Brutus acerbically.

"If it's any consolation," I told him, "I don't think it's going to last long. Usually she snaps out of these things very quickly, and I'm sure it won't be different this time."

"You think?" said Brutus, giving me a hopeful look.

"I'm sure of it," I said.

"Wanna bet?"

I blinked. "Um…"

"Just kidding. I hope you're right, Max. Since this is all very confusing to me, you know."

"It's confusing for all of us," I assured him. Though frankly it wasn't all that confusing. Harriet has always had one driving ambition that has propelled her forward through life and that is to become a world-famous star. A diva, like the divas she admires so much. Unfortunately it's not so easy for a cat to become world-famous. Especially when you don't have any particular talent to speak of. Then again, Harriet would point out that there are a lot of famous people out there who have no discernible talent at all, and she would be right. So it's always possible that at some point she will succeed.

I jumped up onto the couch and settled in for the duration. It had been a trying morning, and I was ready to enjoy a nice long nap. Unfortunately, as would soon become clear, this was not to be.

First the front doorbell rang, and just when Odelia arrived downstairs to open the door, her uncle Alec appeared at the kitchen door and entered. He looked unhappy about something.

"Oh, hey, Uncle Alec," said Odelia. "If you're looking for Chase I think he's next door. He was going to help out my dad with something."

"It was you I was looking for," said Uncle Alec, and his frown deepened even more. Uncle Alec is our chief of police, a large man with beetling brows and a jowly face that wouldn't have looked out of place on a bulldog. He sports russet sideburns that give an indication of the color of hair he used to have on top of his head.

"What is it?" asked Odelia now, clearly concerned that the tidings her uncle was bringing weren't of the joyful kind.

"It's your cousin," he said.

Dooley turned to me. "I didn't know Odelia had a cousin."

"She doesn't," I assured him. At least not to my knowledge.

"Ella?" said Odelia, taking a seat at the kitchen table. "What's wrong with her?"

Her uncle also took a seat and drummed his stubby fingers on the tabletop. "She's in a coma," he said.

"What?!"

"All I know is that I got a call from my sister-in-law late

last night. Her daughter had gone out with a friend and hadn't come home. This was around midnight. So I told her not to worry, that Ella was probably at a party and was having a great time and lost track of time, like a lot of teenagers at that age. But Aurelie said Ella had been acting strange lately, and that while she was waiting for her to arrive home, she had been going through her room and had found a stack of diaries going back years. They were buried under a pile of clothes at the bottom of her wardrobe. So she started reading, even though she probably shouldn't have, and that's when she saw…"

"What?" asked Odelia. "What did she see?"

Uncle Alec gave her a pained look. "Now promise me you won't freak out, honey."

"Uncle Alec, you're scaring me."

"He's scaring *me*," said Dooley.

"Turns out that Ella, when she turned thirteen, was on a quest to find out who her father was. She peppered her mother with questions, and when that didn't bring her any closer to the truth, she decided to do some investigating and try to find out for herself. And she succeeded. Aurelie didn't know about any of this, of course. If she did, she would have put a stop to it, since as we all know Ella's dad isn't the kind of dad any kid needs in their life."

"No, I know," said Odelia.

"Who are these people?" asked Dooley.

"Aurelie is Uncle Alec's late wife Ginny's sister," I said.

"That doesn't make Ella Odelia's cousin, does it?" asked Dooley.

"In a sense it does," I said. "Even though they're not blood-related."

"More like an honorary cousin," Brutus pointed out.

"Something like that," I said with a smile.

"Okay, so Ella found out who her dad was?" asked Odelia. "That's not good."

"It certainly is not," Uncle Alec grunted. "Your aunt Ginny always said Aurelie hit the jackpot when she married Bruno, and not in a good way. So when they finally locked him up and threw away the key, we breathed a sigh of relief. But as we all know a life sentence isn't always a life sentence, and turns out Bruno got out after having served a fraction of that. Lucky for Aurelie, and her daughter, he decided not to stick around and moved to Mexico, where he managed to get in trouble again, and spent another couple of years behind bars. Which is when Ella found out about him and they became pen pals." He grimaced. "Many, many letters, back and forth, all the way up to the present."

"And she never told her mom?"

Uncle Alec shook his head. "Not a word. Which isn't all that surprising, since after reading some of Bruno's letters it's obvious that the man was on a mission to poison the girl's mind against her own mother. At some point he even invited her to visit him in his Mexican prison and suggested she plunder her mom's bank account for that purpose. I don't think that ever materialized, but as you can imagine Aurelie was pretty shocked when she discovered what her ex-husband has been up to."

"Especially since there is a restraining order in place, and Bruno has clearly been in violation of that for years."

Uncle Alec nodded. "Anyway, to cut a long story short, Aurelie called the friend Ella was supposedly staying with, and she said she and Ella haven't been friends for months and she had no idea where she was. So Aurelie called Ella's boyfriend, and he didn't know where she was either. And that's when she called me back. I contacted the hospitals, and discovered that Ella was found unconscious in Hampton Cove Park last night and had been admitted to the hospital."

"Do they know what happened to her?"

"She was strangled," said Uncle Alec, "and left for dead. Possibly her attacker was interrupted before he could finish the job. Even at night that park is pretty popular. An old lady walking her dog found her and called an ambulance. But since Ella didn't have her phone on her, or any ID, the hospital had no way of knowing who she was."

"Oh, God," said Odelia. "Poor Ella. And poor Aunt Aurelie."

Uncle Alec took a deep breath. "The thing is that we think she was meeting someone in the park last night, and now Aurelie thinks it could have been Bruno."

"But I thought he was in a Mexican jail?"

"That's the thing. He's not. I asked around and he somehow managed to escape. There was a prison riot last week, and in the confusion about a dozen convicts got out. They captured most of them, but not Bruno. The slippery fish disappeared, so chances are he's back in the country." He gave Odelia a look of significance. "And knowing him, trouble won't be far behind."

"Bruno wouldn't hurt his own daughter, though, would he?"

"With guys like him you never know," said Uncle Alec with a shrug. "He could be after something—he always is. And if Ella wasn't prepared to give him what he wanted—money, most likely—maybe he lost it and attacked her."

"This is awful," said Odelia. "How is Aunt Aurelie holding up?"

"Not too well. Especially after she discovered Ella's secret diaries and correspondence. She always thought she'd finally gotten rid of her ex, and now it turns out he's been manipulating her daughter behind her back."

"So what are you going to do?"

"I'm going to liaise with the Hampton Keys police to try

and apprehend Bruno," said Uncle Alec. "I've also asked them to put a watch on Aurelie and Ella, but so far they've refused. They claim they're understaffed, and unfortunately I can't use my officers, since obviously it's not my jurisdiction and it's not my case."

"But it's your family," Odelia pointed out.

"I know, which is why I've come to you." He suddenly looked sheepish. "The thing is, I know Bruno, and I know he won't give up until he gets what he wants."

"And what does he want?"

"Two things: he wants to take revenge on his ex-wife, since he figures she's the reason he was sent down. And second: he wants the money he figures she owes him. So somehow, and sooner rather than later—and this is what I've been trying to drill into the head of my colleague over in Hampton Keys—he's going to come for Aurelie one way or another. Which means she's in danger."

"You want us to put her up for a while?" asked Odelia, when her uncle was taking his time getting down to business.

He nodded gratefully. "I already talked to Chase, but he told me to discuss it with you, as there would be a certain risk involved for you as well."

"Why doesn't Uncle Alec put her up himself?" asked Brutus.

"Probably because that's the first place Bruno would look," I said. "He knows Alec, and when he discovers that his ex-wife is gone, he'll suspect she's staying with her brother-in-law. But he doesn't know Odelia, or at least I don't think he does."

We never did have a lot of dealings with Uncle Alec's sister-in-law and that side of the family, after all. Aunt Ginny, Uncle Alec's wife, died fifteen years ago, so the families hadn't been all that close the past couple of years. I had never even met Aurelie, or her daughter. And I certainly had never met this Bruno character.

"Okay, you can tell Aunt Aurelie from me that she can stay with us for as long as she wants," said Odelia.

Uncle Alec's smile was something to behold. "Thanks, honey," he said. "I'm worried about her, you know."

"What about Ella? If her dad attacked her once, he might come after her again."

"Which is why I want her to stay here as well. There isn't a lot they can do for her at the hospital, apparently. And Aurelie has already talked to the doctors, and they agree that she can be monitored at home."

"The only problem is that we don't have a lot of space," said Odelia. "We only have the one extra bedroom."

"That's fine," said her uncle. "Ella can stay in that room, and Aurelie will sleep on the couch for the time being."

"Unless…" Odelia glanced down at us.

"Uh-oh," said Brutus. "Why is she looking at us like that, Max?"

"I don't know," I said. "But I have a feeling it's not good."

"Unless what?" Uncle Alec prompted.

"Ella will probably need a hospital bed, right?"

"I guess so."

"So maybe we can set her up in the living room, so we won't have to move that bed up the stairs, which I think would be pretty impossible anyway. And then your sister-in-law can have the spare bedroom and the cats will simply have to make some space."

As a response to these words, I dug my claws into the couch. My favorite couch. The couch where I did all of my best napping. Where we spent time as a family. Where Dooley and I lay side by side and had such a great time.

"Not the couch!" I said in a choked voice.

"What are you talking about, Max?" asked Dooley.

Brutus grinned. "Have you seen the size of these hospital beds, Dooley? They'll have to get rid of the couch. In fact they'll probably have to get rid of the dining room table, the couch, the armchair, the television—the whole lot."

Dooley's mouth opened and closed a few times. Then he cried, in a perfect imitation of yours truly: "Not the couch!"

CHAPTER 9

$\mathcal{B}$arnaby Blossom had never known a time when his mom didn't interrupt him every time he started to say something. It was so now. He'd just begun to develop his argument when she started talking over him with that high-pitched voice of hers.

"I'm not saying you're wrong," she declared haughtily, "but you're not right either." She cocked her head in his direction. "And when if you were truly honest with yourself you would know that, Barnaby dear."

The way she uttered this endearment would make you think he was the apple of her eye and she was the most loving person on the face of the planet. While in actual fact she had never cared about anyone other than herself, and even now, when Barnaby was a grown man and was running a thriving flower shop, she still acted as if he was a simpleton. A little kid who needed his mom to steer him through life and hold his hand at every possible juncture.

"Mom, I was talking to these people," Barnaby said. Lately he'd started to rebel to some extent, especially when he was addressing clients in his store.

"I know, dearest," said his mother, tying a nice little bow on top of the flower arrangement she had wrapped up, "but you have to admit you were talking nonsense, as usual." She directed an apologetic look at the couple buying the centerpiece. "I'm so sorry. You must think me awfully rude, but it's a fact of life that a boy's best friend is his mother, and that doesn't stop when they get older. If anything it becomes even more so. Wouldn't you agree?"

The couple smiled nervously. Clearly they had become aware of the tension that hung palpably in the air between the flower shop owner and his 'best friend' and mother.

So instead of engaging in a wholehearted endorsement, they uttered polite murmurings that could be interpreted in any way. Of course Barnaby's mother chose to interpret it as an agreement with her argument. "Now I know you think roses are the most romantic flowers in existence," she reiterated her argument, "but they're not, and if you had half a brain you would know that," she chided her son. "The most romantic flower in the world is actually the peony, which is why I'm selling you peonies today and not roses," she stressed as she pushed the finished centerpiece to the fore and admired it with a loving eye.

"It's... very nice," said the man.

"It's lovely," the woman added.

"But I do love roses," said the man.

"Pink roses especially," said the woman.

"There's nothing quite like a pink rose, is there?"

For a moment silence hung in the air, then the woman said in a small voice, "We did ask for roses, didn't we, Jack?"

"We did," said the man in an equally weak voice.

They directed an almost pleading look at Barnaby, who could tell that if he didn't intervene he would lose these customers forever, the same way he'd already lost so many customers before, who felt unequal to the task of contending with his domineering mother, who had a habit of pushing her own ideas and ignoring what his customers actually wanted in the way of their flower needs.

"Okay, let's put this aside for the moment," he suggested, "and why don't I make you a nice arrangement of pink flowers instead? How does that sound?"

The couple immediately perked up to a great extent. "That sounds absolutely wonderful," said the woman.

"Lovely," the man murmured, darting a nervous glance at Barnaby's mother.

The woman stood frozen to the spot, her lips a thin line of disapproval. Finally she slapped the counter with her hands and snapped, "I hate it when people think they know better, don't you?" And after having delivered this statement with the requisite vehemence, she retreated into her inner lair, which was the floral refrigerator where they kept the flowers in cold storage until such time as they were ready to be used for any of the many flower arrangements they had on offer.

He could hear her pottering around in there, moving stuff around and muttering to herself. Clearly her feelings were hurt and she didn't mind who knew it.

"Will Lily be all right, Barnaby?" asked the woman.

"Oh, she's fine," said Barnaby, who was all too familiar with his mother's dark moods when she didn't get what she wanted. "Don't mind her."

"I hope we haven't offended her," said the woman.

"My mother is easily offended," he said before he realized what he was saying. 'Always present a united front as a family,' was one of his late father's recommendations. Barnaby's dad had been a fishmonger, and so he knew a thing or two about how to work with clients. Belatedly he remembered his dad's advice, and smiled. "My mother is very passionate about the store," he explained. "And sometimes she gets carried away when she offers advice. But you don't have to feel obligated in any way. What she said is simply a suggestion. At the end of the day you still decide what you want to buy, right?"

"Right," said the man, eyeing the arrangement that was taking shape under Barnaby's capable hands with admiration written all over his features. "You do have such a gift, Barnaby," he said fervently.

"Oh, you do," said his wife. "My husband wanted to go and buy flowers at the mall. But I told him, 'No way, Jack, we're going to Barnaby, since he's the best. He may be more expensive, but at least his flowers won't wilt after three days.'"

Barnaby smiled a tight smile. If even his most loyal customers were already thinking of transferring their business to the mall he was in big trouble. And he knew he only had his mother to thank for it. Another one of his late dad's axioms was that introducing even the slightest friction in the sales process was already too much and you could lose your customer. And unfortunately friction was his mom's middle name.

"There you go," he said finally, and admired his own handiwork.

"Oh, Barnaby, how wonderful," said the woman, clasping her hands together with honest glee. "You're a genius."

"An absolute genius," her husband agreed wholeheartedly.

When the customers had left, Barnaby took a deep breath and walked into his workshop, where their cool room was also located. When they arrived from their suppliers, who transported the flowers in refrigerated vans, the fresh blooms were transferred to this cool room, before being turned into the lovely bouquets their customers appreciated so much. He found his mother smoking a cigarette and directing a plume of smoke at the ceiling. He had told her many times she shouldn't smoke around the flowers but she just didn't care and did it anyway.

"Mom, you shouldn't smoke in here. It's not good for the flowers. Not to mention when customers walk into a flower shop they expect to smell flowers, not cigarette smoke."

"You know, Barnaby," said his mom, "I hope you're pleased with yourself. After insulting me like that, and humiliating me in front of Jack and Diane."

"I didn't humiliate you, Mom," he said. "You tried to push something on them they didn't want and hadn't asked for. So I simply stepped in and corrected your mistake."

Her nostrils flared at this comment. "I made no mistake. You made the mistake when you decided to insult your own mother's business sense. Most of the time these people don't even know what they want, so I simply help them along. It's what any business owner would do. It's what your father did."

"So when a customer walked into Dad's store and asked for codfish and Dad sold him mackerel instead, would you say that customer was a happy customer? I don't think so. He'd probably think Dad had lost his mind and decide to take his business elsewhere."

"Always arguing with me," his mother muttered darkly.

"Okay, so I'm going to ask you one more time not to smoke," he said. "And please don't argue with the customers next time, all right? When they ask for roses, don't try to sell them peonies. Unless you want to wreck my business."

She bridled at this. "*Your* business? You're forgetting who bankrolled you, Sonny Jim. And who's still busting her ass in here every day. So you better show some gratitude, or else…" She was waving her cigarette at him, and he watched the ashes that had accumulated at the tip of the cigarette with some dread. She was waving them over a rustic arrangement he had made for a local restaurant.

PURRFECT GEMS

"Can you please put that out?" he said. "You're going to ruin that bouquet."

In response she gave him the vilest look possible—a look no mother should give her beloved son, and mashed the cigarette out in the cup of coffee he'd brought in there before he'd been forced to step in and rescue his customers from his mother's ill-advised sales technique. The cigarette made a hissing sound as it was extinguished and he sighed a silent sigh. He'd been looking forward to that cup of coffee—his first of the day.

When his mother left, he poured the spoiled coffee into the stainless steel sink in the corner of his workshop and rinsed it thoroughly. Caffeine was bad enough, he didn't want to add nicotine to the mix. He then stared at himself in the mirror over the sink. What he saw was a thirty-something male with receding hairline, though his curly hair still retained much of the volume of his younger years. His face was essentially a jolly one, kind and friendly, and inspired confidence in his customers and the desire to put in a repeat visit every time the need for buying flowers arose. The only thing still missing from his life was a woman to share it with. When you run a business—any business—and want to do it well, it takes up so much of your time it's hard to muster the energy to have a social life as well. And without a social life it's very difficult to meet new people.

He gave himself a cheerful smile but instead it looked more like a grimace. The only advantage of having his mother in the store was that he didn't have to pay her a lot, since she had her pension and also some benefits after her husband died. Many was the time she berated him for not appreciating all the sacrifices she made so he could keep the store ticking over. And she was right. But sometimes he wondered if he shouldn't simply hire a salesperson instead. It would cost him, but at least they wouldn't insist on driving his customers away.

He took a seat at the long wooden table where he created what he liked to call his art. Like any artist, he put his heart and soul into his work, and it showed. Barnaby's Blossoms was known far and wide as the place to be for all your floral needs. Located right in the heart of Hampton Cove it wasn't too much to say he'd become something of an institution in the thirteen years since he had first opened for business.

He looked up when the door to his workshop opened and, fully expecting to see his mom, he was already hoping he wouldn't have to rebuke her again when he saw that instead it was a young woman who had decided to join him.

"Mr. Blossom?" asked the young woman, who was pretty in a fresh-faced sort of way, with a tilt-tipped nose and cornflower-blue eyes. All this Barnaby had clocked in less than a second, and when his heart made a sort of galloping motion in his chest he fully attributed it to the fact that he had just cut himself on a thorny rose.

"Yes, that's me," he said in a cheerful tone.

"My name is Sarah Mitchell," said the woman, "and I'm responding to the job advertisement in the *Hampton Cove Gazette*?"

He gave her a blank look. "Job advertisement?"

"Yes, the ad said you're looking for a salesperson? I don't have a lot of experience, but I've been temping at the mall as a sales assistant for one of the toy stores." She cast down her eyes. "I'm the one dressed as a clown greeting the people entering the store."

"Okay," he said, blinking a few times. For the life of him he couldn't remember having placed an ad in the paper, unless in his dreams, of course. So maybe this was it? Maybe his dreams had been answered? Or maybe his mom, in one of her more charitable moments, had taken the initiative? So instead of telling the girl he had no idea what she was talking about, he said, "How about a sixty-day trial?"

She looked up with a look of such radiance it almost blinded him. "Deal!" she said, as if it was the best thing that had ever happened to her. And maybe it was. At any rate, it couldn't be worse than having to greet customers dressed like a clown.

CHAPTER 10

*E*zra had given the suggestions of his roommate a great deal of thought. And he had to agree there was some merit in what Jake had said. Wives probably could be rented for a small fee, and so could babies. But the trouble was that he wasn't familiar with the types of outfits that put wives and babies up for rent. He knew they probably existed, but how did you get in touch with them? He'd searched Craigslist and hadn't found a single listing. Also: wasn't this a form of cheating? And wouldn't these detectives Aunt Emily had hired find out and disqualify him?

It was a lot to think about, and as he devoured a sizable slice of pizza, and sipped from a large container of Coke, he figured he might as well consult the man who had come up with the idea in the first place. Unfortunately Jake had gone out. Not to work, as most people do, but to their favorite place in all the world—apart from the apartment they shared: Gandalf's Cave, their local comics store.

Located just around the corner from where they lived in the Bronx, Gandalf's Cave was the ultimate paradise for any comics fan. Sprawled across three floors it stocked almost every single comic that had ever been made and was still in print today, and also a lot of the ones that weren't in print anymore and were considered collector's items. Not that either Ezra or Jake ever bought the latter ones, since they were perpetually in dire straits—financially speaking, that is.

The passion for comics was something that Ezra shared with Jake and if there was one comic they both coveted as if their lives depended on it, it was a copy of The Hump, as published in the year of our lord 1954. It was the year the Hump's creator, the amazing genius Frank Dixon, had reached the pinnacle of his creative powers and had put out the best and most innovative Hump ever made. It had been out of print for decades, of course, and could only be found on auction sites where collectors bid exorbitant sums to lay their hands on a copy. In the last ten years no more copies had become available, and Ezra knew this because he kept tabs on all of the sites. Just in case he ever did see a copy that wouldn't cost an arm and a leg, and he'd be able to afford it. So far no luck, though. And if there was a reason he was giving serious consideration to Jake's crazy notion about hiring wives and babies, this was it: the money from Aunt Emily's inheritance would finally put him in the position where he could buy The Hump issue number 84, where everyone's favorite hunchbacked superhero met his match in his archnemesis Mantis. It was his life's dream—his life's goal, in fact—apart from becoming an NFL team owner, of course. Once he put his hands on that particular comic he could go to his grave a happy slacker.

He was thinking about all of this and more when the door opened and Jake walked in.

"I've been thinking about what you said, Jake," he said, deciding to grab the bull by the horns, or whatever else you did with a bull. "And I think maybe we should do this."

"Do what?" asked Jake, plunking himself down on the couch and starting to unwrap the latest comic he had bought.

"Well, go for the inheritance. Rent a wife, borrow a baby. You know, the plan?"

"The plan?" Jake murmured as he affectionately fingered this latest addition to his extensive collection. He brought it to his nose and inhaled deeply, closing his eyes with relish. "Fresh ink. Is there a better smell in the world? I don't think so."

"The plan, Jake!" Ezra stressed. "You came up with the plan."

"I did?" asked Jake, not paying him all that much attention.

"You did, and I think it's absolutely brilliant. Even though at first I thought you were crazy, now I see it's pure genius. I mean, what are the chances for me to find a wife the normal way, you know, or start a family? Nil. Zero. Bupkis. So I think it's either your plan or it's bye-bye inheritance."

"Bye-bye baby," Jake murmured, still engrossed in his latest purchase. Though it was very well possible that instead of purchasing the tome he had found some other, less legitimate way of procuring the comic, since Jake was just about as broke as Ezra was, or even more so.

"Okay, Jake, so my question is: where can I rent this wife, and where can I find this baby?"

When no answer seemed forthcoming, he yanked the comic from his friend's grip, and positioned himself on the coffee table, looking the man straight in the eye. "Where can I rent a wife, buddy?"

"I was reading that," Jake lamented. "Give it back."

"Not until you tell me where I can rent a wife."

"How would I know? I'm not in the wife-renting business. You figure it out!"

"But I thought you said…"

"Give me back my comic!"

Reluctantly Ezra complied and handed his friend back his much-cherished comic. When he looked closer, he suddenly saw that it was actually THE comic—the one they had both been looking for! It was The Hump issue 84!

"Hey, where did you get that!"

"Don't get your panties in a twist," said Jake. "It's not the real thing. Just an illegal copy I picked up from Ahmad."

"Oh," said Ezra, sagging a little. Ahmad didn't merely sell illegally sourced foldable phones, he actually sold pretty much anything. He still sold DVDs, even though no sane person still owned a DVD player. But he also sold comics, magazines, CDs… And Ezra had to admit that as far as pirated stuff went, Ahmad's stuff was always of the best quality. And pretty cheap, too. Which gave him an idea.

"Do you think Ahmad would know where I can rent a wife?"

"I'm sure he does. Ahmad is God, buddy. The man is plugged in."

"Wanna come?"

"Come where?"

"To talk to Ahmad!"

"Not now. I'm reading."

"You've read this thing a thousand times."

"Yeah, but not printed on actual paper."

"It's just a copy. Probably the same digital file we've got, only printed out. I don't understand why you would want to spend money on this crap."

"It's not crap," said Jake, stroking the comic's tender spine and holding it like a precious baby. "It's The Hump—and in whatever shape or form, it will always be a work of the utmost genius."

"Fine. Finish it and then can we go talk to Ahmad? I need a wife, Jake, and I need one now."

"You got a year," Jake murmured as he took up devouring the comic again.

"See? You do remember," said Ezra.

But his friend was dead to the world once more.

It took Jake all of fifteen minutes to finish the comic and presently the two men set out to talk to their friendly neighborhood pirate king to acquire themselves a wife and a baby.

Ahmad was still on the same street corner where he always stood, his trestle table laden with all manner of stuff. The man had a shifty look in his eyes, which wasn't hard to understand, since the cops could pay him a visit any time, and confiscate the whole lot of his wares.

"Hey, bud," said Jake.

Ahmad directed a broad grin at them. "My best customers!" He exchanged a weird and intricate handshake with both Jake and Ezra, then said, "What can I do for you now? Nice bottle of premium vodka? Some grade-A weed? Comics?" he wiggled his eyebrows invitingly. "Anything you went, Ahmad got, and of the best quality and the lowest price. And if I ain't got it, I can probably get it. So take your pick, or pick my brain, or—"

"Ezra needs a wife," Jake interrupted the flow of words.

"And a baby," Ezra added. "A wife *and* a baby." When Ahmad stared at him with a dumbfounded look on his face, he hastened to clarify, "Not a forever wife, of course. Just for the time being."

"It's complicated," said Jake.

"You want a wife and a baby," said Ahmad, eyeing them as if they'd gone crazy. "Well, I've got a wife, and a baby. Maybe you can take them?" He laughed loudly at his own joke. But when his 'best customers' didn't join him in his merriment, he quickly sobered. "You're serious?"

"Dead serious," Ezra confirmed. "I'm not happy about it, but I need a wife and a kid so I can pocket this inheritance."

"His aunt died, and she was big on the whole temperance, clean living and respectable family thing," Jake explained. "So now Ezra needs to be married with a wife and kid and living the life of the upstanding family man if he wants to stand a chance at touching that money."

Ahmad licked his lips at the mention of the money. "I see," he said, and Ezra could see that he did see, for his eyes were flickering dangerously. "Big inheritance?" he asked as he rubbed his hands together.

"Pretty substantial," Ezra said.

"We talking millions or billions?"

"Honestly? I have no idea," said Ezra. "But apparently Aunt Emily had done pretty well for herself, so I'd bet good money—if I had any money—it's a nice tidy sum. Of course there are four cousins, so we'd have to share the money—at least if the others manage to qualify." One of his cousins had the advantage, since he was already married with a kid on the way. Ezra called that cheating, but what can you do? The lawyer seemed to agree that he was a shoo-in for the cash. His other two cousins were the respectable kind but also the hard-working kind and had always figured they still had years to settle down and get serious about starting a family. That would all change now, probably. And since one of them was a banker, and the other one some corporate honcho, they probably wouldn't have any trouble landing an equally respectable wife in next to no time and start producing offspring, popping it out at a rapid pace. It wasn't fair, of course, since they already had money to burn as it was. In fact Ezra was the only one who didn't own his own place, and didn't even have a 401(k), whatever that was.

"Okay, so do you think you can help us, Ahmad?" asked Jake.

Ahmad was fingering his chin, where a tiny strand of hair grew that with some imagination could be called a goatee.

Once upon a time it had inspired Ezra to grow his own goatee, which was pink and now dangled from his chin like a weird hirsute appendage. "I might be able to get something for you, yeah," he said. "Does it have to be an actual baby, or is it all right if it's a kid?"

"What age?" asked Jake immediately, taking up the negotiations.

"Three," said Ahmad. "You see, my wife's cousin's fella walked out on her and left her to raise the kid all by herself. So she could use a nice chunk of that inheritance if we can come to some kind of an arrangement."

Jake and Ezra shared a look. "I told the lawyer that I didn't have kids," said Ezra sadly. "So if I suddenly show up with a three-year-old in tow he'll probably be suspicious." These lawyer types were shrewd and they could probably do the math. No way was he going to be able to pass this kid off as his own.

"You could always tell him you didn't know about the kid until now," Ahmad suggested. "Happens all the time, bubba."

It was a suggestion, of course, but somehow he had the feeling the lawyer wouldn't go for it and call foul play.

"You don't have anything else?" asked Jake.

Ahmad thought for a moment. "Let me ask around," he finally suggested. "I'm sure there's plenty of women who'd love to be Ezra's wife for a couple of days…" When Ezra raised his eyebrows, he went on, "Weeks? Months?"

"One year," Ezra stipulated. "I need to be married with a kid for the period of one whole year."

"Jeez, your aunt Emily sure knew how to play hardball," said Ahmad. "One whole year, huh? That's going to cost you, bruh."

"I know," said Ezra sadly. "But it's worth it. Probably."

"Imagine if the inheritance turns out to be some measly little sum," said Jake with a laugh. "Wouldn't that be funny?"

But Ezra wasn't laughing. "Knowing that she pretty much ran the Anti-Alcohol League that wouldn't surprise me," he said. Clearly the woman had a screw loose.

"Look, I'll make some calls," said Ahmad. "See if there isn't someone who's willing to be your wife for a whole year." He gave Ezra a grin and slapped him on the shoulder. "Anything for my best customer!"

CHAPTER 11

Things weren't looking very promising for the four of us I have to say. Humans have a habit of pushing things through once they've made up their minds about something. I thought it would be at least a couple of days before this whole business with the hospital bed and the comatose cousin came to pass, but instead it happened very quickly. Uncle Alec had just left when Chase arrived, along with Tex and Marge, and together they started rearranging the furniture and moving stuff around. And so before I knew what was happening, gone were our couches, and gone was our nice and cozy living room!

Another half hour later the ambulance arrived, and four burly paramedics rolled a bulky hospital bed in place and carried the patient in. Ella Marshall looked very pale and very, well, comatose, I guess is the best way to describe it. Her mother had also arrived in the same ambulance, and was hovering around her daughter, very much the concerned and caring mom. Meanwhile it was obvious that the center of attention had already shifted from us to them, and I can't say I was all that happy about it. Look, I know I shouldn't be selfish, and that Ella and Aunt Aurelie needed our humans more than we did, but I still couldn't help feeling a little put out by the way Odelia and Chase went out of their way to accommodate the new arrival. I know Aunt Aurelie is family and all, but still.

"Looks like I picked a bad time to move in," said Footsie, as he watched all this with a baleful eye.

"Yeah, it's not going to get any easier around here," Brutus agreed. "With two extra humans in the house things are going to be very different."

"Gone are the cozy nights in front of the television," said Harriet sadly. "And gone are the happy family times huddled around the barbecue set."

"Barbecue?" said Footsie, perking up. "Did I hear the word barbecue?"

"Yeah, our family loves to barbecue," I said. "Tex especially loves his barbecue set, and I have to say he's improved considerably. He took lessons, and he watched a ton of YouTube videos, and so now he's more or less proficient at the thing."

"He still burns stuff from time to time," said Brutus. "But at least whatever he cooks up is more or less edible. Most of the time."

"Look, I don't mean to pry," said Footsie, who was lying next to us on the kitchen counter, watching the events as they unfolded. And if anyone objected to a rat and four cats lying on top of the kitchen counter, they were far too busy fussing over the patient and her mother to bother. "But is it true that you guys solve cases from time to time? You know, mystery stuff and crime cases and all of that stuff?"

"It's true," said Brutus. "Though it's mainly Max who figures things out. You wouldn't say so when you saw him, but he's actually very clever."

I stared at my friend. Brutus rarely paid me a compliment, so I decided to savor the moment.

"Max *is* very clever," Dooley added. "He's got a very big brain, and once he fires it up it's pretty impressive to watch."

"I do my best," I said humbly.

"No, the thing is that I might have a case for you," said Footsie. "In fact it's one of the reasons I decided to drop by. And then when I discovered that there's an entire maze underneath your backyard, I couldn't help but explore."

"You have a case for us?" I asked.

"Well, sorta," said Footsie. "My human has found herself in a spot of trouble lately."

"You have your own human?" asked Harriet. "But I thought you said you didn't have a human."

"Well, I have," Footsie admitted. "I'm truly sorry about the subterfuge but I didn't want to say it before I got to know you guys a little better. But it's clear to me now that I can trust you with my human's dirty little secret. So here goes." He took a deep breath.

But before he could launch into the nitty-gritty of the thing, Harriet decided to interrupt. "Oh, by the way, I've given some more thought to what you said, Max."

"What did I say?" I asked.

"About changing my name? I think you were right. If I keep calling myself Harriet it's going to confuse people. So I want you all to call me Harry from on."

We stared at her—or him—or it. "Um..." I said.

"Why do you want to change your name, Harriet?" asked Dooley.

"Harry, please," said Harriet—or Harry. "Do you really have to ask, Dooley?"

"Yes, I do," said Dooley. "Cause you have a nice name. And I'm not sure if Harry is as nice as Harriet."

"Why, thank you, Dooley," said Harry, simpering a little.

"Look, Harriet is obviously a girl's name, and since I'm not a girl, I think it's probably for the best if I adopt a boy's name. And I think Harry has a nice ring to it, wouldn't you agree?"

"It does," I quickly said, and the others all agreed that Harry had a very nice ring to it indeed.

"Okay, please excuse me for the interruption," said Harry. "But I thought it was important. Go on, Footsie."

"Thanks, Harry," said Footsie. "Now where was I? Oh, right. My human and her problem. See, the thing is that she's probably one of the nicest and sweetest people on the planet, but she does suffer from one thing and that's kleptomania."

"Klepto-what?" asked Dooley.

"Kleptomania. She likes to steal stuff. It's a compulsion that she simply can't seem to shake. She will enter a store with the intention of paying for whatever she picks up, and she will leave with her pockets stuffed full of items she didn't pay for. It's very annoying."

Especially for the owners of the store, I thought. "So how is that a mystery that needs to be solved?" I asked. "Cause it seems to me it's more a problem for a shrink."

"She did see a shrink for a while, and she made great progress," said Footsie. "In fact she stopped stealing altogether—pretty much."

I cocked an eyebrow. "Pretty much?"

"She was caught again a week ago," said Footsie. "She had pocketed a nice diamond ring, and the owner of the jewelry store wasn't happy about it, so he called the cops, and she was duly arrested, then released on bail—again."

"You mean she has been arrested before?"

"Oh, she's been arrested many times, but mostly for minor stuff. Mainly candy bars, I'd have to say, since she likes candy bars. But this time is different. It's possible she will have to do actual time this time, since the jeweler has decided to press charges. He's also posted the footage on his Facebook page, even though the police told him not to. So now things are looking a little, shall we say dire?"

"Dire sounds about right," I agreed.

"But what do you expect us to do, Footsie?" asked Harry. "We're detectives, not people who can bust convicts out of prison."

"If she did the crime, she should do the time," Brutus grunted implacably. As a cop's cat he mostly takes a dim view of criminals and their criminal behavior.

"She's basically a good person," said Footsie. "And this stealing… it's not because she wants to steal, or that she even needs the stuff. It's a disease. A compulsion. Sarah doesn't belong in jail. It will kill her. What she needs is therapy and lots of it. But good therapists are expensive, and unfortunately she can't afford one."

"I thought you said she was seeing one?"

"It's actually a friend of hers who's studying to be a therapist and who likes to practice on her," said Footsie. "Not really what I would call a practiced practitioner who can make a difference."

"Poor Sarah," said Dooley. "We have to help her, you guys. We have to keep her out of jail."

"I really don't see…" I began.

"Look, I know Chase is a cop," said Footsie, "and Odelia's uncle is also a cop. And his wife is the mayor."

"His girlfriend," Harry corrected him.

"Whatever. These are all people with some pull in this community. If they wanted to, they could tell this jeweler to back off and they could also find Sarah a decent therapist to free her from this compulsion to stuff her pockets with loot."

"When you put it like that…" I said.

"So you want us to put in a good word for your human, is that it?" asked Harry. "Cause I guess we could do that."

"No guarantees," Brutus added. "Obviously."

"Oh, no, obviously," Footsie agreed. "I mean, all I would like to ask is that you talk to Odelia, so she can talk to her husband and so on up the chain of command, and put in a good word for Sarah, cause I'd hate it if she went down for this."

"It would also mean you were out of a home," Harry pointed out shrewdly.

"Gee, I hadn't thought of that," said Footsie, but it was obvious that the prospect of his human becoming a guest of the state didn't sit well with him, and not for purely unselfish reasons either.

"Okay, so we'll talk to Odelia," I said. "And we'll see what we can do. How does that sound, Footsie?"

"That sounds amazing," said Footsie. "Thank you, Max."

"Don't thank me yet," I said. "She's not out of trouble."

The activities in the living room had come to a conclusion, and the large hospital bed now took center stage. It made me feel as if we were in an actual hospital, and not in our own home. But then I guess sometimes you have to drop your own selfish desires and considerations and think about other people and put their needs first instead.

"She looks peaceful," said Dooley, commenting on Ella who was lying, her face as white as the pillow she was resting on, in peaceful repose.

"She looks sick," said Harry.

"She looks dead," said Brutus.

"When is she going to come out of her coma?" asked Footsie.

"Maybe never," said Brutus, voicing the gloomy view.

"I'm sure she'll come out of it very soon," I said. After all, until she did, we wouldn't have our couch back!

Odelia now approached us, and whispered, "I have a very special assignment for you guys."

We all perked up. We might not be dogs, but when Odelia utters the A-word, we sit up and pay attention.

"I want you to keep a very close eye on Ella. And the moment you notice anything out of the ordinary, I want you to tell us immediately."

"You mean when she wakes up?" asked Dooley.

"Not just that. You know that her dad probably put her in this state, right? And that he's probably out there looking for her so he can finish the job? Well, I want you to watch out for any sign of that man, and the moment you see him, you tell Chase and me so we can have him arrested."

"If you like I'll bite him," Footsie suggested. "My teeth are very sharp, and I've been told that my bite is very unpleasant."

I translated the rat's words and Odelia looked doubtful. "Maybe better not," she said. "Unless of course he presents a clear and present danger to Ella. In which case all bets are off."

Footsie grinned widely. "Oh, I hope he shows up! I really do!"

CHAPTER 12

Dooley had a hard time following the recent events as they unfolded. It wasn't that he was the kind of inflexible cat incapable of adapting to change, it was simply that sometimes he didn't fully comprehend what was happening, which made him feel anxious sometimes. So he accosted his best friend Max to explain to him what was actually going on in the house. "So why does Harriet suddenly want to be called Harry?" he asked for instance. "And why is this girl in a coma and why is she staying with us and not at the hospital? And why does Footsie's human steal stuff she doesn't need? This is all very confusing, Max."

"It is confusing," Max said with the kind of reassuring tone in his voice that soothed Dooley so much. "And I'll explain everything to you in just one moment. But right now we need to talk to Odelia, since I have the impression we won't get this opportunity very often from now on, with this new guest staying with us."

Odelia had stepped out of the house and was sitting on the bench on the patio looking out across the backyard. She was taking a breather, and if she had been a smoker, which she was not, Dooley imagined she would have smoked a cigarette, as so many humans do when they're stressed, or even when they're not.

So they approached Odelia to state their case. Footsie was also with them, but Harriet and Brutus had left to relax on their couch—at least they still had a couch.

"Odelia? Can we ask you something?" Max said.

Odelia looked up from her reverie. "Absolutely, Max. What is it?"

And so Max explained that Sarah, Footsie's human, was a compulsive thief, and how that had gotten her into big trouble with a jeweler, who apparently didn't like that she took a nice diamond ring and didn't intend to pay for it.

Odelia's frown told them that this was serious. "I'm not sure what you want me to do about it. If she stole a ring and was arrested it's out of my hands, Max."

"Yeah, but maybe you could put in a good word with your uncle," Max suggested. "The girl needs therapy, not prison."

"Be that as it may…"

It was at that moment that Footsie suddenly burst into a high-pitched squeak that went through Dooley like a knife. It sounded very sad and very disconcerting, and when Odelia had finally traced the source of the sound, she actually got tears in her eyes. "Oh, Footsie," she said, picking up the rat and hugging the creature to her chest. "Don't be sad. Of course I'll have a word with my uncle about Sarah."

Abruptly the rat stopped squeaking, and instead gave Odelia a cuddle. Odelia giggled and seemed to have put her doubts about the rat staying with them behind her. She wasn't even scared or angry at the furry rodent anymore.

"You're a sweetheart, aren't you?" she said. "And the fact that you would be willing to come stay with us to save your human tells me that you've got your heart in the right place.

I'll talk to my uncle and let you know what he says. Is she in prison right now, this Sarah of yours?"

"No, she's home on bail. And she was so sad that I simply couldn't bear it and I vowed to look for someone who could help us deal with this crisis. And since I'd heard about Max and the wonders he performs, I decided to try my luck."

It took Dooley and Max a while to translate all of that, but then Odelia hugged the rat even closer. To such an extent even Dooley had to wipe away a tear.

"So beautiful," he murmured. "I love it so much."

He wasn't sure whether Max liked it or not, for his friend merely grunted something under his breath. Probably he was already thinking three or four steps ahead, like he always did, and had already figured everything out.

"I want you to know that you can stay with us for as long as you want," said Odelia. "Though I'm sure you miss your human, don't you, Footsie? So if you want we can pay her a visit, and then I can tell her what happened?" Then she frowned. "On second thought, maybe better not. She'll probably think I'm nuts for talking to her rat."

"Technically you're not talking to Footsie," Max pointed out. "You're talking to us and we're talking to Footsie."

"All the same," said Odelia with a sigh. "It's not the kind of story I can tell anyone. But I'm still going to pay a visit to Sarah and maybe tell her I heard about the problems she's been having and offer her my support."

"Do you know a shrink she could see?" asked Max.

Odelia thought for a moment. "Personally I don't know anyone. But I could ask Dan."

"Who's Dan?" asked Footsie.

"He's Odelia's editor," Dooley explained. "He's very clever and he knows a lot of people because he's very old."

"He's also a great networker," Max pointed out.

"What's a networker, Max?" asked Dooley.

"It's a person who likes to network," Footsie said, which told Dooley nothing. But since the conversation seemed to have moved on, he decided to let it go. It often happened that conversations moved on and he had to play catch-up, but that was all right. If he remembered later on where he had gotten stuck, he could always ask Max. His friend was never annoyed when he peppered him with questions, and took his time to answer them all, even the very difficult ones.

Odelia checked her watch. "Okay, so why don't we go and see Sarah now? Aurelie can take care of her daughter, and I've asked my mom and Gran to keep an eye on them."

"Okay, great," said Footsie, perking up to a great extent. Dooley was glad he'd stopped squealing, since it was a pretty distressing sound.

Moments later they were all piling into Odelia's car and were on their way to Sarah, Footsie's kleptocratic human.

"Kleptomaniac, Dooley," Max corrected him.

He smiled at his dear friend. "Thanks, Max."

CHAPTER 13

Sarah felt pretty pleased with herself. Her friend, who'd been helping her out on a freelance basis—since she wasn't a licensed shrink but a student—had told her that she needed to take control of her life, since right now it looked to her as if circumstances were controlling Sarah and not the other way around. She also needed to keep moving forward and not get stuck in the past. And when Sarah had asked her how she should go about that, she had told her she should probably get a job first, and then take it from there, rebuilding her life step by step.

Ever since that jeweler had turned nasty and grabbed her by the neck and called the cops on her, Sarah's life had effectively gone off the rails in a pretty spectacular way. She had been arrested, had been kicked out of her apartment, lost her job at the mall, and her boyfriend had told her he didn't want to see her anymore. All of this had happened in the space of a week, and frankly she was still reeling from the fallout of that one ill-advised moment of recklessness.

She hadn't wanted to steal that diamond ring, but somehow it had simply found its way into her pocket, and it had taken until the moment she walked out of the store and the alarm had started ringing for her to realize what she had done.

She had pinched stuff before, of course, but mostly low-value items. Candy bars, mainly. And fortunately she had never gotten into real trouble over it. But this time was different. This time she would probably be convicted and would get an actual criminal record, which would complicate her life in a myriad of ways.

Her parents weren't angry with her, but they were sad, which was even worse. Her mom had cried on the phone last night, and it was all because of what she had done, which made her feel terrible.

So she had called Vanessa, her shrink-in-training friend, who had given her those two pieces of advice. On the credit side of the ledger she had already found a new apartment. On the debit side, her pet rat Footsie had run away from home. She didn't blame him. He was a very sensitive rat and had probably sensed her mood and decided he couldn't cope. Her first priority right now was finding a job, so she could make rent and didn't have to borrow from her parents or her sister, and then to put up flyers to find Footsie and induce him to come home.

So when she walked past the flower shop and she heard a couple discussing the frankly rude behavior of one of the salespersons and telling each other that 'Barnaby should get a professional salesperson instead of that harridan he's got serving his customers now,' she had suddenly decided to take her future into her own hands and had walked into the store.

And much to her surprise, the owner had hired her on the spot! She didn't know why, since she didn't have any references, but then he hadn't asked for any either. He hadn't even asked for her resume, which was meager to say the least. He had simply heard her out, nodded and said, "When can you start?"

It was like a miracle. Like something from a Hallmark movie, which her mom liked a lot and had always forced the rest of the family to watch with her.

And so it was a jubilant Sarah who practically skipped along the street, feeling better than she had felt in a long time. Now if only she would be able to keep her hands to herself and not steal one of Barnaby's blossoms, things just might be fine.

It was at this moment that her phone rang. It was her mom.

"Mom, I've got some great news!" she caroled into the device.

"Oh, that's so great, honey. Listen, a policewoman has been trying to reach you. Can you give her a call? Here's the number." And she rattled off the number.

Which is when her good mood crashed down to earth again and she was reminded of the great dark cloud that hung over her future. What if Barnaby found out about the arrest? He'd probably fire her just as fast as he'd hired her.

Realizing that her future hung by a thread, she called the number Mom had given her. The woman was actually very kind. She said her name was Odelia Kingsley, and she wondered if she could have a word with her as soon as possible.

And so she had hurried home to meet with this Mrs. Kingsley person, wondering what she would have to say that was so important.

When she arrived, she was surprised to find that the woman was accompanied by two cats—a fat orange one and a small fluffy one—and her very own Footsie!

"Oh, you found him!" she cried, clasping her hands together. "I thought I lost him." She knelt down next to her pet rat and hugged him close. "Oh, Footsie. Why did you run away?"

"He was in our backyard," said Mrs. Kingsley. "He's been staying with us, until I discovered that he actually belonged to someone."

Sarah had put up a post on her Facebook when Footsie disappeared, but so far no one had responded. Until now.

"Did you see my Facebook post?" she asked therefore.

Mrs. Kingsley hesitated for a moment, then nodded. "Absolutely. That's how I found you, Sarah. Facebook."

"Oh, I'm so happy he's back! Footsie!"

The rat squealed, as he often did when he was either happy or excited or someone had stepped on his tail.

"I don't know why my mom said you're a policewoman," said Sarah. "Or are you with the police?"

"I'm a reporter with the *Hampton Cove Gazette*," said Odelia. "But I'm also a part-time civilian consultant with the police. Which is how I learned that you were recently arrested for shoplifting."

Sarah quickly sobered. "I was," she admitted quietly.

"Look, the thing is that my uncle is the chief of police," said Odelia. "So I was thinking that maybe I could put in a good word for you. And also…" She bit her lip for a moment. "I don't know how to put this without making it sound as if I'm trying to interfere, Sarah, but…"

"Yes?" she asked.

"I talked to my editor, and he told me about this great therapist he knows. And so I was thinking that if you would commit to therapy to deal with your issue, that would go a long way to convincing my uncle that maybe the best place for you isn't in prison, you know."

Sarah stared at the woman, and felt herself tear up. "You would do that for me?"

Odelia smiled. "I'm glad you don't think I'm imposing."

"Are you nuts? I've been looking for a therapist to help me get rid of this thing. Only…" Her mood sank. "I don't have a lot of money. And therapy is expensive. Though I was just hired by Barnaby's Blossoms as a salesperson, so…"

"I'm sure we can come to some kind of an arrangement with the therapist to treat you for a reduced fee."

She brought her hands to her mouth, and blinked away tears once more. "I don't know what's going on today," she said. "First I found a job, then Footsie came back, and now the therapist. This is so amazing."

"It's Footsie," said Odelia with a smile. "If he hadn't shown up at my place, I wouldn't have started looking for his owner, and then I wouldn't have found out about… the other stuff."

"I'm so embarrassed about what I did," said Sarah. "And to be perfectly honest, I don't know what got into me. One moment I was browsing, you know. Looking at rings and stuff, since my boyfriend had dropped some heavy hints about getting married. And the next I was walking out of the store with a diamond ring in my pocket."

"It's a compulsion," said Odelia. "Tough to beat without professional help. Which is what we're going to get you, Sarah."

She couldn't help herself, but the next moment she was hugging this woman she had never met before. But far from being a stranger, she had the distinct impression that Odelia Kingsley was a dear, dear friend.

CHAPTER 14

Dooley looked a little confused when we were back in the car and on our way home. Finally he asked, "So why isn't Footsie coming back with us?"

"Because Footsie ran away from home to find help for his human," Odelia explained. "And now that he's fulfilled his mission and he's been reunited with Sarah, there's no reason for him to stay with us anymore."

"Oh," said Dooley. "But... I like Footsie. I thought he was going to stay with us for two weeks. That's what Max said."

"That was before he told us that his real reason for wanting to stay with us was to save his human's life," I explained. Dooley stared at me, wide-eyed and much dismayed. "Sarah's life is in danger? But Max, we have to go back and save her!"

"It's not in *danger* danger," I said. "But it is in danger of going off the rails if she doesn't get help for this habit of hers of stealing stuff that doesn't belong to her."

"Yes, that's not a good habit," Dooley agreed, starting to see the picture. "So what's going to happen now?"

"Now she's going to get the help she needs," said Odelia. "And then let's hope she doesn't get arrested again."

"Are you going to talk to the jeweler and convince him to drop the charges?" I asked.

Odelia nodded. "That's the plan, yes. Otherwise there isn't a whole lot my uncle can do."

"You're such a brave soul, Odelia," said Dooley, moved to tears again. It was clearly a very teary day. Between Footsie and Sarah and Dooley, a lot of tears had been shed already.

"Okay, so now there's something you have to explain to me," said Odelia. "What's all this about Harriet changing her name to Harry?"

"Oh, that," I said. "It's just one of those things. Well, you know Harriet. When she gets a bee in her bonnet…"

"Yes, but are we supposed to call her Harry from now on or what?"

"I think it's best if you do," I suggested. "If you don't she might get upset."

"So… she's going to be a male from now on?"

"Yes, she identifies as a male," I said. "At least for the time being. Until she realizes that even as a male she still won't be a star any time soon."

"It's such a pity, isn't it?" said Dooley. "Harriet is so talented, and still she's not in Vegas getting that residency she wants so badly."

I had to smile at that, and so did Odelia. "Harriet—or Harry—isn't getting a Vegas residency because nobody knows about her, Dooley. Only the top talent gets that kind of offer, and only after they've already had a long and successful career. For now Harry is only famous in Hampton Cove Park, and even then she gets more shoes thrown at her head than applause, which isn't a good sign."

"She's hugely talented, though," said Dooley. "When she opens her mouth to sing I get goosebumps."

"I also get goosebumps," I said. "But not in a good way."

We had arrived home, and Odelia was determined to look in on our new guests and see how they were settling in. Turns out Aunt Aurelie was knitting a sweater seated next to the hospital bed, keeping a close eye on her daughter all the while.

"Any sign of Bruno?" Odelia whispered.

"None," said Aunt Aurelie. "And I hope it stays that way!"

"I've talked to my uncle, and he's already put out an alert to look for your ex-husband," Odelia said.

"The Hampton Keys police did that," said Aunt Aurelie.

"I know. But it doesn't hurt if our local police are also on high alert, just in case he gets wise to the fact that you've moved here."

Aunt Aurelie stiffened. "I hope he won't find out."

"I hope so, too. But we have to be prepared for every possible contingency. Someone at the hospital might blab. You never know. So let's be vigilant and make sure that man doesn't come anywhere near Ella, shall we?"

Aunt Aurelie smiled. "I don't know how to thank you, Odelia. If it wasn't for you, I don't know what I would have done."

"At some point he will be caught, and he will go back to jail," Odelia assured her uncle's sister-in-law and placed a hand on her arm and gave it a comforting squeeze.

"Now that Footsie is gone, who's going to bite the bad man when he gets here, Max?" asked Dooley.

"There will be no biting, Dooley," I said. "When Aunt Aurelie's ex-husband gets here—if he gets here—we'll simply alert Odelia and Chase and they will handle him."

"Oh," he said, and sounded a little disappointed. "I was hoping we'd tackle him together, Max. The four of us? I mean, this man did something truly horrible, and he needs to be punished."

"I know, and he will be punished, but not by us."

I noticed how Aunt Aurelie was following our conversation intently. "They seem to be talking to each other," she said finally. "Your cats, I mean."

"Yeah, they talk all the time," said Odelia. "They're big talkers, all of them."

"So funny," murmured Aunt Aurelie, and returned to her knitting.

We snuck out of the house through the pet flap and found Harry and Brutus lounging on the patio, taking in some sun.

"And? How was it?" asked Brutus. Then he glanced around. "And where is Footsie?"

"Footsie left us," said Dooley sadly, causing both Harry and Brutus to do a double take.

"He's dead? But how!" Brutus cried.

"Oh, he's not dead," said Dooley. "But he's going to stay with his human from now on. She's not in prison, you see. And she found a job. And Odelia is going to arrange a therapist so she can stop stealing stuff. It was all very emotional. She was crying a lot, and Footsie was crying a lot."

"And you were crying a lot," I said with a smile.

Dooley grinned a sheepish grin. "I did cry a lot."

"Okay, so we're minus one rat again?" asked Harry.

I noticed how she had changed her voice, and she also looked a little different. It was the way she was carrying herself, with a certain swagger, as if she had been watching too many John Wayne movies.

"Harry, what's wrong with your voice?" asked Dooley.

"My voice? What about my voice?" said Harry, still speaking in a low voice. It took her a lot of effort, I could tell, but she was trying to make it work for her.

"If you strain your voice like that you might damage your vocal cords," Brutus pointed out. "And then you won't be able to sing your solos anymore."

This gave Harry pause. She blinked. "I hadn't thought of that," she said, in her usual melodious voice.

"Brutus is right," I said. "If you keep talking like that you're putting a lot of strain on your vocal cords."

"God, why is it so hard to become a global superstar!"

"If it was easy, everybody would be a global superstar," Brutus pointed out. "But then who would be the audience?"

This gave us all food for thought and I stared at Brutus appreciatively. I had never figured him for a deep thinker, but this was the stuff of philosophers.

"I mean, a global superstar needs a global audience," said Brutus, having noticed our looks of approval. "So if there are eight billion superstars in the world, who's going to listen to them? It's impossible when you think about it."

"It is impossible," I agreed.

"I don't care," said Harry, tilting her head in a very unmanly manner. "I'm going to be a superstar if it kills me."

"I hope not," Brutus murmured, looking much alarmed.

"It's just a figure of speech," Harry hastened to add.

"Good," said Brutus emphatically. "Cause I don't want to lose you, tootsie roll. After all, you are my superstar."

"Oh, sugar bun."

"Oh, honey bunch."

"Oh, pooh bear!"

After this had gone on for a while, they disappeared into the rose bushes at the bottom of the garden, and Dooley and I finally had some peace again.

For a moment we simply lay there, basking in the sun. Then Dooley said, "So maybe Footsie can come and stay with us from time to time?"

"Of course," I assured him. "He can stay with us any time."

"Oh, goodie," said Dooley, well pleased. "We can have a sleepover." Then he thought some more. "Okay, so maybe once Aunt Aurelie's daughter is out of a coma." He thought some more. "And once her ex-husband is in prison again."

"Great idea, Dooley," I murmured, and nodded off. It's possible he talked some more, but the soporific force is strong in me, and whatever comments he had to make would have to wait until such time as I woke up again.

CHAPTER 15

It didn't take Ahmad long to get back to Ezra with a solid proposition. Not only had he found a wife for him, but the wife also had a baby, so that meant he'd hit two birds with one stone, or at least a bird and a hatchling. They had arranged for Ahmad to drop by later that night to introduce the bird—or rather the woman—so Ezra could get acquainted with his future wife and get started on the proceedings.

"I'm nervous," he confessed to Jake, who once again was devouring his favorite comic. "It's not every day that you meet your future wife and your future child, after all. What if she doesn't like me?"

"You're paying her to like you," Jake reminded him. "So you should be all right."

"The problem is: how am I going to pay her?" he said, broaching another topic that had been vexing him to a great extent. "I don't have any money."

"You're going to write her an IOU and then once you get that money from your inheritance you can pay her." He looked up from his perusal of the adventures of the fabulous

Hump, who could slay his enemies with a swing of his formidable bump. Ezra wished he could do the same thing. Life was so easy if you were a superhero. "You better get all this in writing, so there are no misunderstandings."

"I know," he said, sinking deeper into the couch, and wishing this would all just go away. He had always been nervous around women, especially women he liked. And now he was going to meet his wife. Well, not his actual wife, of course, but still. He probably would have to spend time with her, and at the very least he would have to visit the lawyer with her and the baby, and put on a display of marital harmony, which was hard enough when you actually knew and liked the person—in other words when she was your actual wife. But this woman was a stranger. Probably one of Ahmad's many cousins. He pictured a dark-haired woman with Ahmad's coarse features and pockmarked face and winced.

"Do you think we'll have to kiss?"

"Why would you have to kiss?" asked Jake without looking up. "She's not your actual wife, you doofus. It's all fake."

"Yeah, I know, but maybe the lawyer will want to make sure we're husband and wife, and he'll want us to prove it. Ask us to make out in front of him."

"You're an idiot," said Jake with a chuckle.

Idiot or not, he'd better get all that in writing as well. So he picked up his phone, where he had been working on a first draft of a contract between himself and his 'wife' and added the phrase, 'There will be kissing only when and if absolutely necessary.' He thought for a moment and added, 'No tongues.'

He imagined kissing Ahmad and shivered. What a cruel, cruel world this was. Only that morning he had met the girl of his dreams. But before he had a chance to talk to her, she had been whisked away by that most devious of modern inventions: the elevator.

Not that he had known what to say to her. In actual fact he probably would have been as tongue-tied as ever, and she would have simply written him off as a halfwit and gone on her way. So the end result would have been the same.

But still. How glorious if he had spoken, and she would have smiled and flicked that golden hair across her shoulder. The amazing things he would have told her—if only he had managed to cross the threshold of this infernal timidity.

The image of Ahmad drifted in front of his mind's eye again, erasing that of the golden-haired goddess. He winced once more and took out his phone and put the bit about the tongues in bold. He was willing to make a lot of sacrifices to adhere to his late aunt's wishes, but there were limits to what he was prepared to do.

He snatched the bong from the coffee table and decided to settle his nerves by inhaling some of that wonderful weed. And he was just in the process of lighting the bong when a glint caught his eye. It had briefly reflected on the opposite wall, and when he looked over, suddenly he found himself face to face with a man dressed in a trench coat. He stared at the man and the man stared back at him, neither of them moving. Then the man gave him a two-fingered salute and was gone.

"Jake!" he cried, rocketing up from the couch and moving over to the window. "There was a man!"

"Mh?" said Jake, without much excitement.

"A man! On the fire escape! Just now!"

He had reached the window and could see the man clambering down the rickety metal ladder that led to the street below.

"Jesus Christ," he said, bringing a fist to his brow. "It must be the detective the lawyer was talking about. The one who was going to make sure we led the life of the upstanding citizen! And I was just about to take a hit from that bong!"

"Good thing you didn't," Jake murmured.

He swallowed a couple of times. "Maybe we shouldn't be meeting my wife here," he said. "What if the detective is lurking across the street with a pair of binoculars? Or one of those cameras that can see the pimple on your nose from a distance of ten miles? They might even have planted listening devices in the apartment! We could be bugged!"

"We're not bugged," said Jake. He looked up with a frown. "Are we?"

"We could be bugged," said Ezra as he followed the man with a kindling eye. He got into a dark sedan that was parked across the street, but the car wasn't moving. Clearly they were staking out the building!

"Let's ask Franklin to give the room a sweep," Jake suggested. Animation had returned to his form. This whole being bugged thing was having an electrifying effect on him.

"Your NYPD buddy?"

"Uh-huh. I'm sure he knows how to take care of that."

"But what if we're bugged and we do get rid of the bugs? They'll know that we…" He stopped abruptly, realizing that if they were bugged these bozos had heard every word! So he gestured for his friend to follow him into the bathroom.

Jake did as he was told, and once they were in the tiny bathroom, Ezra opened the taps and whispered, "If we're bugged and then suddenly we get rid of the bugs they'll report back to the lawyer that we're not playing by the rules!"

"If we're bugged they will also have heard our conversation about renting a wife and her baby," Jake pointed out.

Ezra's blood ran cold as the realization hit him like a steamroller. "Jesus Christ," he repeated. "This is worse than I thought!"

"Listen, if we were bugged they wouldn't be staking out

the place," said Jake. "I mean, if they knew you were about to meet your fake wife they would have shut us down already. This lawyer fellow would be on the phone to fire you from the program. The fact that he hasn't means they don't have a clue."

"Yeah, you're right," said Ezra. It was some consolation. But still. If they were staking out the place, they would see his future fake wife walk in along with Ahmad, and wonder what the deal was. He relayed his concerns to his friend.

"Relax, bro," said Jake. "They don't have a clue. So what if this lady walks in here tonight? She's your wife! She has every right to walk into the apartment. And so what if Ahmad is also present at the scene? You're allowed to meet friends, aren't you? You've got nothing to worry about."

"You think?"

"I'm absolutely sure of it." He started to remove himself from the scene. "But I wouldn't touch that bong again if I were you. In fact maybe we better get rid of it altogether, along with the booze and the weed and all the rest of it."

Ezra closed his eyes and thunked his head against the doorjamb. "Why did I ever say yes to this thing?"

"Just think of the money, bro."

And so he did think of the money. Though he sincerely hoped it would all be worth it in the end. "Imagine if Aunt Emily leaves me a thousand bucks for my trouble," he said.

"Then you pay the lady a thousand bucks and count yourself lucky that you went through the experience. And who knows? Maybe you'll like her and you'll marry her for real."

"Yeah, right," he scoffed.

CHAPTER 16

The moment of truth duly came, and by then Ezra was so nervous he was sweating bullets. Under normal circumstances he would have smoked some weed to settle his nerves but pursuant to their new policy of getting rid of their stash Jake had simply gathered everything up and dumped it down the garbage chute.

"Got rid of the evidence," he said, looking very pleased with himself. "Let them pin it on us now, huh!"

Eight o'clock on the dot, the buzzer buzzed and Jake buzzed Ahmad and Ezra's new wife into the building. Pacing the apartment like a caged tiger, Ezra had a good mind to call the whole thing off right then and there, but Jake was there to remind him of all of that moola that awaited him on the other side of this torment.

And so in a bid to calm down, he downed about a pound of chocolate, stuffing his face like a maniac, and only calmed down when he was starting to feel sick. Chocolate often had that effect on him.

By the time their guests arrived on their floor, he felt like throwing up. With a supreme effort he managed to pull himself together, and then the door swung open and an ebullient Ahmad walked in, displaying his usual swagger, followed by... the most beautiful girl in the world.

As Ezra stood staring at the nymph he'd fallen head over heels in love with that morning, he had a vague notion that his jaw was dangling a couple of inches below the rest of his face, but then suddenly another bout of nausea came over him and he had to run to the bathroom to throw up.

* * *

IT'S OFTEN hard for a girl to know what effect she has on the other sex. In Sylvie's case this was compounded by the fact that she had, from a young age, felt extremely self-conscious about her appearance. Her mom never stopped pointing out to her that she was too chubby and should limit her calorie intake, which hadn't helped her self-esteem, of which she had very little. But this was actually the very first time that a man had vomited within seconds of meeting her.

Ahmad seemed to think the whole thing hilarious, and so did the roommate, but Sylvie wasn't of the same opinion. In fact it was all she could do not to bolt right then and there. The idea of being a wife for hire was ridiculous to begin with, of course, but then if she wanted to supplement her income there weren't a lot of options available to her. She could take a second job, but that wasn't feasible in this case since she had Julie to think about. The product of an ill-fated affair, the little girl was the apple of her eye, but also the bane of her existence since it limited the possibilities for a second job to a great extent. During the day her parents took care of Julie, but she couldn't very well ask her mom and dad to babysit her in the evenings as well. That would stretch the boundaries of propriety to the breaking point. Already her mom was complaining that she and Dad had had to put their plans on hold and wouldn't be able to do so indefinitely. Dad hadn't quite pictured his early retirement as consisting of a long string of babysitting duties, and was starting to insist more and more that she find some other arrangement. The cruise line brochures scattered around the house and the brochures for trips to Europe were a very unsubtle reminder to Sylvie that this situation couldn't go on indefinitely.

And so when Ahmad had called her out of the blue and had suggested she meet this guy Ezra Burns, she had jumped at the chance. Even though it all seemed a little iffy, if the money was as good as Ahmad said it was, she might be able to afford an actual babysitter, or even regular childcare.

"Okay, so this is Sylvie Mitchell," said Ahmad, once Ezra had returned to the land of the living. He looked awfully pale, Sylvie thought, and she actually felt for the guy. "And this is Ezra Burns, Sylvie. Your new husband." He grinned widely as he said this, obviously having a ball.

Ezra produced a sickly smile and shook her hand. His felt cold and clammy. "I'm so sorry about this," he said. "I had a bad reaction."

"I can tell," she said a little stiffly.

His eyes widened as he correctly interpreted her words. "Not to you! I ate a ton of chocolate before you arrived, and sometimes it makes me sick—literally."

She didn't know whether to believe him or not, but when his roommate nodded seriously, she figured she'd give it another couple of minutes before she bailed. She had known Ahmad for years, and if he said this Ezra guy was on the level, maybe he was. She was still going to tread carefully, though. She had Julie to think about, after all.

"We met this morning, didn't we?" said Ezra now.

"We did?"

"Downtown? I had just met this lawyer representing my Aunt Emily, and you were going up."

She vaguely remembered some guy giving her weird looks, and wondered if this was him. It probably was, since there weren't a lot of guys with blue hair and a pink goatee. If it had indeed been Ezra, it didn't exactly endear him to her.

"It's possible," she said, hedging her bets.

"Oh, it was you," he said, nodding fervently. "I never forget a face, and definitely not yours." He'd gripped her hand and was holding onto it for dear life. She actually had to yank it away from him and gave him a polite smile.

"So tell me about this proposal," she said.

"It's a gem," said Ahmad, not for the first time. "An absolute gem. Listen to this. His aunt was some kind of temperance and clean living freak, and only wanted to leave her substantial fortune to the nephews who could prove they're married with a kid and living the life of the upstanding citizen within a year. That means no booze, no weed, no nothing. And also, they have to hold down a regular paying job. Which means our friend Ezra here has to turn his life around three hundred and sixty degrees."

"One hundred and eighty," said Sylvie. "If he turned his life around three hundred and sixty degrees he'd be back where he started from."

"See? Didn't I tell you she's brilliant?"

Sylvie gave him a weak smile. "So you don't have a job?" she asked Ezra.

"I've got a job, but the lawyer told me Aunt Emily didn't consider being a waiter an actual job. And also Jake's uncle doesn't believe in fixed contracts."

"You work for your roommate's uncle?"

"Uh-huh. That's right."

"And you're not married, no kids, and you like to drink and smoke weed?"

"Not just weed," said Jake with a guffaw.

Oh, God. This was a nightmare. The guy was obviously

some kind of idiot slacker, and so was his roommate. The urge to run became stronger by the second. Ahmad must have noticed her displeasure, for he intervened. "He recently gave up drinking, though, didn't you, Ezra? And smoking?"

"I did! I'm all about clean living from now on."

"And he's got a plan about the job part," Ahmad prompted.

"Absolutely," Ezra confirmed. He was still staring at her like some kind of weirdo stalker, and Sylvie was getting the creeps. "I've got a plan."

Oh, boy. "So where do I fit into that plan?"

"Well, like Ahmad probably told you I need to be married with a kid, and so Jake figured I might as well… you know."

"Rent a wife," said Jake proudly.

"And a baby," said Ezra with a sickly grin. The way he said it made Sylvie's blood run cold. But when she was about to make for the exit and escape with her life, he quickly added, "I'm sorry. That came out wrong. What I meant to say was that I need to establish myself in the eyes of the executor of the estate as an upstanding family man, which means married with kids—or kid. And even though I'm sure in due course I will be married with children, I only have one year. So Ahmad suggested… Well, he thought… I mean, he figured…"

"How much?" she asked coldly.

He blinked at the sudden vehemence of her stare. "How much?"

"How much are you going to pay me for this charade, and what exactly does it entail—and how long will it take?"

"The contract!" Jake hissed. "Show her the contract."

And so Ezra produced a contract he'd drawn up. It stipulated a number she could live with, though the time frame wasn't convenient. "I can't commit to this for one year," she said. "That's way too long."

"Okay, so what about six months?"

"Make it three and I'm yours." She immediately reddened when she realized what she was saying. "I mean—I'll play your fake wife for three months."

"And you'll throw in the baby?" asked Jake. But when she gave him an icy look, he quickly piped down.

"Three months," she said. "Take it or leave it."

Ezra said he had to confer with his roommate, and for a moment the two men stood to one side and carried on a whispered conversation. Finally they returned and Ezra held up his hand. "It's a deal," he announced solemnly.

In spite of her misgivings, she shook hands on it.

Somehow she wondered if she had just made the biggest mistake of her life. Then again, it couldn't be bigger than the mistake she had made when she got involved with Julie's dad. Though at least something good had come from that.

CHAPTER 17

"I miss Footsie," said Dooley. "I didn't think I would, but I do, Max."

"I also miss him, Dooley," I said. To some extent, of course. I mean, Footsie was a rat, and how badly can one ever miss a rat when he's no longer in one's presence? Not that much! Though I had to admit I was wrong about Footsie. I had intuitively understood he had entered our home under false pretenses, and that he had some hidden agenda, but I had never expected that his hidden agenda wasn't as nefarious as I had thought. In fact it had been both benign and touching to a degree. All he wanted to do was help out his human who had found herself in a pickle. Now if that didn't touch the heart, I didn't know what would.

"I don't miss him," said Brutus, who had never been a great proponent of our rat visitor. "I think it's good that he's back where he belongs. With this Sarah person."

"Is it true that she stole a big diamond ring, Max?" asked Dooley.

"That's what she says," I said.

"I'm sure it's all some kind of big mistake," said Harry.

"I'm sure she never actually intended to steal that ring but it somehow dropped into her pocket. It happens. You bump into a display with all kinds of neat trinkets and baubles, and one drops into your pocket. It could have happened to anyone, so I really don't see why Uncle Alec and that jeweler would be so hard on the poor girl."

"At least she probably won't steal any flowers," said Brutus. "Or," he quickly added when Harry gave him a strange look, "accidentally bump into a display of flowers and have them fall into her pocket."

"Where is Odelia going to find a shrink, though?" said Dooley. "Shrinks don't grow on trees, you know."

"Dan knows a shrink," I reminded him.

"Dan is probably seeing a shrink himself," said Harry. "After having been a reporter for over forty years he probably needs one, too." When we all looked at her in a non-comprehending way, she elaborated, "Dan has been exposed to the scum of the earth on a daily basis his entire life. That kind of thing leaves a mark on a person, you guys. A major mark. And so it wouldn't surprise me if he didn't see a shrink on the side. Or even out in the open, since shrinking is all the rage right now. Even Indiana Jones is playing a shrink on television these days."

It was true. Indiana Jones had gone from swinging from the vines in the jungle and fighting the Nazis to shrinking people. Though he did have some experience at one point during his adventures with shrunken heads if memory served.

The four of us were in our home, keeping a close eye on Ella, who was still in a coma, and her mother Aunt Aurelie who was still knitting something that could be a sweater, but it could have been anything, really. She had explained to Odelia how she had taken up knitting again after a hiatus of thirty years, and how she was taking an online course. I sincerely hoped she wouldn't knit the four of us some matching outfits. I think I speak for all cats everywhere when I say we do not like to wear anything close to our skin except our very own fur!

Uncle Alec had dropped by to look in on his niece Ella, and his other niece Odelia had taken the opportunity to consult with him about Sarah Mitchell's fate.

"There isn't a lot I can do, I'm afraid," said Uncle Alec. "Ebenezer and Rebecca Scrum pressed charges, and so there will be consequences for what Sarah did. And even if I could get the Scrums to drop those charges, it's not up to them but up to the DA whether the case goes to court or not. He can decide to prosecute whether the Scrums change their minds or not. Though if they do decide to withdraw their complaint it might get the DA to reconsider, figuring he doesn't have a case anymore. In Sarah's defense, she doesn't have a criminal record. But she was arrested on those previous occasions, so the DA might want to proceed, figuring she's gone too far this time. But whatever he decides, I think your idea of the shrink is a great one. It'll go over really well with the judge."

"She also found a job," said Odelia. "So she's trying to work past her issues and turn her life around."

Uncle Alec grinned as he took a sip from his coffee. "And you got all of this from a pet rat, is that correct?"

"Yeah, Footsie. He had heard that Max is this famous detective, and decided to take his chances and come and pay him a visit. But since he didn't know what to expect, he decided to befriend the natives first." She pointed to the four of us for some reason, causing us to look up in alarm.

"The natives?" asked Harry. "What does she mean by that?"

"No idea," said Brutus.

"I think she means we're native to this part of Harrington

Street," I said. "And also to Hampton Cove, of course. So Footsie figured that if he befriended us, we might be willing to help Sarah."

"Which we did," said Dooley. "So it all worked out for the best. Yay Footsie!"

"Yeah, yay Footsie," Brutus grumbled, though it didn't sound quite as enthusiastic as Dooley's endorsement of Sarah's pet rat.

"Okay, so if you want I'll have a word with the Scrums," Uncle Alec suggested. "And ask them if they won't consider dropping the complaint. Then it's up to the DA whether the case goes to court or not." When Odelia gave him a hug, he added, "I'm not making any guarantees, mind you. Ebenezer Scrum is a tough nut. And he's been robbed before so he's not likely to go easy on any shoplifters after the experience he's had."

"Maybe I should have a word with him?" Odelia suggested.

"Let me have a crack at him first," said her uncle. "And then if he persists, you can talk to him and try your charms on him."

"My very limited charms," said Odelia.

Her husband had walked in, and when he heard that statement, he firmly protested. "You're just about the most charming woman I know, babe. So don't sell yourself short. If you can't persuade this jeweler to play ball, I don't know who could."

"Thanks, babe," she said warmly, and pressed a kiss to his cheek.

Aunt Aurelie looked up from her knitting and smiled. "You're such a lovely couple," she said. "It's a pity it's taken this tragedy for us to get to know each other."

"Isn't that usually the case?" said Uncle Alec as he scratched his scalp. He walked over to his niece, whose face was still as white as the sheets she was wrapped in, and gave a wistful sigh. "What's it going to take for her to wake up again?"

"Maybe we should tickle her feet?" Dooley suggested. "If she's ticklish that might do the trick?"

"I doubt it," I said.

"Yeah, don't tickle her feet," said Brutus. "Or Aunt Aurelie might decide to tickle you, and not in a good way either."

I hadn't realized until now that there is a good way and a bad way to tickle people, but I could see what he meant. From the way Aunt Aurelie had taken position next to her daughter's bed like a sentry, it was clear she would fight like a lion if anyone came close to Ella, even if it was simply to tickle her footsies.

Our very own Grace chose that moment to emerge on the scene. She glanced around, clearly not fully awake yet. She was clutching a teddy bear in one hand and rubbing her eyes with the other. When she saw the big hospital bed and the strange woman sitting next to it, she asked, "What's going on? And what's with the bed and that woman over there?" And so we explained to her in brief terms the story of Ella and her coma. It seemed to hit the little girl pretty hard. "I can't believe any father would do something like that to his daughter," she admitted. "That's just terrible."

"It is terrible," I agreed. "But we don't know if it was really her father who was responsible. It could have been anyone."

"I hope so," she said. "Cause if it was her dad, that would be horrible."

She had toddled over to her own dad, who promptly picked her up and sat her on his brawny arm with no effort at all.

"How long are they going to stay?" asked Grace, looking down on the bed from her new higher vantage point.

"Until she wakes up, I guess," I said. "Or until they catch the culprit and arrest him and lock him up."

"So… what happened to your couch?" she asked, looking around.

"It's gone," said Dooley sadly. "We'll have to do without it for the time being."

"Oh, that's not very nice," said Grace, who clearly felt for us. But then her face cleared. "You could always find a new favorite spot on top of that bed. It looks very soft and very cozy."

We exchanged uncertain glances. "I don't know if we're allowed to lie on that bed," said Harry frankly. "And also, I think if we did jump up, Aunt Aurelie would have our hides for breakfast."

"She'd probably come after us with those knitting needles," said Brutus.

"I think what you should do is organize a sit-in," Grace suggested.

"What's a sit-in?" asked Dooley.

"It's a protest where you decline to move from a certain position until your demands are met," Grace explained. "In this case the return of your couch. Cats have rights too, you know. And also: I love that couch. It's my favorite place in the house."

"Look, you guys," I said, when approving murmurs started to emerge from my friends. "The couch isn't gone. It's in storage for the time being, and as soon as Ella wakes up, it will return. So let's not make a big deal out of this, shall we? Things are difficult enough for Odelia and Chase as it is. Let's not add to their worries."

"The couch is in the garden house," Brutus explained to Grace. "Where it will probably start to mold and rot and attract all kinds of vermin. By the time Ella comes out of her coma, which could be any time between today and ten years from now, it will be an absolute mess."

Grace's expression had gradually darkened as Brutus's harangue went on. "We have to save that couch!" she said now. "It's our couch and if we don't do something, it will be too late."

"What vermin will attack our couch, Max?" asked Dooley.

"Oh, I imagine a family of mice might take residence inside that couch," Harry answered in my stead. "Mice are very partial to the stuffing that's inside a couch, you know. And of course cockroaches, spiders, black beetles, worms… Pretty soon that couch will get little feet and start to walk away on its own." She grinned at her own imagination, but Dooley wasn't laughing. In fact he looked closer to tears than he had been when the departure of our couch had been announced.

"Grace is right!" he cried. "We have to save our couch before it's too late!"

"Can I make a suggestion?" asked Grace. "Let's call this Operation Couch, and call in the assistance of a pro."

"What pro?" I asked.

"Gran, of course! She's the only one in this family crazy enough to go against the edicts as laid down by the likes of Odelia and Chase."

"Odelia and Chase are your parents," I reminded her.

"Which doesn't mean I have to agree with them," the little girl shot back. "No, I say we recruit Gran and task her with the secret mission of saving our favorite couch." She shook a pudgy fist. "It's important to take a stance, you guys!"

"Oh, dear," I said.

CHAPTER 18

Barnaby had never actually worked with staff before, so when Sarah arrived to take up her first shift, he was a little less organized than he would have liked. For one thing he had to train her and show her the ropes, and delegate and all of that stuff. And of course he had to pay her a salary, which would make things a little more complicated on the back end as well. But even though it was going to mean a major headache in many ways, the moment she walked into Barnaby's Blossoms, looking like a fresh blossom herself, all of his qualms were immediately forgotten, and he counted himself lucky that she would have simply entered his life like that—like something from his most fervent and cherished dream.

"So what do you want me to do, Mr. Blossom?" she asked as she stood before him, a blush mantling her cheeks and looking a little nervous herself. Which wasn't surprising, since it was her first day in a new job.

"Um... have you ever worked in a flower shop before?" he asked, not being able to take his eyes off her, which was highly inappropriate behavior he knew, since he was now effectively her boss and she was his employee.

"Not really," she admitted. "But I have bought flowers, and I have handled them. You cut off the stems and put them in a vase. That much I know." She laughed what could only be described as a tinkling laugh, and his insides melted. For a moment so did his brain, but then he managed to pull himself together, and started teaching her the basics of the job that he had been involved in since he had launched Barnaby's Blossoms. The store hadn't been all that successful at first, but gradually more and more customers had found their way to the small shop, and when things had really started going well for him, that's when he had asked his mom to step in and give him a hand. It wasn't perhaps the best idea he ever had, but looking back she had been instrumental in the success of the store. She might not be the best person to put in front of the customers—in fact he had to keep her away from them if he wanted the store to keep attracting people—but she did so many other little jobs around the place she was basically unmissable. A fact she was well aware of, and that she never hesitated to rub in his face.

She came walking out of the workshop now, carrying one of the large centerpieces the Mayor had ordered. When she saw Sarah she halted her steps. "Customers shouldn't be behind the counter," she snapped, not all that friendly.

"Oh, but I'm not a customer," Sarah assured the woman. "I'm the new salesperson Barnaby hired."

"Salesperson? What are you talking about?"

Barnaby probably should have told his mom about Sarah, but he had figured she wouldn't agree, and anyway, it was his business, and so it was his decision. Nothing to do with her. But of course that wasn't how she saw things.

Sarah held out a slender hand. "I'm Sarah Mitchell. Pleased to meet you."

But Mom wasn't going to allow herself to be won over so quickly. "We don't need no salespeople. I'm here and that's all the help my son needs."

"Oh, so you're Mr. Blossom's mom?" said Sarah with a smile. "It's so nice to meet you. So are you responsible for these gorgeous flower arrangements?"

Mom's stern expression didn't waver for even one second. She had crossed her arms in front of her chest and was studying Sarah from beneath lowered eyelids. She looked a little bit like a toad now, Barnaby thought, studying a big fat fly.

"Like I said, we don't need no stinking salespeople," she repeated. "So why don't you buzz off, little lady?"

Sarah's confused look turned to Barnaby, who decided to intervene. "Mom, I've hired Sarah because we urgently need someone behind the counter. I can't keep doing everything myself. Create the arrangements, keep up with the suppliers, and take care of the customers. So I've decided it's time to expand. The store is doing very well, so we can definitely afford it. And with Sarah here I'm sure we will enter a new phase of expansion, which is good for all of us." It was the sales pitch he had been practicing over and over again last night, and which he hoped would go over well. He desperately wanted his mom and Sarah to get along.

"Mh," said his mom, still studying the girl as if she was about to devour her whole, chew her up and spit out her mangled remains. "It's true that we have been doing well," she admitted reluctantly. "And that we can probably use a helping hand. So what are your references, Miss Mitchell?"

"I've worked at the toy store at the mall," said Sarah, a little timidly. Clearly she was as intimidated by Barnaby's mom as he himself often was.

"The mall!" said his mom, as if it was the worst thing Sarah could have said.

"It was just a couple of months," Sarah hastened to say. "And I didn't like it all that much, since I'm not into toys myself, so I didn't really have a feel for the product? But I love flowers, and I always wanted to work in a flower shop. It has been my lifelong dream. And of course yours is the best store in town, and the arrangements you make are just so gorgeous and so, so creative. So I hope you'll let me stay."

Mollified, Mom finally nodded her consent. "I guess we could give it a shot," she said, much to Barnaby's surprise. "Okay, so what do you know about flowers?"

"Not much," Sarah admitted.

"Let's teach you the basics," Mom suggested. "Come with me and I'll show you what you need to know."

Barnaby's jaw had dropped, and as he watched his mom lead Sarah to their inner lair, where the magic happened, he stared after the duo, and secretly hoped Mom wouldn't murder the girl with an ax and turn her into an arrangement herself.

Five minutes later, as he was going over some of the invoices his main supplier had sent over via email, the doorbell jingled and he looked up. When he recognized Ebenezer Scrum, he plastered an ingratiating smile on his face.

"Ebenezer. What can I do for you?"

The jeweler was a regular customer, and came in a couple of times a year. He never forgot his wife's birthday, or their wedding anniversary, and even bought her flowers for Valentine's Day which was rare when a couple had been married as long as the Scrums were.

"Rumor has it that Sarah Mitchell works here now?" said the jeweler as he glanced around with a searching look on his face. "At least that's what one of my customers told me."

"No, it's true," said Barnaby, not surprised that news would have traveled this fast. This was Hampton Cove, after all, and nothing ever remained a secret for very long. "She just started working here this morning. Her first day, in fact. So you won't see her behind the counter for a little while. She needs to be trained in the ins and outs of the flower business first."

"I see," said Ebenezer, drumming his fingers on the counter. Then he suddenly looked Barnaby straight in the eye. "Look, I won't beat about the bush, Blossom. You and I have been friends for a long time, and esteemed colleagues. And if I were in the same situation, I know I would appreciate the heads-up."

"Heads-up? What do you mean?"

"That girl is a thief," said Ebenezer. "I know it sounds harsh, but it's true. I caught her stealing a very expensive diamond ring from my store last week. Of course I pressed charges, and the matter is in the hands of the police now. But I just thought you should know." He pointed to the till. "And to be perfectly honest, if I were you I'd keep her away from that. She may look like an angel, but those hands of hers have a habit of slipping into places where they have no business. I have it on good authority that it wasn't the first time she was caught stealing. Only the others didn't press charges, and I did."

"You have got to be kidding," he said.

"I'm afraid it's true," said Ebenezer.

Just at that moment, Sarah joined them. When she caught sight of the jeweler, her face turned white as a sheet, and for a moment she faltered, then quickly turned on her heel and disappeared back to where she came from.

"See?" said Ebenezer. "Can't even face me. It's the guilt, Blossom. You saw it too, didn't you?"

"I did," said Barnaby quietly. It had been shocking for him to see Sarah's sudden change of demeanor.

"Look, far be it from me to tell a fellow business owner how to conduct his affairs, but if I were you I would let her go. It can only lead to trouble. And also, what will your customers think when word spreads? They won't be easy in their minds when they hand over their credit cards to this girl. And in short order they might start to take their business elsewhere. And I can't say I would blame them."

"Yeah, I see what you mean," said Barnaby, who did see what the other man meant.

Ebenezer tapped the counter, looking vindicated. "You're a smart man, Blossom. I know you'll do the right thing." And with these words, he was off.

For a moment Barnaby didn't move, as his mind was a whirlpool of thoughts and his heart a vortex of emotion. Then he made his decision and set foot for the workshop. He found Sarah there, and also his mother, who was busy showing her the different parts of the flower.

"This is the stem," she was saying. "And these are the petals."

"Mom, can you leave us for a moment?" he asked.

It was a testament to the seriousness with which he had addressed her that his mom didn't even put up a protest but instead left to take charge of the store for the moment.

Sarah didn't look up. Instead her eyes were riveted on her feet. Her cheeks were the color of the roses she was holding in her hand, and it was all Barnaby could do to not give her a reassuring hug. But he was her employer now, and she was his employee, and that kind of behavior was simply out of the question.

So instead he said, "Is it true?"

Sarah nodded timidly. Tears had appeared in her eyes, and were rolling down her cheeks.

"I see." And he did see. Very clearly, even.

She was taking off her apron, and now placed it on the table.

"What are you doing?" he asked.

"You're firing me," she said, looking up for the first time. "So I'm leaving."

"I'm not firing you," he said.

"But Mr. Scrum…"

"Ebenezer Scrum is an annoying busybody who thinks he can boss people around. I've never liked the man, and I like him even less now. So you're not going anywhere, Miss Mitchell. But I would like you to tell me what happened."

And so she told him. Haltingly at first, then with the words tumbling over each other, and also the tears. Finally he nodded. His instincts had been correct. So he offered her a grateful smile.

"That can't have been easy. And I want to thank you for being so honest with me. As far as I'm concerned, the topic is closed. And if Mr. Scrum or anyone else ever bothers you again, please send them to me and I'll deal with them. Okay?"

She nodded, a smile having appeared on her face, like the sun shining through the clouds on a cloudy day. "Thanks, Mr. Blossom."

"Barnaby, please. My father was Mr. Blossom."

"Thanks, Barnaby. And please call me Sarah."

"I will," he said, and for some reason found himself holding her hand. Not understanding how that had happened, he now shook it and then dropped it again. He then nodded at her and removed himself from the scene before he trespassed other boundaries in the employer-employee relationship, such as there are: warm hugs and tender kisses feathered on upturned faces.

If they were going to work together, he would have to eradicate such ridiculous notions. He would also have to put a leash on himself and be firm about it.

It wouldn't be easy, but with some effort he was sure he would manage.

He met his mom in the store, where luckily no customers

had shown up, and she eyed him curiously. "What was that all about?"

"Just a few ground rules we had to establish," he said. "The employee handbook and such."

His mom frowned. "I didn't know we had an employee handbook?"

"We never had an actual employee before."

"And what am I? Chopped liver?"

"You know what I mean, Mom."

"What is an employee handbook anyway?"

"Oh, you know. Stuff about our mission, vision, values, policies… Um… our code of conduct."

She cocked an eyebrow. "Do we have a mission?"

"Sure. Selling flowers. Now please continue the training, Mom. It's very important Sarah finds her footing."

His mom's frown deepened. "I think if there's anyone here who needs to find their footing it's you, sonny boy. Seems to me like you're floating on cloud nine. And if I'm not mistaken this girl Sarah has got a lot to do with that."

He should have known Mom would see right through him.

CHAPTER 19

Sylvie still had her doubts about the deal she had made with Ezra Burns, but it did give her the impetus to walk into her boss's office the next morning and tell her she was quitting her job. Mrs. Woods didn't look impressed. She merely waved an impatient hand and said, "Pack your things and leave. And don't come begging me to take you back cause I won't." She then fixed her with those evil eyes of hers and added, "And you can kiss your severance pay goodbye."

Sylvie hadn't even thought about possible severance pay, knowing she probably wouldn't get any, so she merely shrugged and walked out of her boss's office.

"You were a lousy secretary anyway!" Mrs. Woods yelled after her. "So goodbye and good riddance!"

"Nice," said Sylvie as she emptied her desk.

Her colleague Frankie was tearful. "Now what am I going to do? That woman is going to devour me. She's going to take it out on me, you realize that, right? And when they find my mangled broken body under a bridge you'll know it's your fault." But she was smiling as she said it, wiping her eyes with a Kleenex.

"Why don't you find another job, too?" Sylvie suggested. "I mean, it can't be worse than here, right?"

"I wouldn't be too sure about that," said Frankie. "There are some pretty lousy bosses out there. And at least with this one I know what to expect."

"Better the devil you know?"

"Exactly."

She had told her friend all about Ezra and his dodgy roommate and their slacker ways, and Frankie had expressed great doubt that she would ever see any money. But Sylvie knew she had to do this. She simply couldn't stand working there one more day. She would end up strangling their boss, if she didn't strangle her first, of course, which, judging from the nasty looks Mrs. Woods was giving her was a serious possibility.

The phone rang on Frankie's desk and she immediately picked up, nodding to her friend.

And as Sylvie walked out of the office, she gave Frankie's shoulder a squeeze. 'Hang in there,' that squeeze said. But also: 'I'll see you at lunchtime.'

Walking out of the building with her cardboard box containing her meager belongings in her hands, she experienced both the exhilaration of freedom from the terrible conditions she'd been subjected to for the past years, but also a powerful dread about her future. She couldn't afford not to work, and if Ezra didn't come through, she was well and truly screwed.

So she picked out her phone from the box and put in a call to her 'husband.'

"Yup," said Ezra, picking up on the first ring.

"I need an advance on that payment," she said.

For a moment he didn't speak, then: "How big of an advance were you thinking, exactly?"

"Ten thousand. I just quit my job, and I need to make rent, buy food, take care of my kid. So yeah, ten thousand sounds about right."

"Can we maybe take that down a notch?" he asked tentatively. "To let's say a thousand? Or how about a hundred?"

She closed her eyes. "I knew this was a mistake."

"No, no. It's not a mistake. It's just that I'm dealing with this slight cash flow problem right now? Once that inheritance money comes through, I can pay you what we agreed on. But until then I'm afraid money is tight. Very tight. Very, very, very tight."

"Yeah, yeah, I get it," she said. She would just have to swallow her pride and borrow some money from her mom and dad to tide her over. They wouldn't like it, since they had been saving to go on this big cruise the moment Julie was old enough or until Sylvie finally got her act together and arranged for childcare so her parents wouldn't have to function as her designated babysitters anymore and spend their golden years taking care of their grandchild day in and day out.

"Okay, give me anything you can afford, and then pay me once your inheritance kicks in." She had googled Ezra's aunt Emily, and the woman had been richer than Bill Gates before he started giving all of his money away, so that shouldn't pose a problem. Even if the money was to be divided between the four remaining cousins, as per the stipulations of the will, Ezra would still fetch a tidy sum. Not that he deserved it, since as far as Sylvie could tell all he did all day was hang around the apartment dressed in a onesie, smoking dope and reading comics.

She hung up after Ezra had promised her to do a deep

dive between the couch cushions and retrieve any nickels he could find so she could feed 'their' baby.

The first thing she did when she got home was to call her mom and dad to tell them she was home, and to feel free to drop off Julie. In fact she wouldn't be needing them to act as babysitters anymore. The gratitude and relief were palpable. But then once they had arrived at her modest studio apartment and she broached the subject of a loan, their mood became decidedly less sunny. It took a little while, and there were some recriminations flying back and forth, but finally she managed to secure a loan for the exact amount she had pestered Ezra for, and once her parents had left, and she was alone with her little girl, she relaxed.

It might not be the best decision she had ever made, but it was going to give her more time with the person she loved the most in the whole world, and that made it worth the aggravation and the sense of insecurity.

* * *

Ezra had searched that couch for coins but unfortunately hadn't retrieved the tidy sum of ten thousand his new wife had demanded of him. Ten cents was all he would be able to offer her, in fact.

"Don't you dare give that to her," Jake demanded. "That's our money and she doesn't have the right to come barging in here making demands."

"She didn't barge in here, Jake," Ezra pointed out. "She called me on the phone."

"It's the same thing. She barges into our lives and starts making demands. This almost feels like a hostage situation to me. She's the hostage taker and we're the hostages. Or one of those hostile takeover situations."

"It was your idea in the first place!"

"I didn't think she would actually move in with us!"

"What did you expect? We're going to be married, bud!"

"I know, but that doesn't mean I can't protest about this gross violation of our personal space."

"It'll be fine," Ezra assured him. "It's only for a couple of months and then she's out of our lives again."

"I'm not sure I'll be able to stand it," said Jake as he dropped himself down on the couch and tucked one leg beneath his butt with some effort. He shook his curly head and looked shell-shocked. "I mean, living with a baby is supposed to be hell. These things cry all the time, man. And they spit food on you when they eat. And they projectile vomit when they're upset. And you have to give them so much attention! This is going to turn our lives into a living hell, I just know it."

"It's a baby, not a vampire. And it won't turn our lives into a living hell. Sylvie is going to take care of that baby, so it's got nothing to do with us."

"But it's going to live here, man! It's going to be such a trip! And can you please leave my stuff alone?"

Ezra, contrary to his deepest instincts, had taken to cleaning up a little, since he felt really embarrassed about the state of the apartment. As per their arrangement, Sylvie was going to give up her own flat and move in with them. She had also demanded that Jake move out, since it wouldn't look good if the detectives his late Aunt Emily had hired would find a roommate living with them—a newly married couple. But at this point Ezra had put his foot down. He couldn't throw Jake out on his ear. Also, Jake paid half the rent, so it wasn't as if they could afford to kick him out either. And besides, a lot of young couples share their living space with other people. Real estate came at a premium in New York. Even in the boroughs that used to be amongst the cheapest ones in the city, like the Bronx or Brooklyn, it was almost impossible to rent an apartment at a price anyone but a millionaire could afford. So they would just have to make do for the time being.

One thing that was going to change was that Sylvie and Julie would take Ezra's room from now on, and Ezra would shack up with Jake, something else the latter had vehemently objected to but that simply would have to be done. Ezra and Sylvie might officially be getting married, but that didn't mean they were actually going to share a bed together. That would probably be, like, prostitution or something.

And so when Sylvie arrived about an hour later, she found Ezra in the midst of cleaning out his room and transferring his precious belongings—amongst which were about a thousand comics of various descriptions and value—to Jake's room.

"Why don't you sell a couple of those?" she suggested as she picked up a Spider-Man comic from the stack and leafed through it.

He immediately grabbed it out of her hands before she creased it, and snapped, "No way. Do you know what I had to do to get my hands on this?"

"You mean you bought all of these? How do you actually make enough money to afford this crap?"

His finer feelings seriously hurt, he still managed to retain a sense of dignity. And so it was with a quaking voice that he said, "It's not crap. It's the highest art form in existence, and the most precious possessions I have ever owned." If he had the money to rent a safe deposit box at the bank, he would put his most expensive and rare comics in there, but unfortunately that wasn't the case. So for the time being he kept them in his room. Or Jake's room.

It was true that he wasn't making as much as he could have if he actually applied himself, but then he also helped out at Gandalf's Cave and that took up most of his free time. Not that Sylvie would understand.

"Okay, so where are we?" she asked.

"Right here," he said, and showed her her new lodgings.

She sniffed the air. "What's that weird smell? Like old socks."

"I'll air it out," he said.

"In fact the whole place smells weird," said Sylvie. Then her eye fell on a poster depicting a cannabis leaf. "You better get rid of that, Ezra. I'm not having you guys smoke that stuff around Julie."

"We did get rid of it," he assured her. "It all went down the garbage chute."

He eyed the infant Sylvie had brought briefly, and thought it was the ugliest baby he had ever seen. It looked like an old person, only in the body of a young person—or something. And it was staring at him with unwavering interest, as if Ezra was the most interesting thing it had ever seen.

"Is it a boy or a girl?" he asked.

"Can't you tell, 'Dad?'" asked Sylvie as she picked the infant up from the couch where she had placed it for the time being and hoisted it up in her arms.

"Actually, no," he admitted. Since he didn't have any siblings who had kids of their own, he had never really been around kids, so this whole baby thing was definitely a new experience.

"It's a girl," said Sylvie as she pressed a kiss to the kid's cheek. She then sort of rocked her in her arms and said, "This is your new daddy, baby. What do you think?"

In response, the kid's face sort of crumpled and she started wailing like a fire engine. Her face turned red and the noise she made was out of this world.

Immediately Jake came stomping out of his room. "What's with all the noise? I can't focus on my game!"

"And this is your uncle Jake," said Sylvie, pointing to Ezra's and her roommate. "Uncle Jake is very happy to see you. Are you happy to see him?"

But the kid screamed even louder than before. Jake rolled his eyes. "Whatever," he said, and disappeared back into his lair to continue slaying dragons—or babies.

Sylvie smiled. "We're going to get along great, I can feel it."

"Does she do that a lot?" asked Ezra, putting his fingers in his ears. "Cry, I mean," he added when Sylvie gave him a quizzical look.

"All the time," said Sylvie. "Day and night."

Ezra groaned. "You're kidding, right?"

"Just a little bit," said Sylvie.

CHAPTER 20

"Are you sure about this, Max?" asked Dooley, not for the first time I might add.

"Unless Odelia decides to put a car full of police officers out in front of the house, this is the best we can do," I said.

And since Uncle Alec didn't see the need to pay good money for a car full of his officers, Odelia had asked us to keep an eye out and make sure that we alerted her and Chase at the first sign of trouble.

"Do you have any idea how expensive overtime pay is?" Harry repeated Uncle Alec's justification for the fact that he wasn't going to put a contingent of cops watching his niece's house around the clock.

"And besides," he had added, "Bruno has no idea his ex-wife and daughter are holed up at your place. So he won't be dropping in on you in the middle of the night."

"I wouldn't be so sure about that," Chase had replied. "The man escaped from a Mexican prison, so he's proven himself to be both resourceful and ruthless. Frankly I think we can expect anything from the guy."

"He's not going to come," Uncle Alec insisted, whether he believed it or not.

And so it was up to the four of us to take the first watch. And also the second watch, and however many watches there were after that. But first things first: we had an urgent and very important meeting arranged with Gran, and so instead of watching the house, as we had promised, we decided to use the cloak of darkness to set up a different campaign entirely. One that involved a couch, a garden house and Odelia's grandmother, not necessarily in that order.

We met in front of the garden house, and much to our surprise discovered that Gran wasn't alone. She was accompanied by her son-in-law.

"Hey, you guys," said Tex pleasantly. The good doctor had decided to dress in black from head to toe: he was wearing a black cap on his head, a black turtleneck sweater, black jeans and even his shoes were black.

"What is he doing here?" asked Brutus. Then he realized something. "He's not going to prevent us from taking what is rightfully ours, is he?"

It was true that Tex was the official and rightful owner of the garden house, so in all likelihood he had found out about our nefarious plan and was going to put his black-clad foot down and reduce our plan to the scrap heap of history.

"He's going to help us out," Gran declared instead. "It's his garden house, and he doesn't like that this stuff is taking up so much space."

"I want to practice my art," Tex declared, spreading his arms. "And I can't do that when there's couches and all kinds of furniture blocking my personal space."

"Is he still painting those freggies?" asked Brutus.

"No, he's moved on to portraits," said Gran. "In fact he promised to paint my portrait next. Isn't that right, Tex?"

"Absolutely," said the doctor magnanimously. "Once I've

got full access to my atelier, I'm going to paint your portrait."

"I'm looking forward to it," Gran revealed. "Once it's done I'm going to hang it in my bedroom. I might even have more than one made so I can give it out to my friends as presents."

Tex nodded approvingly. "It's going to be my masterpiece. I can feel it in my bones." He held out his hand, thumb and pinky finger extended, then squeezed one eye tightly shut and sort of measured Gran's face. "You've got one of those faces," he murmured meditatively.

"One of what kind of faces?" asked Gran eagerly.

"I'm not sure. I have to paint it to know it," said the master mysteriously. "But I'll let you know in due course."

"First we have to get this junk out of there," said Gran, rubbing her hands. She wasn't dressed in black but in her usual tracksuit. The one she had selected for the occasion was gray with a pink stripe. It was also fluorescent, which probably went against the code of the nocturnal marauder. Then again, since she was marauding her own property, she might get away with it.

"So what are we going to do with all of this stuff?" asked Tex once he had accessed his garden house and stood regarding Odelia and Chase's property. There was a couch in there, an armchair, a coffee table, a dining room table, a couple of chairs, a rolled-up carpet and other paraphernalia.

"I suggest we take it to Scarlett's place," said Gran. "She's got a garage but she doesn't own a car, so she uses it as a storage space."

"And does she have it? Space, I mean?" asked Tex.

"Oh, I'm sure she does. And if not, we simply stack stuff up. I find that you can always create more space by stacking stuff up. You simply have to get creative, and channel the Lego spirit."

"What's the Lego spirit, Gran?" asked Dooley.

"Stacking, Dooley. It's all about stacking."

I wasn't sure this was necessarily true, but it definitely sounded good. And if it saved our precious couch from mold, rats, cockroaches, black beetles, worms and other vermin of the undergrowth, I was all for this Lego spirit.

And so the long slog began. For the occasion Tex had borrowed a trailer from a patient, and for the next half hour or so, Gran and the doctor transferred the contents of the garden house to this trailer, stacking to their heart's content. We would have lent a helping paw, but unfortunately cats haven't yet mastered the art of walking on two paws, and neither has evolution supplied us with opposable thumbs necessary for stacking stuff. So all we could do was give instructions and directions and generally offer words of encouragement. Harry, especially, was very good at the latter. She barked and cajoled and cursed like a sailor, all part of her new persona of Harry the tough and hardened male. At one point I saw her direct a wad of spit on the ground. It irked Gran, the only one who could understand her, to a great extent. Finally she must have had enough, for she picked Harry up and locked her in the car so she wouldn't bother her anymore.

The drive over to Scarlett's place proceeded in silence, Tex and Gran too tired to speak, Harry too insulted to offer more words of encouragement, and the rest of us too afraid of her wrath in case we did open our mouths to speak.

Finally she decided to put her righteous anger aside and offer a few nuggets of wisdom. "You should have freed me," she grumbled. "You could see I was in trouble and you just sat there and did nothing."

"How were you in trouble, Harriet?" asked Dooley.

"Harry! My name is Harry! And if you had paid attention you wouldn't be asking me these stupid questions, Dooley. Wasn't it obvious? I couldn't breathe! I was locked up in a closed car without any air. I was suffocating!"

"You weren't suffocating," Gran piped up from the front seat. Tex was driving, and she was offering him directions to Scarlett's apartment. "There's plenty of air, even in a closed car."

"I was choking, Gran," Harry insisted in the gruff tones she had adopted and that she figured went along with her new persona.

Gran turned. "What's gotten into you all of a sudden? You didn't use to be so bad-mannered and ill-behaved."

"I'm not ill-behaved," Harry insisted. "I'm simply being me. Harry. The new star on the firmament of show business."

Gran frowned in confusion. "Harry? You mean you've changed your name?"

"Harry is a male now," said Brutus. "So he changed his name from Harriet to Harry since it seems better fitting." He didn't look happy about it, and failed to hide that fact.

Gran's reaction was not what any of us would have expected. She started laughing and didn't stop until we had reached Scarlett's place. It didn't help improve Harry's mood, and by the time we arrived, the temperature in the backseat was close to double-digit subzero temperatures.

"I'm Harry," she lamented once we were out of the car and our humans once again resumed their task of transferring furniture from one location to another. "But nobody seems to take me seriously. Even my own human is laughing at me. Why is that, Max?"

"She's not laughing at you," I said carefully. "She's laughing with you, since she loves you so much, and she's so happy for you."

Her face cleared. "You think so?"

"Oh, absolutely. Can't you tell between a mocking laugh and one of excitement and relief? Cause that was the kind of laugh Gran was laughing. She's so happy that you're Harry now that she simply couldn't control herself."

Harry's face lit up with a wide smile. "Oh, Max, you're making me so happy right now."

I noticed she had dropped the gruff demeanor and the gravelly voice and was back to talking like her original self. She didn't even spit on the floor. So I patted her on the back. "I think you're doing great, Harry. And I for one am glad that you finally decided to live your true self. The real you, you know."

"I know," she said, simpering a little. "I've always wanted to live my true me, but I guess I was afraid of what people would think. But now that my big secret is finally out, you can't believe how relieved I am. And how happy."

Brutus, who looked the absolute opposite of happy, grumbled, "I'm also happy. So very, very happy."

While the humans were channeling the Lego spirit and enjoying their stacking, the rest of us entered Scarlett's apartment, where we encountered Clarice. The former feral cat looked in fine fettle.

"Have you gained weight?" asked Harry, studying the feline in surprise.

"Just a little," Clarice admitted happily. "It's the good life, you guys. Though I have to say Scarlett exaggerates. She keeps stuffing my face with food every chance she gets. If this keeps up soon I'll be too fat to walk."

"You'll never be too fat to walk," I assured our friend.

"No, but look at these spindly legs and that big belly. Do I look weird to you?"

"You look fine," I said with a smile. It was wonderful to see Clarice flourish.

"Do you still eat rats?" asked Dooley.

"I haven't eaten a rat in twenty days," said Clarice proudly. "I mean, who needs rats when you get gourmet food from the best sources? I get different stuff every day. Food from all over the world, in fact. I don't know where she gets it, but I'm not complaining. This is the most fun I've had in years."

It seemed a given that Clarice was settling in all right with her newly adopted human, and since she had also joined cat choir, we now saw more of her than ever. She had changed, not merely in her outer appearance, but also her personality had gone through a remarkable shift. No longer was she going through life growling and snapping at everything and everyone. She was happier, her mood sunnier, and so her demeanor was a lot more pleasant. She even shared the limelight with Harry now, both singing soprano solos from time to time.

"Oh, but I won't be singing solos anymore," said Harry when the topic came up in the course of our conversation. "You see, I'm a male now, so I'll sing the tenor parts."

"Or the bass," said Brutus in his deep, low voice.

Clarice grinned. "You're pulling my paw, right? Is this the famous cat choir humor? Very funny, Harriet."

"The name is Harry now," said Harry with a touch of hauteur. "And my pronouns are he/him/his."

Clarice's grin took on a touch of bewilderment. "Now you're starting to scare me."

"Don't be scared," said Harry. "It's normal for there to be a period of adjustment, and that's fine. But from now on you will refer to me as Harry, is that clear?"

Something of the old Clarice suddenly shimmered through the new facade. A glint of malice glittered in her eyes all of a sudden, and she licked her lips as if she had seen a nice juicy rat and was about to pounce. "So you won't mind if I take the starring role in cat choir, right?"

"Um..." said Harry, not quite knowing how to respond.

"That's great. I always wanted to be a diva, you know. The one and only diva of cat choir. So I'll sing all the solos from now on."

"But I can sing solos," said Harry quickly. "The tenor ones."

"You know as well as I do that there are no other solos… *Harry*," said Clarice. "Only the soprano sings the solos, and since you're not a soprano anymore, that's all me. Me, me, me. You're simply part of the furniture from now on. The backing vocals, so to speak, while my star shines bright."

Harry looked crestfallen at this. "I-I guess," she finally said.

"So you don't mind if I break the news to Shanille tonight that from now on I'm the star of cat choir and you're part of the chorus?"

"Well…"

"Great. You won't regret it."

Oddly enough it seemed to me that Harry already did. And to a great extent, too. But of course she couldn't say anything, since Clarice was right. Tenors didn't do solos, and neither did bass singers or altos for that matter. At least not in cat choir. The only one who had ever done a solo was Harry, since she wanted to shine. But shine she would do no more.

"There's no shame in taking a supporting role," Dooley assured our friend. "In fact I saw a Discovery Channel documentary the other night that reminded me of you, Harry. It said that the only way a soprano can truly shine is when she's contrasted with the rest of the choir. So a soprano needs the others and the others need the soprano. It's a symbolic relationship."

"Symbiotic," I murmured.

"Exactly," said Dooley, warming to his subject. "So now that Clarice is our lead soprano, you will be able to support her as a tenor, and make her star shine even brighter!"

Harry's face was turning more and more into a death mask. Like the ones worn by the ancient pharaohs of Egypt.

Only Harry was still alive. But it was as if the spark had gone out of her, and she was growing more and more still. Finally, like a volcano, she erupted. "Will you just shut up, Dooley! You talk and talk and talk and talk—you never stop!"

"But…"

A shrill sound made me wince. It sounded like a steam kettle that had gone on the boil. When I looked a little closer, I discovered that it actually came from Harry, who was screaming at the top of her lungs! If this had happened to those pharaohs it would have heralded a miraculous resurrection. In Harry's case I had the impression she was going through some sort of mental breakdown. When she finally stopped screaming, there was a kind of ringing in my ears which was very uncomfortable, and Harry was staring at me with unadulterated rage.

"This is all your fault!" she yelled.

I was taken aback to some extent. "What are you talking about?"

"You put me up to this. You said that it's a tough world out there for us females, and that males get all the breaks!"

"I don't think it was me who—"

But suddenly she threw her head in her neck. "I resign," she said.

"Resign? From what?" I said.

"From everything! From cat choir, from this family, from this group of lousy friends. I quit!" She started to walk away. "Oh, and also: from now on I'm Harriet again. Pronouns she/her/hers!"

And then she was gone. When we hurried after her, we discovered she had left the apartment through the pet flap in Scarlett's second bedroom. We ventured out, but of Harriet there was no trace.

She had effectively quit!

CHAPTER 21

Harriet felt a little upset. Or maybe a lot. All she knew was that she felt tricked somehow. That life had played a mean trick on her and now she was suffering the consequences. And as she walked away from Scarlett's apartment she wondered where she was going. The fervor of her fury had propelled her out of that pet flap and down from the balcony to street level, but that initial burst of rage had presently expended itself and she had no idea what to do next.

As she turned a corner, she suddenly bumped into a lone figure who stood smoking a cigarette and leaning against a lamppost. The man was accompanied by a large dog that looked positively frightening. It was one of those dogs that liked to chew up smaller animals just for fun. But as she recoiled, the dog spoke.

"Excuse me, miss, but are you from around here, by any chance?"

"I am," she said cautiously, reluctant to go anywhere near the ferocious beast.

"Oh, that's such a relief," said the big dog. "I've been trying to get in touch with someone, you see, but I don't know my way around this place. I'm not from around here, but then I guess you can probably tell." He smiled an embarrassed smile. "My name is Boris, by the way, and this is my human Bruno."

"Bruno? Your human's name is Bruno?"

"That's right. Bruno Watts. Why? Do you know him?"

"Not really," she said, studying the human figure. He looked a little rough around the edges, she thought, and his appearance was unkempt. Almost as if he hadn't washed or changed his clothes in days. He was wearing a khaki shirt that had holes in it, and his jeans had also seen better days.

The dog had followed her look, and now said, "I have to apologize for the state he is in. He had a pretty nasty shock, you see, so he hasn't been himself lately."

"Does Bruno have a daughter, by any chance?" asked Harriet.

The dog's face lit up. "How did you know?"

"Oh, just a lucky guess."

"It's the daughter I'm looking for, you see," Boris continued. "Her name is Ella, and I have this awful feeling something really bad happened to her."

"And why would you think that?"

"Well, Bruno was supposed to meet her, you see. They had arranged a time and a place, but when he arrived there, the girl was a no-show. Bruno waited around for a while, but finally he left, figuring she had changed her mind. But the strange thing is that she hasn't answered his texts, even though before they would text all the time."

"What do you think happened, Boris?" she asked.

"I have absolutely no idea, and neither does Bruno. The only thing I can think is that Ella's mother found out and stopped Ella from meeting her dad. They are divorced, you see, and they don't get along well, the father and the mother."

"So you were there when Bruno went to meet his daughter?"

"I was there," Boris confirmed. "And she never showed up. We must have waited maybe two hours, but finally Bruno gave up." Boris lowered his voice. "Don't tell anyone, but Bruno has been having some trouble with the law. So when a policeman showed up in the park, we had to beat a hasty retreat, unfortunately."

"What kind of trouble is he in?" asked Harriet.

"Oh, nothing important," said Boris vaguely. "So can you help us? Do you know how we can find out where Ella might be?"

"I don't know her personally," Harriet began, causing the dog's face to sag. "But I could always ask around."

The dog immediately perked up again. "That would be so kind of you. Bruno really loves his daughter, you see, and he hasn't seen her in a very long time. So he's very anxious to finally meet her and find out if she's all right."

Harriet studied the dog, then decided he was either on the level or a very good liar. "Okay, so where can I find you?" she finally asked.

"You mean, are we staying at a hotel? Well, we're not, actually. And this is where this same trouble with the law plays a major part. We're staying with an old couple at the moment, who are renting us a room on a weekly basis." He gave her the address, and she memorized it.

"Okay, you can expect to hear from me soon," she said.

"Is that a promise, Harriet?"

"It is," she assured the dog.

Bruno had finished his cigarette and threw the remnants into the gutter. Then he gave Boris's leash a yank. "Let's go, you stupid mutt," he growled.

Boris smiled apologetically. "Like I said, he hasn't been himself lately. Please don't hold it against him."

"What did I tell you!" Bruno yelled. "Let's go!"

Another yank, and Boris waddled after his master. "See you soon, Harriet!" he yelled.

"Yeah, see you, Boris," she yelled back.

After the duo had rounded the corner, she hurried back to Scarlett's apartment. She climbed the tree that led to the balcony next to Scarlett's, hopped across the breach and was soon entering the pet flap. She encountered Max, Brutus, Dooley and Clarice, and also Gran, who looked puzzled.

"I was just about to go look for you!" said the old lady. "The others told me you ran off? That you quit?"

"What are you talking about?" she said. "I didn't run off." She then smiled. "You guys, I just met Boris. And guess what? His human is Ella's dad! And I have an address!"

* * *

AFTER HARRIET HAD LEFT—or was it Harry?—we were all in quite a state. Brutus wanted to go after her immediately, but I told him that maybe it was better to let her cool off a little first. Harriet does get worked up from time to time, which is a consequence of the passion with which she attacks life. But her moods mostly don't last very long.

"But we have to find her!" Brutus cried.

"And I say she'll snap out of it," I countered.

"Snap out of what?" asked Clarice, who was languidly licking her claws. "She seemed like the usual Harriet to me."

"So is it Harry or Harriet, Max?" asked Dooley. "Cause I'm having a hard time keeping up."

"We all have a hard time keeping up, Dooley," I said. "But I think it's Harriet."

"And what's with these pronouns?" asked Dooley. "What did she mean by that?"

"Beats me," I said.

"I have some pronouns for you," said Clarice. "From now on I want to be identified as non-binary, and my pronouns are they/them/their. So please don't misgender me or I'll claw your eyes out, is that understood?" We stared at them, but then they laughed. "Just kidding." They giggled—or was it she—or even he? "You should have seen the look on your faces! Priceless!"

"This is all very confusing," said Dooley, and I think he spoke for all of us when he said it.

"I'm glad that Harriet is Harriet again," said Brutus. "Not that I mind all that much that she was Harry, but I'm just not into dating dudes, you know. Even though technically she never was a dude. I mean, not really, if you see what I mean. I mean, her bits were still the same. Right? Am I right?" He looked pained and I gave him a pat on the back.

"Her bits were still the same," I agreed. "And so were her pieces."

"What bits are you talking about, Max?" asked Dooley.

Brutus and I shared a look of panic. "Um…"

"The thing is, Dooley," said Clarice, "that males and females have different bits and pieces. And as luck would have it—or as nature intended it if you want to take the broad naturalistic view—those bits and pieces fit perfectly well together. You see, whereas males have a—"

Brutus and I both cleared out throats in a loud fashion, interrupting this no doubt fascinating biology lesson which nevertheless I didn't think was appropriate for one as young and innocent as Dooley, and Clarice looked up, a little disturbed.

"Okay, so males have a pe—"

Once more Brutus and I cleared our throats loudly, causing Clarice to look even more annoyed.

"Maybe you guys should have a sip of water," she suggested. "Clearly there's something stuck in your throat. A fishbone, maybe." She took a deep breath to resume her lecture, with Dooley waiting patiently for the answer to his question about Harriet's particular bits and pieces. "So one more time. The male of the species possesses a—"

Which is when Harriet suddenly burst upon the scene, surprising us all. She looked both radiant and very excited. When Gran hurried into the room, no doubt having heard the pet flap flap, she was as flabbergasted as the rest of us. We had told her all about Harriet's tantrum, and to see our friend act as if nothing had happened was as surprising to her as it was to us.

Then again, Harriet will be Harriet, whatever her pronouns may be—or whatever is going on with her bits and pieces.

CHAPTER 22

"Boss?"

Barnaby looked up from the stack of bills he'd been checking. Sarah had appeared at the door of his office looking a little nervous. "Yes, what is it?" he asked.

"Do you think I could get tomorrow morning off? It's just that my sister is getting married. She just called to tell me the news."

"Oh, sure," he said easily. "I didn't know you had a sister?" There was a whole lot of her he didn't know. In fact probably everything. Not that he wouldn't mind getting to know her better, but he figured he would—over time, of course.

"Yeah, she lives in New York, though she comes out here from time to time. The funny thing is that I didn't even know she had a boyfriend."

He smiled. "Must be one of those *coups de foudre*. You know, like love at first sight?"

"I don't think so. She never mentioned the guy before. And we're very close, so if she had met him and fallen in love she would have told me." She shrugged. "I guess I'll find out tomorrow."

"You'll probably be gone all day. And then there's the wedding reception and the party. Maybe you better take the next day off as well," he suggested.

"No, that's fine. There won't be a big party. It's just the thing at City Hall and then we'll all have lunch at a restaurant, I guess. Anyway, I talked to my mom and she sounded pretty shocked so I don't think she knew either."

"It all sounds very romantic," he said, settling back in his chair. "Is she older or younger than you, your sister?"

"We're the exact same age. We're twins," said Sarah. "Which is why I find this all so baffling, since I normally have a great intuition about what happens in her life, and it's the same way with her. But this time I didn't have a clue. She was married before, you see, but it didn't work out. The guy was a brute, and we were all glad to see the back of him. She did have a kid with him, my niece." She smiled, and the thought of her niece made her eyes sparkle. "She's the apple of Sylvie's eye, and frankly the rest of the family as well. She's just the sweetest little girl."

"How old is she?"

"Twelve months."

"I'm sure your sister will be very happy with her husband," he said. "Like I said, it must be love at first sight, and they simply couldn't wait to get married."

"Mh," said Sarah, and didn't look convinced. She eyed him for a moment, then said, "Can I ask you a personal question, boss?"

"Sure, shoot."

"So your dad was a fishmonger, right?"

"That's correct."

"And he passed away a couple of years ago?"

"Yeah, he passed away thirteen years ago now. It was very

sudden," he said, recalling the dreadful event. He'd been on his way to work when the news came that his dad had suffered a heart attack while emptying a container of salmon into the display counter and fallen into the counter himself. Mom had found him like that, and later said he looked so peaceful and so relaxed she thought he was asleep at first. Later it turned out he had died on the spot. At least he hadn't suffered, and according to Mom he had died in his favorite place: among his beloved fish.

"And you never thought about taking over the business?"

"I didn't. I spent a lot of time in that store growing up, and helped out my dad during the holidays and the weekends, but the fish bug never caught on. I guess I wasn't made to sell fish." He smiled. "I'm a vegetarian, so I don't even eat fish. I don't even like the smell."

"Oh, me too!" she said. "I'm also a vegetarian. So did you always want to sell flowers?"

"As a matter of fact I did. I know some people think it's strange. I know my mom never liked the fact that I wanted to open a flower shop."

"She came around then, since she works with you now."

"I guess she did," he said. "She would have preferred if I took over my dad's fish business, though. But at least flowers is better than nothing. And it's better than what I was studying to become."

"Which was?"

"A lawyer." He grimaced. "Which was my dad's idea, actually. I never liked it, though, and dropped it as soon as I could. I actually finished college, and even worked at a law firm for a while, but I hated every minute. And then when my dad died, I decided to drop the whole thing and open a flower shop instead. It just brought the fact home to me that life is too short to postpone the things you want to do." He eyed her wistfully for a moment, then restrained himself with the reminder that he was ten years older than she was—not to mention her boss.

"Do you..." She eyed him timidly all of a sudden. "Are you married, boss? It's just that your mom clammed up when I mentioned it, so I just wondered..."

"I was engaged to be married once," he said. "But nothing ever came of it." His bride-to-be had fallen in love with the wedding planner a week before the wedding, and he'd been forced to call the whole thing off. She had gone on their honeymoon, though, but had taken the wedding planner instead of him. It was a painful episode he'd rather not be reminded of. Then again, if Sarah asked him, he felt obliged to answer her truthfully, even if it made him look foolish.

But after he had told her the story, she didn't laugh, like most of his friends did. Instead she looked a little sad. "That wasn't very nice of her," she said. "And then to go on your honeymoon with another man—that was really mean."

"The honeymoon had been paid for," he explained. "And she had already arranged to take time off from work. So she figured she might as well go."

"I still think it's mean of her to put you through something like that," she said.

"Yeah, well. What's done is done. And it was a long time ago."

"When was this?"

"A week before my dad died."

"Oh, God," she said, bringing a hand to her face. "So while your ex-fiancée was enjoying your honeymoon with your wedding planner, you were burying your father?"

He nodded. "It wasn't the best time of my life."

"Oh, boss," she said. "It must have been terrible."

He shrugged. "You know what they say. What doesn't kill you makes you stronger. And it did inspire me to finally take the leap and quit the law firm and set up Barnaby's Blossoms.

So at least something good came out of all of that. I probably wouldn't have had the courage to turn my life around otherwise."

"It is true that adversity sometimes inspires us to move forward with our lives," she said, nodding. "Like me with this whole… jewelry business."

He nodded, reluctant to dwell on that but still curious.

"You see, Odelia Kingsley got me in touch with a shrink, and I just had my first session yesterday. And as I walked her through what happened, I still find it hard to believe that I took that ring. I mean, I've been involved in some minor incidents before, but never as major as this. Usually it's candy bars. But this?" She paused as she contemplated the enormity of what had happened. "This is on a completely different level. And it's not as if I'm even interested in jewelry. I'm not."

He had noticed that she didn't wear rings or bracelets or even a pendant or earrings, which had surprised him.

"My sister is exactly the same. She's not into material possessions either. Though of course with the baby she has to make sure she makes a living, but apart from that, neither of us are into fancy clothes or jewelry or whatever."

"Did you want to buy something at Scrum's Baubles?"

"I was looking at the rings. My boyfriend had dropped some heavy hints about getting married, so I figured I might as well take a look at some of the rings. He mentioned that he knew the Scrums, and his family were regulars there, so…"

"So what did your boyfriend have to say when you were arrested?"

"He broke up with me by text." But instead of looking sad about it she actually looked relieved. "Sylvie said I'm better off without him. If at the first sign of trouble he decides to bail on me and doesn't even have the guts to talk to me face to face, it probably wasn't meant to be."

"I agree with your sister," he said with a smile. "So what happened in the store that day?"

"That's what's so strange. Nothing happened, at least not that I can remember. I asked if I could take a look at the engagement rings, and mentioned that I was Grant Richardson's girlfriend, and this woman behind the counter became really annoyed with me for some reason. She didn't like it when I took my time to check out the rings, and kept sighing a lot and rolling her eyes at me. So finally I decided I'd had enough and left. Which is when the alarm started blaring and her husband grabbed me by the neck and they both started screaming at me. It was all very embarrassing, especially since there were other customers in the store at the time." She took a deep breath. "And then the police showed up and I was arrested."

Barnaby frowned as Sarah told the tale. He'd been holding a pencil in his hand and noticed he'd almost snapped it in half. The whole story upset him to a great extent. Not just the way this Grant Richardson had treated her, but also the Scrums, who he had never liked all that much to begin with. "And that's when they found the ring in your pocket?"

"That's the weird part. I don't remember pocketing that ring. But I must have, for the guy grabbing me by the neck fished it out of my pocket immediately. It's almost as if I had some kind of blackout or something. The shrink says it's not uncommon, and I guess she knows what she's talking about, but it's still odd."

"It is odd," he said. "Though I have to say I find the way the Scrums treated you beyond the pale. And also your boyfriend. The way he…" He ground his teeth a little. "I mean that's just…" At that moment the pencil did snap.

"I know, right?" said Sarah softly. "Looks like we both picked some pretty lousy partners." Then she realized this social faux pas with her new boss, and blushed. "I'm sorry. That came out wrong."

"No, it came out exactly right," he assured her. "We did have lousy partners."

They both smiled, and for a moment they enjoyed the companionable silence that hung between them. Then the store bell spurred them both into action once more. Sarah to attend to their customers, and Barnaby to pore over his books.

Before she left his office, she said, "Good talk, boss."

"Yeah, good talk," he agreed.

He had returned to his books when Sarah stuck her head back in. "Um… can I ask you a favor, boss?"

"Only if you call me Barnaby."

"Gotcha. Could you keep an eye on Footsie for me?"

He blinked. "Who's Footsie?"

"He's my pet. And if you tell me I should simply leave him at the apartment while I'm gone, I'll tell you he's the kind of pet who doesn't like to be left alone. He gets nervous when he's all by himself. He's very sociable that way. A real people's pet. And since he already ran away once, I don't want to take any chances."

"Okay, I can take care of Footsie for you," he said. "Why not?"

"Oh, that's so kind of you, bo—Barnaby. He won't give you any trouble, I promise. And I'll give you a bag of food for when he gets hungry. And I'll also leave you his bag of toys to play with."

"Don't give it another thought," he said magnanimously. "I'll keep him here in my office and I will keep a close eye on him." He smiled. "So is Footsie a sweet little kitty or a cute doggie?"

"Neither. He's a rat," she said, and quickly ducked out again.

CHAPTER 23

"So... just to make sure," said Dooley. "Harriet is Harriet again, right?"

It wasn't the first time he'd asked the question, and I had a feeling it wouldn't be the last time either. "As far as I can tell she's Harriet again," I confirmed.

Harriet was busy in Scarlett's kitchen telling Gran about Bruno and Boris, which allowed the rest of us some time to reflect on these recent events.

"I think it doesn't matter what she calls herself," said Clarice. "Whether it's Harriet or Harry, deep down she will always be the same cat, which is how it's supposed to be. And besides, she probably knows best who she is or wants to be, correct?"

"I guess so," said Brutus dubiously. It was obvious from his expression that he had gone through some tough times while Harriet was trying to figure out who she was, and even now he still wasn't feeling on sound footing again. I patted him on the back. "It'll be fine, Brutus. Maybe Clarice is right, and whatever Harriet does or whatever she decides, deep down she'll always be the Harriet we know and love."

"I hope so," said Brutus. "Though I have to say it's all been very confusing. I mean, I went through a similar episode myself, where I didn't know whether I still wanted to be Brutus or not, and it's made me more susceptible to these vagaries of life and the notion that at our deepest core maybe who we think we are isn't always who we really are, if you see what I mean?"

We all stared at him, and I have to confess that I didn't really see what he meant at all. I still nodded sagely, though, and so did the others. Brutus seemed content to leave it at that, and so was I. I mean, I may be something of an amateur sleuth when the mood takes me, but what I'm not is a shrink, even though I know that even pets might need counseling from time to time—if such a thing exists.

Harriet had returned from the kitchen, where she had informed Gran about the latest regarding our comatose guest and her criminal father, and when Gran joined us, she had the kind of determined look on her face we all knew too well.

"Uh-oh," said Brutus, and I think he captured the mood to a T.

"It's neighborhood watch time, you guys," said Gran. "So are you coming with me?"

"Of course," I said immediately. Even though I'd wanted to join cat choir and see if Harriet would sing the soprano part or the tenor part or any of the other parts, it was probably more important to join Gran while she went about securing the safety and comfort of Hampton Covians everywhere.

Scarlett had already grabbed her purse and was ready to join her friend.

"Are you going dressed like that?" asked Gran.

"What's wrong with this?" asked Scarlett, glancing down at herself. She was wearing a woolen skirt and a nice silk blouse that revealed the lacy bra she had on underneath. "Am I overdressed, you think?"

"A little," said Gran. "We're going on a stakeout, honey, not a fashion show."

"Okay, so let me slip into something more comfortable," said Scarlett, and hurried away again.

Tex had returned from the bathroom and was smiling. Clearly the mission involving his garden house had managed to put his mind at ease. "I think tomorrow I'll paint you, Vesta," he said.

Gran was taken aback by this. "Me! You mean I'd have to pose for you?"

"Not necessarily. I can always paint you from memory. But if you would like to pose that would probably be best. There's something about the interaction between a model and the artist that brings out the best in me," he said, his face having taken on a contemplative aspect.

"I won't have to pose in the nude, though, right?"

The contemplative expression made way for one of sheer horror. "Oh, no!" he said, holding up his hands to stave off the disaster he saw with his mind's eye. "I'm not that kind of painter, Vesta. As you very well know."

"What I know is that you used to pose in the nude," said Gran with a touch of cheekiness.

Tex became rigid. "Those days are gone, so please don't remind me. Been there, done that."

"Well, of course I'll pose for you," said Gran, "but I would have thought you'd want to paint a portrait of your wife first."

"I already did," said Tex cheerfully. "In fact I painted several. But she doesn't seem to be satisfied with any of them, so I decided to try something else for a change." He sighed wistfully. "Shall I tell you about my big dream?"

"Please do," said Gran with a glint of mirth in her eye. "Don't let me hold you back, buddy."

"What I would like to do—and accomplish in my lifetime—is to paint portraits of all the people of Hampton Cove."

"All of them?"

"All of them," said Tex resolutely. "It's going to take me a while, but at the end of the day it's going to represent a body of work I can be proud of. A body of work that will stand the test of time. And with a little luck it will establish my name as the Hamptons' premier artist."

"You have some competition there," Gran reminded him. "The name Pollock ring a bell? Or de Kooning?"

Tex made a throwaway gesture with his hands. "Oh, but those were contemporary painters. I want to be a painter in the classic tradition. Like Vermeer or Rembrandt, you know. Or Caravaggio. One of the greats."

"Well, if it makes you happy," said Gran. "And keeps you from doing mischief," she whispered to us with a wink.

We all smiled. Tex wasn't exactly known for getting up to all kinds of mischief. Then again, she was right. If painting made him happy, it might be a good idea. Even though his project seemed a little grandiose to me.

"So when are you going to paint me?" asked Harriet.

"Harriet wants to know when you're going to paint her," said Gran.

Tex looked at Harriet uncertainly. "Um…"

"I mean, if you're going to paint all the residents of Hampton Cove you can't stop at painting people," said Harriet. "You have to paint the pets, too. And there are a lot of pets in Hampton Cove. Thousands, probably, when you include all the pet rabbits, gerbils, fish, rats, mice, parrots…"

Gran dutifully translated Harriet's words to Tex, who looked more and more flustered. "The thing is that I'm not sure if I'm cut out to be a painter of pets," he finally revealed. "I mean, it's so hard to capture the soul of a pet on canvas—if animals even have a soul, that is. So maybe I'll leave that to some other deserving artist." He gestured to Gran. "Maybe you can do the honors, Vesta. You like pets, you even talk to them."

"Oh, I'm not getting into all of that stuff," said Vesta. "Like you said, been there, done that. And I'm definitely not getting into the racket of painting pets."

"Why not?" Harriet challenged her. "I'll bet there's good money to be made with pet portraits. Every pet owner will probably pay through the nose for a portrait of their pet, providing it's done well. They'll give it pride of place in their home, and they will cherish it forever."

This had Gran thinking, and finally she nodded. "You know, maybe you're onto something there, Harriet. Maybe there is some value in painting pets for fun and profit."

"See?" said Tex, perking up to a great extent. "I knew you'd see the light. It's a great feeling to be able to give something of yourself to the world, Vesta. To be an *artiste* in the true sense of the word. And now if you'll excuse me, I think I'll walk back and start another painting. I suddenly feel the muse calling to me."

"Let it call," said Gran. "We've got a house to stake out."

"That's not on my agenda, I'm afraid," said Tex cheerfully, and before Gran could stop him, he walked out the door.

"Where is he going?" Gran demanded.

"He says he heard the muse calling," said Dooley. "Though I have to say I didn't hear anything. Did you guys hear this muse calling?"

"It's a metaphor, Dooley," I explained. "Nobody is actually calling, except the urge for the artist to put his brush to canvas and create great art."

"I hope he doesn't paint me from memory," said Harriet, sounding a little worried. "I've seen Tex's paintings, and they're terrible at the best of times. So I can only imagine what he'll do when he tries to paint something from memory."

"He's not going to paint you, sugar plum," said Brutus. "Didn't you hear what he said? He's not into painting pets, because we don't have a soul."

Harriet bridled at this. "What is he talking about? Of course we have a soul! We probably have more soul than any human I know! I call it discrimination. And if he doesn't paint me soon I'm going to file a complaint with the Equal Employment Opportunity Commission. Let's see if he still won't paint me then!"

"Go easy on Tex," was my advice. "He's just starting out as a painter. I'm sure once he's further along in his career, his work will improve, and you'll stand a better chance of having a portrait that actually does you credit, instead of the childish daubings he'll create now."

She thought about that for a moment, and finally nodded. "I guess you're right. If I allow him to paint me now, it's just going to look terrible. So I'll let you go first, Gran."

"I'm not the first one," Gran grunted. "Apparently he's been painting Marge, and some crappy stuff, too, by the sound of it." She clapped her hands. "But what are we standing around here jabbering about my son-in-law the failed artist? We have a job to do and we have to do it now!"

Scarlett had reappeared, this time dressed in a pantsuit that didn't look all that different from Gran's.

"Ooh, look at us!" said Scarlett. "We could be sisters!"

"We are sisters," Gran agreed. "Sisters from another mother."

This had Dooley stumped, and for the next five minutes, while we all descended the stairs and then filed into Gran's car, he peppered me with questions about Gran's mother and Scarlett's mother and whether they were the same person or not, and if they were, why did Gran and Scarlett look so different?

I was used to fielding my friend's questions, and so I finally managed to convince him that Gran and Scarlett weren't actually sisters at all, but that the notion of being sisters somehow appealed to them for some deep-seated psychological reason. He still didn't understand, and frankly I didn't either. Humans are hard to plumb, after all, and like I already explained, I'm not a shrink!

"Aren't you going to ditch the trailer?" asked Scarlett, referring to the contraption that rattled on behind us as Gran put the car in gear.

"No time," said Gran as she stomped on the accelerator and the car jumped away from the curb with a force that slammed us all against the backseat.

"Where is Clarice?" asked Harriet suddenly.

"She said something about cat choir," I said.

Harriet opened and closed her mouth a few times, then said, in a voice that betrayed her annoyance, "Bet she'll try to take my place as the lead soprano. Oh, the treachery." At this point she demanded that Gran stop the car and let her out.

"Where are you going?" asked Brutus.

"To cat choir!" said Harriet. "No way am I going to let this back-stabbing traitor take my place as the leading soprano!"

"Wait, I'll come with you," said Brutus.

The upshot was that it was just me and Dooley, along with the two sisters from another mother, who continued their journey to the house where Bruno and Boris resided. Somehow I would have felt more at ease if our friends hadn't bailed on us. Then again, it was just the one guy with the one dog, so how bad could it be?

CHAPTER 24

We arrived at what could only be described as not a very nice part of town, where the houses were small and a little dilapidated, and the streets weren't as nicely asphalted as they could have been. I saw patches of green sticking out from between the paving stones that constituted the sidewalks, and I saw houses that had been boarded up and sprayed with graffiti.

"Charlene should really deal with this neighborhood," Gran grumbled. "It's a disgrace to our lovely town."

"It isn't very nice here," Scarlett agreed. "But then she can't be expected to make every part of town as nice-looking as the next. People also have a responsibility to keep their neighborhood clean, and their houses," she added as she took a keen look at one particular house that looked old and saggy.

"This is it," said Gran. "At least according to Harriet it is."

"Too bad she decided not to join us," said Dooley. "She already met this Bruno fellow, so she could have provided the introductions."

"We're just going to stake out the place for a while,

Dooley," I reminded him. "We're not actually going to talk to this Bruno—or to Boris."

"Oh, too bad. I thought we were going to barge in there and demand some answers. Like: what was he thinking when he put his daughter into that coma?"

"Boris claims that Bruno was never anywhere near his daughter," I told my friend. "And that he was with Bruno the whole time, so he would know."

"He was probably lying. We both know what dogs are like. They're so loyal to their masters they would lie through their teeth if they thought it would help them."

It is true that dogs are known to be extremely loyal to their humans. But as Harriet had told the story this Boris had actually sworn high and low that he had never left Bruno's side, and that the man hadn't actually come face to face with his daughter. That in fact his daughter had simply stood him up that fateful night.

It was all very puzzling, and I hoped we would get some answers soon.

"Okay, so what is our mission statement?" asked Scarlett eagerly.

"We're simply going to keep an eye on the place," said Gran. "And make sure this guy doesn't come anywhere near his daughter."

"But I thought you said he's innocent. Or at least that's what his dog claims?"

"We all know what dogs are like, Scarlett," said Gran. "They would lie through their teeth if they thought it was in the best interests of their masters."

"See!" said Dooley triumphantly. "That's exactly what I said!"

"Okay, so maybe you're right," I admitted. "And maybe Gran is right. But I still would prefer to defer judgment until we've actually met this Bruno and heard it from his own lips."

The best thing would be for Ella to wake up from her coma, of course, and for her to tell us what had actually happened. As it now looked, she might be the only one who could provide us with the truth.

So we settled in for the duration, and Gran took out a bag of chips and started snacking on them.

"I wish you wouldn't do that," said Scarlett.

"Do what?"

"It's very tempting, Vesta, and you know I'm on a diet."

"You're always on a diet," said Gran. "And I don't even see why. You've got a great figure."

"Why do you think I've got a great figure? Because I'm always on a diet!"

"Still. One bag of chips isn't going to make a difference."

"Oh, but it will," Scarlett assured her friend. "One leads to another, and then another, and before you know it, you can't stop. No, it's better to go cold turkey and simply don't touch the stuff at all."

"Suit yourself," said Gran, sticking another potato chip into her mouth and crunching down on it.

The scent of the chips spread through the car and Scarlett groaned in agony. "It's not very kind of you, Vesta," she lamented. "It's like drinking beer in front of an alcoholic. You wouldn't do that, would you?"

"Of course I would. Why do I have to deny myself the pleasure of drinking a beer just because the other person can't keep himself under control? It's not my problem."

"That's a very selfish way of looking at the world," Scarlett pointed out. "And very mean of you."

"It's not mean. It's just the way things are." She sat up a little straighter, warming to the topic. "Look, suppose, for argument's sake, that you're addicted to chocolate cake, and you've been trying to stop. Now do you really expect me not to eat chocolate cake anymore, because you have an issue? That doesn't seem fair to me."

"I would ask you, as a friend, not to eat chocolate cake in my presence," said Scarlett. "There's plenty of opportunity for you to eat cake when I'm not there. So yeah, if you continue shoving your cake in my face I'd become very upset."

Just like she was upset that Gran kept stuffing her face with chips right now. Finally Gran grimaced and put the bag away. "I'm sorry. I guess you're right. That is a little inconsiderate of me."

"A little? How about a lot?"

"I know, I know. I have a tendency to get a little selfish from time to time and I have to learn how to modulate that."

We all stared at the old lady. "Who has kidnapped Gran and put this new person in her place?" was how Dooley worded our astonishment. Even Scarlett seemed surprised.

"You're becoming awfully mellow and wise in your old age, honey," she said.

"I try to be," said Gran virtuously. Then she shrugged. "I guess this business with Ella has really gotten to me. Life is short, you know. And you never know what will happen next, or how many good years you've got left. So why waste them on rubbing people the wrong way? I mean, look at us. We used to fight like cats and dogs, and now we're best friends. And isn't this a lot nicer?"

"It is a lot nicer," Scarlett confirmed.

"Gran is acting weird, Max,'" said Dooley.

"I think she's acting like a grownup," I said. Which was a nice change of pace at any rate.

The front door of the house we were watching opened and a man appeared. He looked disheveled and was dressed slovenly and he answered exactly to the description Harriet had given of Ella's dad Bruno Watts.

"That's him!" I said. "That's Bruno!"

"Yee-hah, the game is afoot!" Gran cried, as she started up her car. Unfortunately for us, the man seemed determined not to use a car as a means of transportation, but was simply going for a walk.

"What do we do!" said Scarlett.

"There's only one thing we can do," said Gran. "Walk!"

And so we all got out of the car, and moments later were following along in Bruno's wake—following the man and hoping we wouldn't be seen!

The art of surveillance is exactly that: an art. It takes skill and it takes a certain discipline. Unfortunately our humans possessed neither. Scarlett and Gran didn't bother to split up, for one thing, but simply walked side by side. I could have told them that it would have been better if they covered both sides of the street, and kept their distance. So when Bruno crossed the street, one of them would simply be behind him, while the other person hung back on the other side of the street, not conspicuous at all.

Now, when Bruno crossed the street, looking left and right, of course he immediately spotted the two similarly dressed old ladies, who also crossed the street, and who had their beady eyes glued to the back of his head like a poultice.

I groaned, for I had noticed that Bruno had noticed that he was being followed. Talk about a beginner's mistake!

But since he wasn't bothered with Dooley or myself, at least we'd be able to keep track of him, even if he managed to lose his tail in the form of the matching tracksuit duo.

And this is exactly what happened: suddenly Bruno ducked into an alleyway, broke into a run, and soon disappeared out of sight, even as Scarlett and Gran followed suit.

"Where is he!" Gran cried.

"Where did he go!" Scarlett yelled.

And so it was up to Dooley and me to keep up the

surveillance, which we did by putting our noses to the ground, then breaking into a little sprint ourselves, and catching up with the man on the next street, where he was glancing over his shoulder from time to time, and generally setting a brisk pace.

"Where are Gran and Scarlett?" asked Dooley.

"They couldn't keep up," I said, panting a little. I'm a cuddly cat, you see, built for comfort, not speed, and all this running about like a headless chicken wasn't doing me any favors. But I had a mission to complete, and I was going to complete it, no matter what.

It took Bruno about half an hour, but finally I had the impression we were on familiar ground.

"I think I recognize this street," said Dooley.

"Me, too," I said, glancing around. And then it hit me. "This is our street, Dooley!"

"Oh, dear," said my friend. "He knows where we live!"

And so he did. Moments later we arrived at our very own home, and Bruno was leaning against a lamppost, smoking a cigarette and staking out our home the way we had staked out his. Looked like the roles had been reversed!

The lights inside had been doused, as they should, since everyone was probably asleep by now, and I wondered what to do.

"We should tell Odelia," said Dooley.

"I know, but by the time we tell her what's going on, Bruno will probably have skedaddled."

"So you tell her, and I'll keep an eye on Bruno. Or the other way around."

I thought for a moment, and figured this was an excellent idea. "You go and tell Odelia," I suggested. "So Chase can arrest the guy." If it was true that he'd escaped from a Mexican prison, there probably was a warrant out for his arrest.

And so Dooley crossed the street and disappeared around the back of the house while I stayed rooted to the spot. I wondered what Bruno's game plan was. Why he had decided to stake out the house. I also wanted to know how he had discovered his daughter's new location, since no one was supposed to know where she was. Then again, Bruno probably had contacts, and those contacts had contacts, and at the end of the day it's a fact of life that people blab, especially for the right price. Someone at the hospital must have talked, or maybe someone at the police precinct. At any rate, we had a situation that needed to be dealt with, and right speedily, too!

A curtain moved on the second floor, and I knew that either Odelia or Chase was doing the moving. Bad idea! Bruno must have noticed, too, for he stiffened and pushed himself away from the lamppost and moved back, out of the circle of light the lamp spread on the pavement below.

I moved back along with him, and as he ducked down into a bush that borders the front yard of one of our neighbors, I found myself very close to the man indeed.

Next thing I knew he had taken out his phone and was furiously texting. But as I approached in an attempt to read what he was texting, Bruno suddenly turned and directed his phone at me, and I was caught in the bright light of the screen!

He cursed, and I could tell he would have thrown his phone at me if he could. So instead I decided that my cover was blown, and hurriedly removed myself from the scene.

Bruno seemed to figure the same strategy was advisable for him, and when I looked over again, the man was gone.

CHAPTER 25

*B*arnaby hadn't known what to expect when his new employee told him she owned a pet rat. He'd never known anyone who even liked rats, let alone owned one and actually kept it in their home and allowed it to run riot. So when Sarah dropped off her rat that morning, before leaving for New York to attend her sister's wedding, he felt a slight frisson of resentment mingled with fear at the prospect of having to spend the day in the company of the creature.

But all in all he had to admit the rat was exceptionally well-behaved. It didn't try to chew up his papers, or pee on the floor or leave droppings in the store. It had its own litter box where it did its business, and its own bowl of food where it liked to nibble on kibble, and on the whole the experience wasn't entirely as disagreeable as he had expected.

At least not until his mom walked in and came eye to eye with the creature. He didn't know who screamed the loudest: his mom or Footsie. The rat actually produced a squealing sound that reminded him of the kind of horror movies he used to like, and his mom... Well, she simply jumped on top of his desk and stood screaming her head off for about a minute before exhorting him to 'Kill the rat! Kill it! Now!'

"I can't," he explained. "It's Sarah's pet rat Footsie."

"There ain't no such thing as a pet rat!" she declared, still standing on top of his desk and eyeing Footsie as if he was evil personified. The rat himself had calmed down and was simply sniffing the air, presumably taking a whiff of Mom's particular aroma so he would recognize her later. He could see him exert his tiny rat brain trying to figure out what that crazy lady was doing and whether she represented a menace to him or not.

"He's not dangerous, Mom," he assured his mater. "He won't bite or anything. In fact he's pretty docile."

"You have got to be kidding me!"

"No, I'm serious. Sarah had to attend the wedding of her twin sister so she asked if I could keep an eye on Footsie while she's gone."

"That girl is crazy. There's no other explanation. Completely nuts!"

"I don't think so. I've googled the phenomenon of the pet rat and they're actually pretty intelligent creatures. And once they're domesticated they're cute and lovely."

"It's staring at me, Barnaby. It wants to hurt me, I can tell."

"Oh, get down from there before you break your neck," he said, though the prospect of his mom breaking her neck actually provided him with a tiny sliver of anticipatory pleasure for which he immediately felt guilty.

He assisted his mom from her high perch, and while she still kept a close eye on the rat, at least she wasn't resorting to a more radical solution like grabbing a pair of scissors and snipping off its head.

"You have to do something about that girl," Mom said now as she took a seat.

"Do what? What are you talking about?"

"I caught her last night trying to filch some roses. Actually putting them into her backpack. When I caught her she said they were wilted anyway, and we were going to throw them away. But I ask you: is that a way to behave? Imagine what she'll steal next. Stationary, or the contents of the cash register? I know we should never have hired a known kleptomaniac. She simply can't control the urge. Before you know it she'll rob us blind and don't tell me I didn't warn you!" she finished, wagging her finger in his face.

"I'm sure it's just as she said: that we were going to throw those flowers out and she figured she might as well take them home."

"I don't trust her," Mom grumbled. "And I would like you to reconsider, Barnaby. I talked to Rebecca Scrum yesterday, and when she heard that you had actually hired Sarah, she was outraged. She said she would tell all of their customers never to set foot in here again until that no-good girl is gone."

Barnaby shrugged. "That's their business."

"No, it's our business," his mom pointed out. "If we lose customers over this…"

"We might lose a couple of customers, but only the ones who aren't prepared to give a person a second chance, and frankly speaking I don't even want that kind of customer."

"That's a very shortsighted way of thinking, Barnaby, and you know it."

"All I know is that she's doing a good job, and the customers like her."

"Mh," said Mom, and Barnaby could tell that she agreed with him on that, albeit very reluctantly.

"Look, it's going to take some getting used to, for sure, but we need the extra help, Mom, if we want to expand. And I like the way she's handled herself so far."

"You won't like it so much when she takes off with the

cash register and the contents of that safe." She was pointing to the safe that was built into the wall and where Barnaby kept the daily receipts until such time as he could deliver them to the bank.

"She won't take off with the contents of the safe," he assured his mom. "For one thing, she doesn't know the combination, and for another, I don't believe for one second Sarah is capable of such a thing. She's a kleptomaniac, not an actual thief."

"It's the same thing and you know it," Mom insisted. "But I see what's going on here. You've got the hots for that girl, haven't you? And don't you try to deny it. I've seen the way you look at her, and it's obvious she's got you under her spell." She shook her head. "Your dad was exactly the same way. He would hire a salesgirl based on her looks, and even though she didn't know a cod from a haddock he wouldn't allow me to get rid of her until we lost half of our customers to the competition. Mark my words: once you realize your infatuation is costing us more customers than we're gaining, you'll sing a different tune. Let's hope it won't be too late by then."

And with these tidings of doom, she left the office, but not before giving Footsie another look that could kill. Barnaby had to hand it to the creature: he took it in stride a lot better than Barnaby did.

"So what's your secret, little buddy?" said Barnaby, addressing the rat. "How do you manage to remain so calm and resist the urge to strangle my mother with your bare hands?" Then he realized that a rat doesn't have bare hands. It does have teeth, though, and very sharp ones at that. "Okay, all kidding aside: you have my permission to dig your teeth into her ankles next time she looks at you like that."

And it could have been his imagination, but the rat actually seemed to smile.

***

IT HAD TAKEN Sarah a little time to arrive at the City Clerk's Office, where her sister's marriage was being officiated, but she got there just when the minister, or the official, or whatever he was, called the parties into his office to commence proceedings. It was a pity she hadn't arrived sooner, she thought, for she would have liked to meet her future brother-in-law before they tied the knot. As it was, her first look at the man wasn't all that favorable. Far from being the handsome prince she had imagined, he looked more like a troll. A droll troll, admittedly, but still a troll. He was short and squat and he had a funny round face that reminded her of a pancake. On the fringes of the pancake some sprigs of hair sprung out. On the top the hair was blue for some reason, and on the bottom his goatee was pink. All in all he looked more like an alien than an eligible bachelor, or a man her sister would ever fall in love with. But there they were, on the verge of getting married.

Sylvie's baby was also there, being held by Sylvie and Sarah's mom, who didn't look all that happy either. In fact when Sarah looked a little closer her folks looked shell-shocked. As if their eyes had just witnessed a terrible sight and their brain was having trouble processing it.

She sidled up to her mom as they were led into the main hall where the wedding was to take place.

"Who is this guy?" she asked her mom. "Have you met him?"

"No, we haven't," said her mom stiffly. "This is actually the first time we've laid eyes on Ezra."

"Oh, is that his name?"

Mom nodded. "I wonder if it's his real name, though. I mean, what kind of name is Ezra? It sounds so... weird."

"Where did he and Sylvie meet? Do you have any idea?"

"She told me over the phone they met at a comics convention. Which strikes me as odd since your sister has never read a comic book in her life. But I can only repeat what she has told us."

"A comics convention, huh? So this guy Ezra is a comics artist?"

"Your guess is as good as mine," said her mom.

They had taken their seat on the wooden benches and her dad leaned in. "I think he looks like a drug dealer."

"He does look a little like a drug dealer," Sarah agreed. "Though we shouldn't judge a book by its cover, Dad."

"I'm judging *this* book by its cover," her dad insisted. "And I'm not liking what I'm seeing, to tell you the truth."

Mom's lips had turned into a thin line of disapproval. Clearly she was in full agreement with her husband.

"So what's going on with you, sweetie?" asked Mom. "How is your new job?"

"Oh, it's fine. I've got a great boss, so that's nice. He actually agreed to take care of Footsie for the day."

"The animal hasn't died yet?"

"No, Mom. Footsie is alive and well."

"Such a shame," Mom murmured, perhaps a little harshly. She was rocking Julie on her knee, and the little girl was studying her aunt with glittering eyes.

"You look happy, don't you?" said Sarah, giving the little girl a gentle tap on the nose.

"She's too young to understand that her mother is squandering her future on a bum," said Dad.

"Is he a bum, though?" said Sarah. "How do you define a bum?"

"That," said Dad, pointing to his future son-in-law, "is my definition of a bum."

"He's a waiter," Mom said.

"Ezra works as a waiter?"

Mom nodded. "At least that's what Sarah told me."

"Sylvie."

"Right," said her mom vaguely. It wasn't the first time Mom confused her two daughters. "I asked her what he did for a living, and at first she kind of hemmed and hawed, then finally she told me he works at a diner. But he's got ambitions to be an artist."

"An artist? What kind of artist?"

Dad leaned in again. "A con artist!" he hissed.

But then the official requested them all to be quiet and the proceedings commenced. At a certain point he asked if there were any objections to the union of Sylvie and Ezra, and Sarah could tell that her dad had trouble keeping his mouth shut, but the moment passed, and before long her sister was duly married and had become Mrs. Ezra Burns, as the man's name turned out to be.

The meeting was adjourned, and Sarah streaked forward to give her sister a hug and her heartfelt congratulations. She was surprised, therefore, when she found her sibling standoffish and stony-faced, and when her new husband ambled over, looking as happy as any groom had a right to be, his new wife gave him a look of such loathing that the man instantly ambled off again, his exuberance having received a considerable dent. There had been no kissing involved at any point in the proceedings, Sarah now remembered.

"Is everything all right between you and Ezra?" she asked therefore.

At which point her sister lowered her voice and said, "Not here. Not now."

Interesting. And surprising.

CHAPTER 26

Sylvie hadn't enjoyed the best time as the future Mrs. Ezra Burns. Not only had she found her new home resembling a pigsty more than an actual livable habitation, but she had also found Ezra's roommate Jake Barker an exceptionally obnoxious individual. It was clear that when the man had suggested the scheme to his friend he had never expected it to impact his own life to such a degree.

"Well, what did you expect?" said Sylvie. "Where did you think Ezra was going to live with this new wife of his? On a cloud?"

"I just think the space is too small for the three of us," Jake had insisted stubbornly. "Especially with *that* thrown into the mix." 'That' turned out to be Julie, and the way Jake had looked at her little girl had raised all of Sylvie's hackles and she had come very close to giving the man a slap across the face that would have spun his head around a couple of times like in one of his beloved comics.

Instead she had simply stalked back into the bedroom she now shared with Ezra and plunked herself down on the bed and wondered if this was the worst decision she had ever made in her entire life. And considering she had had a baby from a man she now hated almost as much as she hated Jake, that was quite a feat.

Ezra had ambled into the room looking sheepish. He obviously didn't like being caught between his new roommate and his old one, but that couldn't be helped.

"Jake is not a bad guy," he insisted after he had sat down on the bed next to her. "He just needs a little time to get used to the situation, that's all."

She angrily wiped away a tear and said, "We all have to get used to the situation, but that doesn't mean we have to be obnoxious about it."

"I know," said Ezra, and gave her a pained look, then looked away again. "Can I just say I think you're very brave, the way you're dealing with this? I don't think I could have coped quite as well as you are doing if I had a kid to think about."

"It's not 'a kid,'" she insisted. "Her name is Julie."

"I know, I know. Julie. And she's a sweet kid, too."

She bridled a little, but refrained from making a comment. "Okay, so what do you think should happen next?"

"What do you mean?"

"I mean: how are we going to organize ourselves?" When he still continued to look mystified, she spelled it out for him: "If these detectives are keeping such a close eye on us, as you seem to believe, it's probably important that they know we're sleeping in the same bed. This bed is very small, Ezra. There's no way we're both going to fit in here, unless we snuggle or spoon. And even then it's not going to be very comfortable."

His face had turned a bright red at the thought of either snuggling or spooning with her, and she couldn't blame him. He probably hated the prospect of having to share his personal space with a complete stranger, confirmed bachelor that he was.

"Um... I guess I hadn't thought about that," he admitted. "So... maybe I'll get on the horn with Ahmad and ask him to get us a double mattress."

"Do you buy all your stuff from Ahmad?"

"Not all my stuff. Just, you know, the weird stuff."

"A double mattress is weird?"

"It's unusual. I mean, I've never slept on a double mattress before. Or shared my bed with a person... for more than one night." He gave her a shamefaced look, his face even redder than before, and in spite of herself she had to laugh.

"It's all right, Ezra," she said. "I'm a girl, not a live grenade. I'm not going to go and blow your head off."

"Oh, I wasn't afraid of that," he insisted. "Just, you know."

"Yeah, I know," she said. "Okay, so you better get that mattress, so we can both get a good night's sleep, and I'll start tidying up a little." So she wouldn't get septic shock. He got up from the bed and she suddenly thought of something. "Do you keep any drugs around the apartment?"

"Oh, no. Absolutely not."

"You're sure? It's just that I don't want Julie accidentally inhaling something, or swallowing something, or generally being exposed to anything that might be harmful or toxic."

"We threw it all down the garbage chute," Ezra declared proudly.

"I remember you told me about that. I thought you were kidding."

"Oh, I wasn't," he assured her. "We got rid of everything. The booze, the bong, the weed. The whole lot. Gone. No one can trace it back to us, even if they tried."

She eyed him with a touch of compassion. "If they really wanted to, they could trace everything back to you, Ezra."

His eyes went wide as saucers. "They can?"

"Of course. Did you wipe down that bong before you threw it down the chute?" When he shook his head, she said, "Have you ever heard of fingerprints? Or DNA?"

He clasped both hands to his face in a look of horror. "What have we done!" And before she could stop him, he was running from the room. She could hear a shouted conversation being carried out in Jake's room, and the next moment both men were racing out of the apartment, slamming the door behind them, presumably on their way down to the basement to destroy the evidence of their debauchery for real.

She smiled and got up from the bed.

Finally. Some peace and quiet.

She returned to the living room, where she found Julie seated on the couch and watching an NFL game for some reason, and picked her up. This was going to be quite the challenge, and she desperately hoped the money Ezra had promised her would materialize in the end. If not... She had no one but herself to blame.

Sarah stared at her sister in abject horror and shock. "You did what?!" she cried, then quickly piped down again when the eyes of everyone in the restaurant turned to them.

"I admit it wasn't one of my brightest ideas," said Sylvie ruefully. "But what else was I going to do? I hated my job, my boss hated me, I was dying. And Mom and Dad kept nagging me about finding some affordable childcare solution so they could finally leave on that cruise they've been planning for when Dad took early retirement. So I cracked. I admit it. I buckled under the pressure. When Ahmad approached me with this cockamamie idea of making a big pile of money by simply playing wife to a friend of his, I figured it would be easy money."

"But it's not?"

"No, it's not. First off, it's not guaranteed that there will ever be any money, and second, Ezra is supposed to find a job, but so far all he's done is goof around and play video games with his roommate. They did get rid of all of their booze and dope, but you should see the apartment. It's an absolute dump. I've tried to make it inhabitable, and baby-proof, but it isn't easy when you're living with two men who are basically still children themselves."

"He does strike me as pretty immature," Sarah agreed as she watched Ezra get into a potato-eating match with his best friend and roommate, stuffing as many potatoes as they could into their mouths at the same time. Mom and Dad watched the scene with inscrutable faces, but Sarah could tell their opinion of Ezra was sinking to a new low.

"He's a baby," said Sylvie with a sigh. "Julie is probably more mature than he is." She rested her head on her hands and groaned. "And I married the guy!"

"It's only a fake marriage, though, right?"

"Didn't you hear that guy from the Clerk's Office? The marriage is real, all right, and if I ever want to get out of it I'll have to divorce Ezra."

"Which is part of the contract, correct?"

"It is part of the contract, but that doesn't mean it's going to be easy. This guy…" She gestured in the direction of her husband, who was now balancing a piece of pork on his chin. "He needs to stay married for one year. So even though I only agreed to do this for three months, it's very well possible I'll be forced to go the whole nine yards and stick to the routine for a whole year. Otherwise no inheritance. And no money for me."

"Maybe it will be worth it in the end?"

"Somehow I doubt it," said Sylvie. "The thing is that this Aunt Emily had a certain person in mind who she wanted to leave her money to. A person who holds a steady job, who's married with a family, who's not a drug addict or an alcoholic. In other words: a responsible adult."

They both looked over to Ezra, who had stuffed red peppers in his ears and nostrils and was trying to hold his breath for as long as he could.

"It's a disaster," Sylvie concluded. "An absolute disaster."

"If I were Aunt Emily I wouldn't leave my money to your husband either," Sarah agreed. But when her sister dissolved in wails of despair, she patted her back. "There must be some benefits, though, right? Or otherwise you wouldn't have agreed with this crazy scheme."

Sylvie wiped her nose with a napkin. "He is kind," she admitted. "And he does seem to have a talent for the arts. When I was cleaning out the apartment I found a bunch of drawings stuffed into a portfolio folder and they were pretty good. But when I asked him about it he said he'd given up on that and claimed he simply wasn't good enough."

"So he wanted to become a comic artist at one point?"

"He did. And I think he's got the talent, but what he lacks is the drive, and the stamina. And I think his roommate has got a lot to do with that. I think Jake brings out the worst in him."

"Can't you get rid of this guy?"

"His name is on the lease."

"Maybe you and Ezra could move? You can always claim it will look a lot better for these so-called detectives?"

"Nothing so-called about it. They're actually watching us. Do you see those two guys over there?"

Sarah looked over, and saw two men dressed in trench coats, wearing sunglasses indoors. "Uh-huh?"

"I swear I saw them when I left the apartment to go for a

walk last night. They were in a car parked in front of the building. And when I walked out, one of them got out of the car and followed me all the way to the park and back."

"This is crazy, Sylvie." Then she decided her comment wasn't helpful, and she changed tack. "Okay, so if this is going to be your life for the next year or so, you need to take control of the situation. Which means getting rid of the roommate and straightening out your husband."

"Good luck with that," Sylvie muttered despondently. "I can't even get him to get us a decent mattress. Last night I slept on the bed—which smells like weed and unwashed socks, by the way—and my husband slept on the couch."

"Just give him an ultimatum," Sarah suggested. "Tell him that if he doesn't sort himself out, you're leaving."

Sylvie stared at her. "But then I won't get anything."

"Who cares! You move out, find another job—one that either pays enough so you can afford childcare or even better: a job that actually provides childcare to its personnel—and divorce the guy. Chalk it up to bad choices."

"Bad choices. Now that's an understatement."

"If you want I'll talk to him."

"No, that's fine," said Sylvie, holding up her hand. "I'll deal with Ezra. He is my husband, after all."

Sarah saw that a look of resolve had come into her sister's eye, and was shining brightly now. "I'm going to do it," she said. "I'm going to give him an ultimatum. Either he straightens himself out, or I'm leaving him. How long do you think I should... Never mind. I'll figure it out." She smiled. "Gee, thanks, sis. I should have talked to you sooner."

"Why didn't you?"

Sylvie gave her a sheepish look. "I figured you wouldn't approve. That's why I didn't tell Mom and Dad either. In fact I still haven't told them—and maybe I never will."

"They won't hear it from me," Sarah promised her twin.

"Thanks," said Sylvie warmly, and they shared a sisterly hug. Then she sighed. "Time to get real." And so she got up and walked over to her husband, whose face had turned beet-red and who had tears in his eyes. Sarah could have told him that putting peppers in your nose is never a good idea.

CHAPTER 27

After our run-in with Ella's dad, the atmosphere in the house was electric. When Odelia told Aunt Aurelie about what happened, the woman was up in arms and was demanding we organize a manhunt and arrest her ex-husband right now.

It wasn't difficult to convince Odelia's uncle to do exactly that, and after he had conferred with his colleagues from Hampton Keys, he agreed that Bruno should be arrested and sent back to a Mexican prison to finish serving his sentence.

But when his officers arrived at the scene, the bird had already flown the coop. Which didn't surprise me a great deal. Bruno must have realized he'd been caught, and as the clever jailbreaker he was must have decided to skedaddle.

Aunt Aurelie was beside herself with worry, and wanted to find a different address to stay with her daughter. She also argued that nowhere was safe for them until her ex-husband was placed under arrest. The man had proven himself both cunning and resourceful, and unless Uncle Alec could provide a safe house for her, he might find them again. He had done it once, so he could probably do it again.

The meeting as it took place on the patio, since they didn't want Ella to have to witness the frenzied discussions, was heated to a degree, and as Dooley and I watched on, my friend asked, "So is it true what Aunt Aurelie says? Can people in a coma hear everything that's happening around them?"

"In some cases it has proven true," I said. "And in others not. But since it's hard to know whether Ella is in the former or the latter category, it's probably wise not to discuss such a sensitive topic in front of her."

"So Aunt Aurelie is right," Dooley concluded.

"Yeah, she is."

Harriet and Brutus had also joined us, and contrary to Dooley and me they both looked well-rested and relaxed.

"Cat choir was glorious," Harriet said. "I actually ended up performing a duet with Clarice, if you can imagine."

I could imagine, but that didn't mean I wasn't happy I had missed the recital.

"And I provided backing vocals," Brutus said proudly. "It was amazing. Even Shanille agreed we should continue as a trio. Our voices are so much attuned."

"Is that a fact?" I said, trying to overhear what our humans were discussing, which was hard with Harriet and Brutus regaling us with their tales of success.

"I think we should organize a tour," said Harriet. "I will take first billing, of course, with Clarice's name in fine print below mine, and Brutus in even finer print at the bottom."

"Why is my name at the bottom?" asked Brutus.

"Because you're providing backing vocals," said Harriet. "Try to keep up."

"But I thought we were going to be an actual trio," said Brutus, much disappointed.

Harriet eyed him strangely. "Haven't we always agreed that I'm the main star in this family? Which means your task is to make me look good, sweetie. And you can't do that by taking central billing on my poster."

"Okay," said Brutus, but he didn't look happy.

"It's the way of the world, snickerdoodle," said Harriet. "There can only be one star, otherwise people get confused."

"Maybe we can start a band?" Brutus suggested. "A band has more than one star, right?"

Harriet laughed a tinkling laugh at such naiveté. "Even a band has one star, smoochie poo. The singer is the star. I mean, do you even know who the drummer is in any successful band? At the most people are familiar with the lead guitar player, but that's as far as it goes. No, there is only one star, otherwise it gets too much for people to remember. And that star is me," she concluded emphatically.

Brutus sighed. "I guess you're right," he said finally.

Harriet glanced up at the human contingent. "What are they talking about?"

"Whether they should move Aunt Aurelie and her daughter to a safe house," I said. "To protect them from her ex-husband?"

"Oh, that," said Harriet with a light shrug, and walked off. Clearly she wasn't as interested in the story as she was in her name in bold atop her own poster.

I glanced over to Brutus, who looked a little downcast. "Cheer up, buddy," I told him. "Harriet will never be a star. There will never be a tour. So there will never be a poster and she will never get top billing."

He looked up, a hopeful gleam in his eye. "You think?"

"Absolutely. The only cat in cat choir who can actually sing is Clarice, and she's not interested in being a star. And besides, no human I know is even remotely interested in listening to cats sing. Far from wanting to put their hands together when they hear us sing they want to grab the nearest shoe and throw it at our heads."

"It's true," he admitted, "that Harriet was knocked off her perch by a size-twelve shoe last night, but she figured it was that person's way of telling her how much they enjoyed her performance."

"It was the customary way in which humans express their strong desire for us to shut up," I said.

Brutus was actually smiling at that. "She made quite the tumble, too," he said, giggling at the recollection. "It would have hit Clarice, but she ducked just in time and it hit Harriet in the face instead."

"Clarice is smart," I said. "And she has amazing reflexes."

"She does," Brutus agreed. "That cat is fast as lightning. It has to be seen to be believed."

"Clarice is amazing at everything she does," said Dooley, who is a big fan of Clarice. "She can sing, she can duck shoes, she can eat rats…"

Which reminded me. "Have you heard anything from Footsie?"

Both of my friends shook their heads.

"Time to pay him a visit then," I said. I was eager to find out the latest about his charge, Sarah the shoplifter, and hoped both Footsie and Sarah were doing well.

And on that note I decided to tune into the conversation once more.

"Okay, so I think we can all agree that Bruno showing up here last night has given us all a big shock," Odelia was saying. "But it's important that we don't panic and make any rash decisions."

"So what do you suggest?" asked her uncle.

"I suggest Aunt Aurelie and Ella stay here, but we improve security. The important thing is that we catch Bruno, so we can send him back to prison where he belongs. If we move you now, Aunt Aurelie, you'll never feel safe, and you will always be looking over your shoulder. But if you stay here, and we make sure you're safe and protected, and keep an eye out for Bruno, we can put an end to this threat once and for all."

"You mean use us as bait?" asked Aunt Aurelie. "I don't know, Odelia. It sounds very unsafe to me."

"It doesn't have to be," said Chase. "If we watch the house around the clock—and we can arrange that ourselves, without any input from the department—we make sure that Bruno doesn't come anywhere near you. And we grab him as soon as he shows his face here again."

Aunt Aurelie didn't seem convinced. "And who's going to watch the house twenty-four-seven? Bruno is a very violent man, Chase. You don't know who you're dealing with. He won't allow you to arrest him that easily."

"I know, but I think we have enough manpower to apprehend him." He looked around the table, where Odelia's entire family was seated, with the addition of Scarlett.

Gran was the first to pipe up. "We found him once—"

"And lost him," Scarlett murmured, earning herself a warning look from Gran.

"—so we can find him again. Count on the neighborhood watch to take the first shift."

"And Tex and I can also pitch in," Marge suggested. "I may not be a cop, and neither is Tex, but if push comes to shove we simply wake up Chase, who is a cop."

"I talked to Charlene," said Uncle Alec, "and the moment you lay eyes on Bruno, you call me and the department is at your disposal to apprehend the man. So please, people—and I can't stress this enough—no heroics, is that understood?" He was looking at his mother for some reason when he spoke these words.

"Why are you looking at me like that?" asked Gran.

"Do you understand what I'm saying, Ma?"

"Perfectly," Gran insisted. "So we see the guy and we

pounce. Bam!" She slammed the table with her palm, making us all jump up, as well as a few cups and saucers. "And it's the end of the line for Bruno whatshisface."

"No, no, no!" said Uncle Alec, shaking his head. "Okay, so I'll explain it again."

"No need," said Gran, holding up her hand. "The neighborhood watch has received its orders, and my troops are on high alert."

"Your troops…" Uncle Alec sighed deeply.

"Me, Scarlett, Francis Reilly and Wilbur Vickery will be happy to apprehend this man for you, sweetie," Gran assured Aunt Aurelie. "And we'll try not to rough him up too much, I promise."

For some reason Aunt Aurelie didn't look entirely reassured.

CHAPTER 28

Barnaby couldn't help but feel exhilarated knowing that today was the day Sarah would be back at the store. He had always enjoyed going to work—contrary to most people he knew who hated getting out of bed in the morning he actually jumped out of bed, grateful for another day. But ever since Sarah had come into his life there was a pep in his step and a smile on his lips that had lent life a new quality. As if his world was suddenly a little brighter than before, a little sunnier and a little more joyful now that he knew that Sarah was in it.

Sarah had called him last night and asked him if he didn't mind taking Footsie home with him since she had decided to stay the night at her sister's place. "There are some things I need to take care of here," she had told him, and he had assured her he understood.

"So you are having a party, huh?" he said. "You can't have a wedding without a wedding party, Sarah."

"Yeah, I guess you were right," she said.

So he had taken Footsie home with him, and it had to be said that the animal had behaved exemplarily. Footsie had gratefully accepted a few nuggets of food from his plate, had actually snuggled up to him when he was watching television, and had slept next to him in bed. In fact it wasn't too much to say he was actually going to miss having the little fella around, as odd as that might sound.

He arrived at the store and opened the roll-up security door with an easy sweep of his hand, then entered the store and punched in the security code. He then walked straight through to his office and installed Footsie on top of his desk, exhorting the sweet creature to take a nice nap. Footsie squealed its cute little squeal in response, and Barnaby returned to the store proper to start cleaning up a little, and preparing for a day of welcoming customers and selling flowers.

It was about half an hour later that Sarah finally showed up, arriving even before Barnaby's mom, which was quite a feat. Only when he looked up, he thought he saw double, for there were two Sarahs smiling back at him.

He did a double take and blinked a few times, trying to clear his vision. "Wha-wha-wha..." he stammered.

"Hey, Barnaby," said one of the two apparitions. "This is my sister Sylvie. Sylvie, meet my boss, Barnaby Blossom."

"Is that your real name?" asked the second apparition.

"It-it is," he confirmed. He had been teased relentlessly all through high school, just like his dad before him and his granddad before them. But he had survived, just like all Blossoms had survived. And now it was a blessing, since he actually sold blossoms for a living. "I forgot you're twins," he said, finally catching on.

"That's correct, sir," said the second Sarah.

"Barnaby," he said automatically as he came to terms with the phenomenon. The two were virtually indistinguishable, though when he looked a little closer he saw that Sarah's face was just that tiny bit rounder, and Sylvie's a little more elongated. And Sarah had a cute little mole on the right side of her neck and Sylvie didn't. Also, Sarah was the woman he loved, of course, and Sylvie wasn't.

"Okay, so here's the thing, Barnaby," said Sarah. "My sister is looking for a job. She's going to move to Hampton Cove, you see, she and her husband Ezra. For the time being they'll stay with me, of course. But I was wondering…" She bit her lip nervously, a habit that Barnaby found extremely endearing.

"You're hired," he suddenly heard himself say. "No problem." And he even managed to produce a smile!

The two sisters gaped at him. "You mean…" Sarah began.

"You mean I can work here?" asked her sister.

"Absolutely," Barnaby confirmed.

Before they could talk more, though, his mom arrived on the scene, regarding both Sarah and Sylvie with that usual malevolent gleam in her eye. "Oh, you're back," she said, none too friendly. "I thought we got rid of you." She grinned. "Just kidding. So is this the sister who got hitched?"

"This is the sister who got hitched," Sarah confirmed, but she wasn't smiling. Clearly she liked Barnaby's mom as much as Mom liked her, which was to say not at all.

And that's when Barnaby suddenly saw the light. He'd been wondering how he was ever going to afford paying Sylvie a living wage when the store wasn't doing that much business—yet. But now he knew exactly how.

"Mom, how about you don't come in today?" he suggested.

"What are you talking about? I'm already here."

"So maybe you can go home again."

"Don't talk nonsense, boy."

"I mean it, Mom. You know I love you very much, but this was always going to be a temporary arrangement. So maybe now the time has come to end it."

Mom stared at him, looking quite taken aback. Then she turned a nasty look at Sarah. "This is her doing, isn't it? She put you up to this!"

"Sarah has nothing to do with this," he said. "This is my decision."

"You ungrateful piece of—"

"You could still help out around the store, Lily," said Sarah. "On a voluntary basis maybe? What do you think, Barnaby?"

"You've got some nerve!" Mom spat. "You come waltzing in here as if you own the place and you tell me what to do!"

"It's just a suggestion," said Sarah quietly.

"You can put your suggestions where the sun don't shine!"

"Oh, rude," Sylvie said.

Mom turned on her. "And you!" she said, pointing a shaking finger at the woman. "You!" But apparently her string of invective had run its course, for she merely gave Sylvie a look that could kill, then turned on her son again. "We'll talk about this later," she announced, and waltzed into the workshop.

"Mom, I think it's best if you leave now," he said, hurrying after her. But when his mom wheeled on him, he added, "I mean, I think we'll manage without you from now on. I will manage without you from now on." When his mom didn't speak, but just stood there, her eyes blazing, he said, "Look, I appreciate what you've done, I really do, but I think it's time we both moved on, don't you? You never liked flowers in the first place, and you can't stop complaining about the customers, the business, my work ethic, the way I like to do things…"

"If you can't take a little bit of criticism…"

"I can, but not if it's a non-stop tirade from morning till night. And not if you're going to drive the best salesperson away that I've known so far."

"You mean that little imp?"

"Yes, I mean that little imp," he said with a smile. "And please don't say anything else that you might regret, Mom," he added when she got ready to really lay into Sarah. "Cause you're talking about the woman I love."

They both stared at each other, and Barnaby was probably as shocked as his mother, for he hadn't realized he was about to say what he had just said.

He heard a noise, and when he looked up, he saw that both Sarah and her sister stood looking at him, and both had put their hands to their mouths.

He blinked. "I-I-I don't know why I said that, Sarah. I-I-I know it's terribly inappropriate. Extremely so, in fact. And I want to apologize right now."

"No need to apologize," his mother grumbled. "Any idiot can see that you're smitten with the girl." She sighed. "Okay, so maybe you're right."

He wondered if he had heard right. "Did you just say—"

"Yeah, yeah. No need to rub it in. It's true that I hate flowers. I like fish. I've always liked fish. At least fish serves a purpose. Flowers are just decoration. You can't even eat them. And unlike fish they stink. So maybe it's time to call it quits. I just wanted to help you out when you started this place and I've got the experience dealing with customers and you don't. But now that you've got Sarah, I guess I might as well retire since you obviously don't need me anymore."

And as she started to walk away, Sarah stepped to the fore. "I just wanted to tell you that you've taught me so much, Mrs. Blossom."

"I have?"

"Absolutely. I didn't know the first thing about flowers when I started working here. So you actually taught me everything. And I want to thank you for that."

And before anyone could stop her, she actually hugged the irascible woman.

For a moment Barnaby expected the world to explode or the ground to open up beneath their feet and suck them all up. But nothing happened. Except that his mom patted Sarah on the back.

"You're not too bad yourself," she finally said, which was high praise coming from her. And then she was off. "You know what?" she said. "I've never had a day off in my life. I've been working from the day I turned sixteen and I never stopped. So maybe it's time for me to stop and—"

"Smell the roses," Sarah quipped.

Mom wagged a finger. "Cheeky," she said, but there was a hint of a smile on her lips.

They watched her leave, and somehow Barnaby had the impression she actually looked glad. Then he turned back to Sarah. "Forget what I said," he implored.

"Do you want to grab a coffee later?" asked Sarah.

He frowned. "But I'm your employer. We can't…"

"Oh, don't be so stuffy, Barnaby," said Sylvie. "It's the twenty-first century. You can have a coffee with an employee. Isn't that right, sis?"

"Absolutely," said Sarah. "A coffee and more, in fact. Like dinner, maybe?"

Barnaby's knees had gone a little weak. "But-but-but…"

"Just say yes would be my advice," said Sylvie. "Sarah may look like an innocent little nymph, but she always gets what she wants. Just look at me. Yesterday I was in New York, weeping and moaning at my wedding, and today I'm here, and so is my husband. And if you knew Ezra you'd realize that is something of a miracle. But somehow Sarah talked him into it, and she talked me into it, and here we are, ready to start a new life. At least for the next year."

"How about dinner and a movie?" Sarah suggested.

Barnaby smiled. "Only if you let me pay."

"Are you kidding? Of course you're paying. You're my boss, remember?"

And so it was arranged. Dinner and a movie, and an entirely new existence for Barnaby Blossom.

CHAPTER 29

We had it on good authority that Sarah Mitchell, Footsie's owner, now worked at Barnaby's Blossoms, so that's where we decided to go. The neighborhood watch had things well in hand at home, and so we weren't urgently needed there. Also, I figured Ella's father would probably think twice before showing up at our home so soon after almost having been caught.

"Do they only sell flowers here, Max?" asked Dooley when we had arrived at the flower shop and stood admiring the window display, which was filled with flowers.

"Yes, that's why they call it a flower shop, Dooley. Because they only sell flowers."

"But can they actually make a living selling flowers? I wouldn't think flowers are big business."

"They're not big business, per se," I agreed. "But there will always be people who like to buy flowers. And then there's the special occasions, of course, like birthdays, Mother's Day, Valentine and such."

"Oh," he said. "I hadn't thought of that." He was quiet for a moment, then said, "So why doesn't anyone ever buy us flowers, Max?""

"Probably because there's no such thing as Cat's Day," I told him, only half in jest.

"Too bad. There should be a Cat's Day, just like there's Mother's Day, Father's Day, Secretaries' Day… In fact there seems to be a day for everyone except us."

"There are dog days," I pointed out. "But I guess that's not the same thing."

"It's not fair, Max. It just isn't."

"Every day is Cat's Day, Dooley," I said. "Didn't you know that?"

He smiled at that. "You're so clever, Max. I hadn't thought of it that way. But you're right. Every day is Cat's Day."

We entered the store, and saw that Sarah was behind the counter. But then we saw that she was also rearranging some of the flower arrangements in the store, and so we got a little confused. Which is when I realized that Sarah either had a double or a twin. Probably the latter, though, I thought when we had studied both women a little more closely. Which is when either Sarah or her twin caught sight of us and crouched down next to us.

"You're Odelia's cats, aren't you? Looking for Footsie? He's in Barnaby's office."

"You must be Sarah," I said, well pleased. "And that woman over there is your sister?"

"Sis, I'll be in Barnaby's office for a moment," said the woman. "Can you mind the store?"

"Sure thing," said the doppelganger.

"Yes, you're Sarah," I said, pleased that my hunch was correct. Sarah led us to the back of the store, and then into an office. Behind the desk a man was seated who looked very busy indeed. But when Sarah walked in, his face lit up with a smile and he beamed at the new arrival.

"Hey you," he said in a husky sort of voice.

"Hey yourself," she said in equally husky tones.

"If I'm not mistaken," I told Dooley, "I think Sarah has found love."

"Or maybe love has found her," he suggested.

"That's another possibility," I agreed.

"These two are probably looking for Footsie," Sarah explained. "They're Odelia Kingsley's cats."

"Oh, the reporter who's helping you out?"

"One and the same," said Sarah.

Barnaby studied us for a moment, and I had the impression that either he was suffering from constipation or else he had just had a bright idea. At any rate, Sarah left again, and before long a furry creature stirred on the corner of Barnaby's desk. When the creature looked down at us, I recognized him as Footsie.

"Oh, hey, you guys!" he said, clearly happy to see us.

"I just thought we'd drop by and see how things are going," I said.

Footsie gracefully hopped down onto a lower table and then onto the floor. Though when I say 'hopped' I should probably say it was more like a sliding motion, or as if water was being poured from a can. Rats are really graceful, and very fast!

"As you can probably tell things are fine," he said. "Sarah got this job at the store, and somehow she convinced her sister to join her, so now there's two of them, and Barnaby is just the greatest person. I stayed with him, you know, when Sarah was in New York for Sylvie's wedding, and we had a lot of fun together."

"And if I'm not mistaken pretty soon wedding bells will ring out again, am I right?" I cocked a meaningful eyebrow but he didn't get it for he gave me a decidedly blank look in return.

"What wedding, Max?" he inquired.

"Well, Sarah and Barnaby's wedding, of course."

"Are you sure? Nobody told me anything about that."

"Nobody told me either, but it's obvious, isn't it? Those two are in love."

"I wouldn't know about that," said Footsie. "I mean, he has asked her out to dinner, but we all have to eat, right? So I don't really see how that has anything to do with love."

"When a man asks a woman out on a date, love is usually the driving force," I explained.

"Though it could also be lust," Dooley added, causing me to give him a look of alarm. "Gran once told me," he said. "When Scarlett was wondering if she should ask Wilbur Vickery out on a date."

I shivered. I couldn't imagine any woman going on a date with Wilbur, who owns the General Store in town and is also part of the neighborhood watch, and enjoying it—whether for love or lust. "Okay, so it doesn't matter," I told Footsie. "What matters is that Sarah is happy and that you're happy."

"Oh, we're both happy, all right," said Footsie. "Though we'd be even happier if that arrest business went away."

"The Scrum thing," I said. "That's still hanging over Sarah's head?"

"It is. And things are getting worse. Now the Scrums have started some kind of campaign to boycott the store and force Barnaby to fire Sarah, since they figure Barnaby shouldn't hire a thief since it's bad for business or something."

"They really don't like her, do they?" said Dooley.

"They hate her," said Footsie. "Especially Rebecca Scrum has been going out of her way to say nasty stuff about Sarah to anyone who will listen. It's having an effect on sales, too. Barnaby won't admit it, but he's losing business, since people won't buy from Sarah, figuring she's some kind of criminal and she should be in jail."

"Oh, that's too bad," I said, wondering what we could possibly do about this. "But Barnaby isn't giving in?"

"No, he's not. At least not so far. He has dropped his mom from the personnel roster, but then his mom never liked flowers anyway. She says they smell bad. Which is surprising to me, but anyway, that's a different matter altogether. What's important is that Barnaby doesn't give in to the pressure, but at some point I think he will have to."

"When he starts losing too many customers."

Footsie nodded. "So you see. Not all is well at Barnaby's Blossoms."

"I'll talk to Odelia again," I promised our murine friend. "Maybe there's something she can do."

"She could ask Charlene to mediate," Dooley suggested. "She has done it before, remember?"

"Excellent idea, Dooley," I said. The Mayor does have a vested interest in preventing the shopkeepers that represent our local business community from blackballing and boycotting each other. That kind of behavior serves no one.

So we said goodbye to Footsie with the promise we would take his case in paw, and headed for Odelia's office. And we had only arrived there when Barnaby walked in! He must have been right behind us and we hadn't even noticed.

"Mrs. Kingsley?" the shopkeeper inquired as he poked his head into her office. "Could I please have a word with you?"

"Absolutely," said Odelia, gesturing to a chair in front of her desk. "Barnaby Blossom, right? You're Sarah Mitchell's boss?"

"That's correct," said the flower salesman as he cautiously took a seat. "And I also hired her sister Sylvie. But that's not why I'm here. There seems to be some kind of campaign going on to force me to fire Sarah. The instigators of the campaign are Ebenezer and Rebecca Scrum."

"Owners of Scrum's Baubles," said Odelia, nodding.

"I know you've been helping Sarah get her life back on track," said Barnaby. "So you know all about the charges the Scrums have leveled against her. So what I have to say may sound a little strange. But from what I'm hearing the main driver behind the campaign is actually Rebecca. Now I talked to Sarah, and she told me that she doesn't remember putting that ring in her pocket. She remembers handling it, but not stealing it."

"But then she left and the alarm went off and the ring was in her pocket."

"So…" He blinked a few times. "Like I said, this may sound strange, but…"

"Yes?" said Odelia encouragingly.

"Please don't say anything to the Scrums, but I had this idea—call it a hunch—that maybe Sarah never did steal that ring in the first place."

"What do you mean?" asked Odelia, furrowing her brow.

"Okay, so I may be way off base here, but I get thieves in my shop all the time. We all do. Every shop in the world deals with shoplifters. But I never make a big fuss about it. Not like the Scrums. So does a diamond ring cost more than a bunch of flowers? Sure. But still. It just strikes me as odd that Rebecca would go on some kind of campaign and target Sarah. Almost as if this is personal for her."

"So let me get this straight. What you're saying is that you think Rebecca Scrum framed Sarah somehow?"

"Like I said, it's a crazy theory. But isn't it possible?"

"It's always possible," Odelia allowed. "But why would she do that? What would be her motive?"

"I don't know," said Barnaby, sitting back. "That's why I came to you, since you have a reputation for dealing with that kind of stuff. And this business with the shoplifting, it's having a profound effect on Sarah. She's trying to put on a brave face, but I can tell it's eating away at her peace of mind. Not to mention my profit margin, since Rebecca is doing a good job driving my customers away."

"Basically she's blackmailing you," said Odelia, nodding. "Get rid of Sarah or we will destroy you."

"In effect that's what she's doing," Barnaby confirmed. "I'm not going to fire Sarah, though. Never. But something has to be done. I already talked to Rebecca, but she insists she's merely trying to protect people from being robbed. And she's also doing this for me—or so she claims."

"She has a strange way of looking out for you."

"Yeah, by ruining me," said Barnaby sadly.

"Okay, leave this with me, Barnaby," said Odelia. "I'll see what I can do."

When the man had left, Dooley turned to me. "He stole our thunder, Max. He completely stole our thunder."

I smiled. "Not quite," I said. "We still have a few details we can supply Odelia with." And so we filled her in on what we had learned from Footsie, and I could tell that our human was concerned.

"What do you suggest, Max?" she asked finally.

"I suggest you contact Charlene," I said, reiterating Dooley's idea. "So she can organize a mediation session between Barnaby and the Scrums. And I also suggest Dooley and I sniff around Scrum's Baubles and try to figure out what's going on. If Barnaby is correct, the Scrums have set Sarah up, and we need to know why."

And so it was decided. Dooley and I would try to find out what was going on with the Scrums, and Odelia got on the horn with the Mayor to start a mediation process.

"So sad for Barnaby," said Dooley. "He's getting married to Sarah, so he can't fire her, but if he doesn't fire her, the Scrums will keep going until he goes bust. It's not fair, is it?"

"Which is why we need to act fast, Dooley," I said. "And turn things around before it's too late."

This wasn't about shoplifting anymore. This was about economic sabotage and payback. But payback for what? And who was the intended target? Barnaby or Sarah? Or both? It was a mystery, and we intended to find out.

CHAPTER 30

The task we had decided to undertake was not an easy one, since not all humans love cats to the same degree that our own humans love us. And as far as I could tell these people, the Scrums, didn't even own any cats —or dogs. So how were we ever going to get close enough to spy on them? Now if we had been flies—the proverbial fly on the wall comes to mind—this wouldn't have posed any problem whatsoever, but I don't know if you've noticed but cats are somewhat larger than flies, and also, cats can't fly, or walk on walls.

Still, we were both determined to get to the bottom of this mystery. The first step was to stake out the place and get a good overview of our new surroundings. Get the lay of the land, if you will, or the lay of Scrum's Baubles. And to that end we traipsed over there and took up position across the street. As luck would have it our good friend Kingman didn't live far from the store, so we decided to pop in for a quick chat with the voluminous cat and ask his opinion. As you may or may not know, Kingman knows everyone who's anyone in Hampton Cove, and a lot of nobodies, too. So when in doubt, he is the first one we turn to for advice.

We arrived at the General Store and saw that our friend was seated in front of the store as usual, glancing up and down the street and generally keeping an eye on proceedings. If ever a cat qualified as a watch cat Kingman would be my pick.

"Hey, buddies," he said when we came walking up. "Have I got news for you."

"Oh, what a coincidence," said Dooley. "Because we also have news for you!"

"Let's hear what Kingman has to say first," I suggested.

"It may have escaped your attention," Kingman commenced his tale, "but your Gran has asked Wilbur and Father Reilly to stake out your home tonight. Apparently there's some major criminal on the loose who plans to attack you guys!" He eyed us with the satisfaction of one who has just delivered a piece of startling news.

Unfortunately for him we already knew all about this mission that Gran had accepted to undertake, but I still gave him credit for having discovered it so soon. Then again, never underestimate a cat who spends his days inhabiting some prime piece of real estate in the most popular store in Hampton Cove, located right in the heart of town at that.

"Okay, so what's your news?" asked Kingman, slightly deflated when we didn't exactly fall from our perches at his news.

"We're staking out Scrum's Baubles," I said. "Because the Scrums have been badmouthing Sarah Mitchell and Barnaby Blossom, and so we're trying to get to the bottom of what's going on." I explained how Barnaby had asked Odelia to look into the matter, and how she had asked us to put our feelers out and see if we couldn't be instrumental in figuring out what the Scrums were up to, exactly.

"I don't know about this shoplifting business," Kingman confessed. "But I do know that Angela Scrum is dating Sarah Mitchell's ex-boyfriend."

"Is that a fact?" I said. And this time his information did grip me to a great extent.

"Yeah, they just started going out last week, and already there's talk of marriage," Kingman revealed. "Oh, and Angela's parents are over the moon. In fact Ebenezer was in here yesterday and he couldn't stop blabbing about it to Wilbur. Said he'd invite him to the wedding if he could provide them with some of his finest wine for the reception. They've got their eye on a caterer, you see, but they're not happy about the price tag, so they're trying to find ways of reducing the bill, since wine is a big-ticket item at any wedding, along with the food."

"And the dress," Dooley pointed out.

"Yeah, I guess," said Kingman, whose main interest has always been food, not garments in any way, shape or form.

"So they're talking wedding bells, huh?" I said, trying to get the conversation back on the right track.

"Oh, sure. Turns out this kid Grant Richardson's family is pretty loaded. His dad is a judge in the New York Supreme Court or something, and his mom is a college professor. So the Scrums can't stop pinching themselves."

"College professors aren't usually rich," I pointed out. "Or judges."

"I know, but the Richardsons are old money, so the wealth they've gathered was made probably a hundred years ago or something. Well, you know how it goes: some dude makes a killing, then he transfers it to the next generation, who add their little bit to the pile, and so on and so forth, and by the time you come to the present day, that initial pile has turned into a gigantic mass of dough."

"Unless one of the intervening generations has decided to

spend it all," I said. "Which happens more often than you might think."

"Oh, I know," said Kingman. "But the Richardsons managed to avoid that particular contingency, so now they own pretty much the entire East Coast, though it could also be the West Coast, of course. Or maybe even both of them, and all the coasts in between. Anyway," he said after a pause to collect his thoughts and get back to the gist of his argument. "The Scrum girl is marrying into a big pile of money, and her parents are over the moon."

"So why is Ebenezer Scrum trying to get his wine on the cheap?"

"Because that's the kind of guy he is," said Kingman with a shrug.

"Kingman," I said, placing a well-meaning paw on my friend's shoulder, "you helped us out more than you can imagine."

"I did?" he said, his face morphing into an expression of the utmost delight. Kingman's great joy in life, apart from eating, is helping out his friends. "I thought I had a scoop for you with the neighborhood watch thing, though I should have known you'd be *au courant*. But this is even better." When we made to leave, he added, "If you like that story, I've got about a dozen more where that came from."

"Later, Kingman," I said. "First we have to save a girl from an uncertain fate, and hopefully hear some more wedding bells ring out soon."

"You're a true romantic, aren't you, Max?" said Dooley as we went on our way. "All that stuff about wedding bells, I mean," he added when I didn't immediately respond.

"It's all so very clear to me now," I told him. "It's all about human nature, isn't it? It always is."

"Yeah, humans do love their wedding bells," he agreed. "It must be the sound. It cheers you up, you know. Although I find that they're often too loud. It's all fine and good to ring those bells, but why do they have to be so loud, you know?"

And as he babbled on about the lack of self-control most bell-ringers seem to have, I felt like a dog with a bone. Not an actual dog with an actual bone, of course, since I'm a cat, and I don't even like bones, but you understand my meaning.

We soon arrived at Scrum's Baubles, and took up position across the street so we could keep an eye on things, and check the comings and goings. Customers came and went, some with big smiles on their faces, presumably after they had bought some minor or large trinket, and others less so, possibly they were the ones who had to pick up the bill.

"Diamonds are expensive, aren't they, Max?" said Dooley. "And so is gold and silver. And I don't even understand why. I've seen diamonds and they look just like any piece of cut glass. And gold is just a kind of metal and so is silver. So why do people still want to buy that stuff?"

"I have no idea, Dooley," I confessed. "Except that humans seem to attach a certain value to these things for reasons that are very hard to determine."

"Value is in the eye of the beholder, Max," said Dooley, and I glanced over and gave him a look of appreciation.

"That's very deep, Dooley," I said. "Did you hear that on one of your Discovery Channel documentaries?"

"No, I heard it from Gran this morning, when she was looking at a painting Tex made of Marge. She said it looked like crap, but Marge seemed to like it. Which is when Gran said that the value of something is in the eye of the beholder, in this case Marge. She also said Marge probably said she liked it because the painting made her look younger than her actual years, which is always flattering."

"I think humans like gold and silver because they're rare metals," I ventured. "And when something is rare for some reason they attach more value to the thing."

Dooley thought about this for a moment, then said, "Is that why they attach so much value to human kindness? Because it's so very rare?"

I grinned. "I guess so, though it's hard to put a price on kindness. It's one of those ephemeral things it's tough to grasp and put in a jewelry box."

"Which makes it even more valuable," Dooley said.

"You're turning into an actual philosopher, my friend," I said. "Pretty soon *you* will be the college professor or the Supreme Court judge."

For at that exact moment a young couple had exited the store, and I thought I recognized the young woman as Angela Scrum. And since she was admiring a ring on her finger, and the young man was kissing her cheek, I had a distinct impression here walked Hampton Cove's next power couple.

"Let's follow them," I suggested, acting on a sudden hunch.

The couple was in no great haste as they walked along the sidewalk, laughing and talking animatedly, and looking very much like the epitome of a couple in love.

"They look very happy, Max," said Dooley.

"The girl is probably happy because her boyfriend has just bought her a giant ring," I said. "Which means he probably proposed to her. And the guy is happy because she said yes."

The couple passed by a bridal boutique, and the girl admired one of the dresses in the window, pointing out certain details that seemed to appeal to her. Then she looked down at the price tag and did a double take. At which point the guy stepped up and assured her that money was not an object. She seemed satisfied at that, and simpered a little, kissing him fervently, which made him grow a couple of inches, jutting out his chest like a peacock. When they walked on, he was actually crowing with pride, and her cheeks were glowing with pleasure.

We followed them to a nearby coffee shop, where they proceeded to take a seat at a table outside. Dooley and I took up position underneath the next table, and settled in for the duration, like the seasoned spies that we are.

"So let's talk dates," said the girl.

"I've always thought a spring wedding is a great option," said the guy. "Summer is too hot, and most of our guests would be very uncomfortable and so would we. Autumn is too sad, winter is too gloomy, so spring is in!"

"But there's so much we still have to do," said the girl, "and before you know it, summer is here."

"We could always get married next year," the guy suggested, but when the girl jutted out her lower lip and produced a professional pout, he quickly amended this view and said, "So maybe with the assistance of a great wedding planner we could still make it May." When her pout deepened, he suggested, "June?"

She beamed. "I always wanted to get married in June!"

"Oh, Angela," he said.

"Oh, Grant!" she said.

Kissing ensued, and Dooley and I turned our eyes away out of respect for the couple's privacy. Also: watching humans kissing is not exactly my favorite pastime. The way they use different parts of their anatomy frankly makes my stomach turn, but that could just be me, of course.

"We're actually getting married!" Angela exclaimed, once again studying the ring on her finger as if it was the most wonderful thing that had ever happened to her. Which surprised me, since she had probably grown up around these baubles.

Grant Richardson, still looking like a peacock, couldn't

have been more pleased with himself. "Wait till I tell my folks. They'll be over the moon."

There was a slight diminution of exuberance as the topic of the judge and the college professor were introduced into the conversation. "Do you think so?"

"You know they adore you, darling. They'll be thrilled when I break the news."

"I hope so," said Angela, suddenly nervous. She kept staring at the ring, trying to draw strength from it, but the prospect of being introduced to her betrothed's parents as their future daughter-in-law obviously didn't excite her as much as the actual wedding did.

"I know so," he assured her as he put a hand on the nape of her neck and tickled it with his index finger.

"Why does he do that, Max?" asked Dooley.

"Humans like it when they're touched in specific parts of their anatomy," I explained. "They're called erogenous zones and they derive a certain pleasure from it."

"Do we also have these erroneous zones, Max?"

"Erogenous," I corrected him. "And I'm sure we have. Like when Odelia rubs our heads or tickles our chins?"

Dooley smiled. "I like these enormous zones, Max. I like them a lot."

The conversation between the couple had moved on, and so we tuned back in, lest we missed something important, which, as the couple talked, I was starting to feel was less and less likely.

"I'm so glad I found you again," said Grant as he kissed the inside of his future wife's hand. "And to think I almost made the biggest mistake of my life. Good thing your parents stepped in and prevented me from throwing my life away."

There was a certain stiffening in the limbs that affected Angela when she said, "You mean Sarah, don't you?" She lowered her eyes and frowned. "You know I don't like it when you mention that girl, Grant. I don't like it at all!"

"I know, and that's why I won't mention her again," he promised. "Just that I'll always be grateful to your mom. If she hadn't told me who Sarah really was…"

At this Angela's pretty smile broke through the clouds. "To think you almost married a convicted felon. If my mom hadn't told you that Sarah Mitchell was a dangerous kleptomaniac, you would have actually married her?"

"Oh, absolutely. But now that I come to think of it, it's more my mom and dad's influence, you know. They absolutely adored Sarah, especially my mom."

"Oh, your mom adored Sarah, did she?" said Angela, and once again her smile was wiped away as with a squeegee and a chill slipped into her tone of voice.

"Absolutely crazy about the girl. Said she was the best thing that ever happened to me." A dreamy sort of look had stolen over the young man's face as he threw his mind back to what could have been. "She even told me that Sarah was going to be the making of me as a man—whatever that means. Mom always has these weird ideas. I guess it's the college professor in her. Too brainy for her own good. I told her I'm already a man, so what is there to make, huh?" He laughed a careless laugh. Until he suddenly became aware that thunderclouds had gathered over their little gathering, judging from the look on his fiancée's face.

"I told you I don't like to talk about that woman," she said, and this time her pout was even more pronounced than before. She had even folded her arms across her chest, a clear nonverbal sign she was deeply unhappy with the direction the conversation had taken.

"I'm sorry," said Grant immediately. "Let's not talk about her ever again. That thieving little minx is my past, and you're my future, and as Mom never stops reminding me, we should focus on the future, not the past."

"Your mom is a very sensible woman," said Angela. "Tell me more about her. In fact tell me everything there is to know about your mom and dad." Her demeanor had suddenly changed again, and she was looking at him with an eager look on her face. "I want them to like me, you know. I want them to like me as much as they liked Sarah."

"Oh, but they didn't like her *that* much," said Grant, suddenly aware that he had inadvertently entered a minefield that might be hard to extricate himself from.

"You told me that your mom loved Sarah. That she thought she was going to be the making of you as a man."

"I'm sure she was exaggerating," he hastened to say. "Mom is an eccentric. She has these weird ideas. She teaches philosophy, so that should tell you something."

"I think I've heard enough," I told Dooley.

"I just hope they won't start kissing again," said my friend as we both got up. "I hate it when they kiss and make these weird noises."

And since I couldn't agree with him more, we left the coffee shop and the couple to the mind games they seemed to enjoy so much. Somehow I got the impression that their life together as a married couple might not be a bed of roses.

"So what have you discovered, Max?" asked Dooley.

"I've discovered that Rebecca Scrum sabotaged Grant and Sarah's relationship so she could get him to marry her daughter instead," I said. "So it wouldn't surprise me if she planted that ring on Sarah, and then 'discovered' it when she left the store."

"So Sarah never stole that ring?"

"Sarah never stole that ring," I confirmed.

But how to prove it? That was another matter entirely!

CHAPTER 31

As it turns out, proving that the Scrums had set up Sarah wasn't as hard as I thought it was going to be. It was simply a matter of confiscating the hard disk that contained the CCTV footage of the store and taking a closer look at it. After I had told Odelia what I thought was going on, she called her husband, who immediately sprang into action and called on the Scrums, claiming he was investigating the complaint they had filed against Sarah Mitchell.

The couple was delighted that the police were finally taking them seriously, and when he asked to grab the hard disk so he could investigate the matter more deeply, they didn't bat an eye.

Which just goes to show that some people are simply not equipped with the criminal gene. If Rebecca had thought things through, she would have deleted that hard drive. As it was, the footage of the day of the incident clearly showed how she surreptitiously snuck that ring into Sarah's pocket while her back was turned, only to triumphantly retrieve it later when the alarm had alerted her of the presence of the expensive trinket where no expensive trinket should have been.

The end result was the full exoneration of Sarah, and when Chase and Odelia drove down to Barnaby's Blossoms to give her the good news, it wasn't hard to be touched when Sarah broke down in tears at these glad tidings.

"I thought I was crazy!" she exclaimed. "I thought I'd had one of those blackouts, you know. I knew I didn't take that ring, but still it was there."

"You're not crazy," Odelia assured her. "You were framed."

"But why?"

"Yeah, that's what I would like to know," said Barnaby.

We were in the man's office, where the emotional scene played out. Present was also Sarah's twin sister Sylvie, who did indeed look like her spitting image, a fact that caused Dooley to stare at her in quite a brazen fashion.

"Before he got involved with you," Chase explained, "Grant Richardson dated Angela Scrum for a while. The Scrums were already thanking their lucky stars that their one and only child was going to marry into such a prominent family. So when he broke up with Angela and started dating you they were upset, to say the least."

"They must have heard about the pickpocketing thing," Odelia continued, "so that's when an idea struck Rebecca, who seems to have been the brains behind this operation to smear your name and get Grant to break up with you. She figured if she could get you in trouble with the law, the son of a judge wouldn't think twice about breaking up with you. And that's exactly what happened."

"I never would have thought the Scrums capable of such a terrible thing," said Barnaby. "I mean, I've always known them to be protective of their daughter, wanting the best for her, but this is on a completely different level of duplicity."

"Yeah, they clearly went too far this time," said Chase. He

eyed Sarah closely. "So do you want to file a complaint against them? They tried to ruin your reputation."

"How about ruin Sarah's life?" said Barnaby.

"And your business," Odelia added.

Sarah thought for a moment, then shook her head. "I don't think I will. I want to put this whole thing behind me as soon as possible. Though I would like you to write about it in your paper, Odelia, without implicating the Scrums. Otherwise people will always think of me as the girl who stole that diamond ring."

"Of course," said Odelia. "But it would help if you would file a complaint and the police could investigate further. As it is, the DA might decide to pursue the matter anyway, whether you file a complaint or not."

"I hope he won't," said Sarah, looking worried. "It's going to become this big thing, which is exactly what I don't want. And besides…" She glanced up at Barnaby. "As strange as this may sound, I'm actually grateful now that this happened. If it hadn't, I would probably be married to Grant right now, and looking back on things that isn't what I want."

Barnaby's face had taken on a darker tinge of scarlet for some reason, and judging from the way his Adam's apple kept bobbing up and down he had something stuck in his throat. "I'm also glad it happened," he said in a choked voice. "Simply because…" He rooted around for something more to say, and finally concluded, a little lamely I thought, "Well, simply because."

Sylvie laughed at this, causing both Odelia and Chase to regard her a little strangely. Clearly they hadn't caught on yet that young love had asserted itself once more, this time taking Barnaby and Sarah into its warm but fickle embrace.

"Okay, so I'll write the article," Odelia promised. "And I'll clear your name."

"The Scrums won't be pleased," Chase warned.

"Well, that can't be helped," said Odelia.

"I think I have a better idea," said Sylvie, speaking up for the first time. "Why don't we go over there right now and talk to Rebecca Scrum?"

"You mean me and you?" asked Sarah.

"That's right. We confront her and demand an apology. If she refuses, Odelia can write her article revealing her as the source of the evil gossip about that ring. And if she does want to apologize, we ask her to retract her accusations, and spread the news the same way she spread that gossip. Admit she was wrong."

"It's an idea," Chase agreed. "That way Sarah's reputation will be restored, Rebecca Scrum will be forced to eat crow—"

"And Grant Richardson won't be forced by his judge dad to break up with another girl," Odelia said in conclusion.

"This Grant guy got over you pretty quick, sis," said Sylvie. "How long did it take him? A day? A week?"

Sarah grimaced. "Which proves my point. Rebecca Scrum actually did me a favor. I would never have been happy being married to that man." She directed a quick sideways glance to Barnaby, and her cheeks flushed again and so did those of her boss. It was cute to watch. I just hoped they wouldn't start kissing, for I'd already suffered enough of that particular display of affection for one day. When I glanced up at their hands, though, I could see that their pinky fingers were briefly touching, before parting again.

Dooley must have seen it too, for his eyes widened. "Max, you were right. They're an item! Sarah and her boss are a couple!"

"I told you."

"But… isn't that forbidden? She's working for him!"

"I don't think there's a law against employers and employees dating," I said. "Thought it might be one of those gray areas you always hear so much about."

"I hope she won't buy her engagement ring from the Scrums," he said. "Rebecca Scrum just might try to frame her again. She seems to have a bad habit in that department."

"I don't think she'll ever try to frame anyone ever again," I said. "Not unless she wants to destroy the business she and her husband have built up." As it was, I wasn't sure Scrum's Baubles would survive the coming storm, even if Odelia didn't write her article, and if the DA's office didn't think it worth their while to prosecute. As far as the wedding between their daughter and Grant Richardson was concerned, I had a feeling that might go ahead as planned. From what I had learned during our brief moment of surveillance, those two deserved each other.

We left the store feeling pretty happy with ourselves. Sarah's reputation was restored, and the boycott campaign the Scrums had waged against Barnaby's Blossoms had effectively been lifted.

As we walked out, a colorful individual walked in. His hair was blue, he sported a pink goatee, and he was dressed in a yellow onesie in the shape of a unicorn.

"I didn't know it was Halloween already, Max," said Dooley.

"It's not," I assured him. But since we had more important things on our mind, like assisting Gran in guarding Ella Marshall, I forgot about the colorfully dressed young man and focused on the task ahead.

* * *

Ezra didn't know whether he should be happy or sad. He had always loved living in the Bronx, and had thought he would live there forever. All his friends were there, and so was his family. So when Sylvie's sister Sarah had suggested they move to Hampton Cove, this small and inconsequential hamlet in the Hamptons, at first he had put his foot down firmly. But when Sylvie put things more clearly and had actually offered him an ultimatum: move to Hampton Cove or I'm divorcing you, he had to admit defeat against the united brainpower of the Mitchell twins.

Jake hadn't been happy. In fact he had been outraged that his buddy was leaving. But if he was going to land that big fat inheritance he saw no other choice. And even though Jake promised him he could always find another woman he could 'rent,' Ezra wasn't so sure about that. If the experience with Sylvie had taught him one thing, it was that it wasn't easy to find a woman who was willing to marry him and throw her baby into the deal. Also, the kind of women Jake suggested he contact were all escorts, and not the type of girl Aunt Emily or the detectives her lawyer had hired would approve of. Plus, none of them had babies.

And so it was a reluctant Ezra who had packed up his stuff and moved out to the sticks. Their new lodgings had the added disadvantage that they featured not one but two Mitchell girls, and that Sarah, even though she didn't have a baby, owned an actual rat. And a big one, too! It was going to take him a while to get used to shacking up with two women, one baby and one rat. But when he contemplated buying a one-way ticket back to the Bronx, it was the thought of all of Aunt Emily's money that kept him rooted to the spot.

It was only one year. And how long is a year? Not long, right? He was a survivor. He could survive living with two women who looked exactly alike, a screaming infant and a hairy rat who looked at him as if he was a yummy snack.

He walked into Barnaby's Blossoms, the place where both his wife and her sister worked, and crossed a couple accompanied by two cats. He shook his head. Clearly there was something in the water in this place, where everyone and their mother owned some type of pet. Personally he didn't like pets—any pets, and that included babies.

The moment he walked into the store, he knew something important must have happened, for the mood was jubilant to a degree. Frankly he didn't actually care what it was, as long as it didn't affect him and his prospects of becoming a very rich man somewhere down the line. But he had been raised to be polite, so he asked Sylvie what was going on.

"Remember I told you about my sister being accused of stealing a diamond ring? Turns out she was framed. The person framing her wanted her daughter to marry Sarah's boyfriend. And now everything is out in the open."

"Sarah has a boyfriend?" he asked, directing a not-so-friendly look at his sister-in-law, who he held responsible for supplanting him from his beloved Bronx to this godforsaken place.

"She did, and he was loaded, and this couple wanted him to marry their daughter instead, so they framed Sarah and now the guy is engaged to marry the daughter."

"Sounds like a solid scheme," he said.

When Sylvie gave him a vicious look, he realized he must have said the wrong thing. In his defense, it was very hard to know what to say in front of her, since she was so easily insulted, almost as if being offended was a lifestyle choice. "Where is Julie?" she asked. "Weren't you supposed to babysit her?"

Darn it. He knew he'd forgotten something. "Um… She's right outside. I just didn't think it was safe to bring her in."

"You didn't think it was safe to bring Julie into a flower shop? Why? We don't handle toxic substances here, Ezra."

"No, I just thought better safe than sorry, you know," he said, backtracking. Soon he was out the door and running in the direction of the apartment they shared with the jewel thief—though apparently she wasn't a jewel thief after all.

When he arrived home, he was relieved to discover that Julie had fallen asleep in her cot. And when he checked her pulse, he discovered she was still alive, which would please his wife. Moments later the door opened and Sylvie walked in, looking a little wild-eyed. She made a beeline for Julie and picked her up.

"I can't believe you forgot her," she snapped.

"I didn't forget her!"

"Don't give me that crap," said Sylvie. "I followed you here. You were running like a bat out of hell, and I didn't see any sign of Julie."

He hung his head. "It's not easy being a dad," he said. "It's easier for you, since you've had her for a while, so you had time to get used to her, but it's all new to me. One day I'm a single guy, and the next I'm married with a kid. I haven't developed the instincts!"

She softened. "I suggest you develop them fast. Cause you can't just leave a baby alone at home, Ezra. It's not like in the movies. They can't take care of themselves."

They'd watched a fun movie last night, where a baby escaped from its cot and went on all kinds of adventures, including but not limited to crawling up a tall building under construction and messing with a couple of gangsters. It was pretty entertaining, but Sylvie had to close her eyes several times. Almost as if she was watching a horror movie.

"Look, maybe this was a bad idea," said Sylvie, not for the first time. "Clearly I didn't think this through when I agreed to get married to you so you could land that inheritance. You're not ready to be a husband and a father, Ezra, not even if it's just pretend. So perhaps you should go back to the Bronx, and I'll stay here with my sister."

"But I don't want to go back to the Bronx," he said, even though every fiber in his being told him that he did. "I want to stay here. With you and Julie and your klepto sister. Look, I can change," he told her. "I promise you I will change."

"Okay," she said dubiously. "So show me some of your new work."

"Oh… kay."

When Sylvie discovered that Ezra once had ambitions to be a comic artist, she told him he should start drawing again. Even though she professed to be an absolute amateur when it came to the art of comics, she said she was shocked by how good his stuff was. And so she insisted he picked up the baton again—or the pencil as was the case—and tried to break into the business of creating art.

Only so far the only art he'd perfected was the art of procrastination. Not that he would ever admit it to her. So he took out some doodles he made ten years ago, and showed them to her.

"Oh, but these are absolutely lovely, Ez," she said.

He looked up in surprise. It was the first time she'd used the diminutive, and he liked the way it sounded. "It's nothing," he assured her. "Just some doodles."

"Well, they're lovely doodles," she said. She placed her hands on his shoulders and looked deep into his eyes. "Keep up the good work. I believe in you."

He blinked as he stared into those blue eyes of hers. They were green-flecked, he now saw, and he wondered why he hadn't noticed before. Probably because ever since she had come into his life she had been berating him for being such a slacker, or been overwhelmed taking care of Julie and telling him to clean up his act and stop playing video games and help her out instead. Being married to the most beautiful girl in the world had somehow dulled the effect she had on him. Until now.

"T-thanks," he said, and out of some kind of suicidal tendency suddenly decided it was a good idea to try and kiss her. The kiss landed where it should have, but he instantly realized it was a bad idea when she went completely still.

Finally he removed his lips from hers, and stammered an apology. "I-I'm sorry," he said. "I guess I've been under a lot of pressure and…" He produced a weak smile and cast down his eyes, then removed himself from the scene.

Now what was he thinking, kissing his wife? He must be out of his mind. And it was as he was staring out of the window of the bedroom he now shared with Sylvie that he suddenly thought he recognized a particular car that was parked in front of the house. In the car two particular men were seated, and if he wasn't mistaken, it was those two detectives, one of whom he'd caught on his balcony!

Just then, Sylvie came barging into the bedroom.

"You've got some nerve!" she cried.

But he immediately put his finger on her lips and gestured at the window.

Under his finger she was still trying to express her displeasure with his kissing initiative in the most vehement terms, but then she followed his gaze, saw the car, and her anger dissipated as if transformed by magic.

"Oh," she said when he removed his finger. "So they followed us, huh?"

"Yeah, they did," he said somberly.

She stared at the car for a moment, then suddenly grabbed him by the ears, and planted a wet smooch on his lips. His mind went blank, which was par for the course, since as a rule his mind was pretty blank to begin with, but this time was different. He actually enjoyed this particular blankness, and the kiss, of course.

When finally she broke the kiss, he was reeling, and if she hadn't steadied him, he would for sure have fallen.

"T-t-that was nice," he stammered. "C-c-can we do it again, please?"

And so they did it again. And since the bed was right behind them, they found themselves tumbling into it, and before long they were doing the kind of stuff people did when they were newly married and determined to give their little girl a little sister or a little brother.

CHAPTER 32

When we arrived home we were gratified to discover that everything was as we had left it: Ella was still in a coma, and her mother was still watching over her like a hawk and knitting away at a frenetic pace.

"When she wakes up and sees the sweater her mother has knitted, Ella will be so happy," said Dooley.

"Or immediately fall back into a coma," said Brutus, who didn't seem to put a lot of faith in Aunt Aurelie's knitting qualities.

Dooley eyed Harriet a little uncertainly. "So… is it Harry or Harriet today?"

"Today it's Harriet," said Harriet blithely. "And I think it will probably stay that way for the foreseeable future. I liked the experience of being a male, though. I have to say that you guys have got it easy."

The three of us exchanged a look of confusion. "What do you mean?" asked Brutus finally, taking the bait.

"Life is a lot tougher on us females," said Harriet. "We have to cook, clean, take care of the kids, and take care of your emotional needs as well. Talk about a full-time job."

"But... you don't have babies," said Dooley.

"And you don't cook and you don't clean," said Brutus.

"And what about these emotional needs?" I asked.

Harriet made a deprecating swish of her tail. "Oh, you know what I mean. Life is simply a lot easier when you're a man. So it was fun while it lasted, but in spite of all the hardships we females have to endure, I'm still glad to be myself again."

"Okay," Dooley said carefully, and he had the kind of look you often see on the faces of bomb disposal specialists.

"So what happened while we were gone?" I asked, hoping this topic of Harry/Harriet was finally closed for good.

"Nothing," said Harriet with a wide yawn. "Comatose people sure are boring. They don't talk, they don't move, in fact I wonder what they do do, you know."

"Not much," I ventured. "Since they're in a coma."

"Oh, well. At least we got a visit from Kurt Mayfield, who brought some flowers." She gestured to a bouquet of flowers on the side table, courtesy of Barnaby's Blossoms. "And Marcie Trapper also dropped by, and she brought those." She gestured to another bouquet, also courtesy of Barnaby's outfit. "In fact a lot of neighbors came in and dropped off stuff for Ella."

"That's probably not good," I said. "Since her presence here is supposed to be a secret."

"The secret is out now," said Harriet. "So I guess we'll have to deal with it."

"But no sign of Bruno Watts?" I asked.

"Nope. Hasn't shown his face around here yet. And I hope it stays that way. We don't need the drama, do we?"

At that moment the doorbell rang, and Aunt Aurelie hurried to the door. But before she could reach it, Gran suddenly popped up as if sprung from a trap. She was holding what looked like a can of pepper spray in one hand

and a baseball bat in the other and urged Aunt Aurelie to step aside. She then proceeded stealthily to the front door, looked through the little peephole, and seemed to relax.

"False alarm!" she yelled. "It's not your criminal ex-husband, Aurelie!"

Aunt Aurelie shook her head in distinct disapproval. "Well, I never," she muttered. "So who is it?"

"Beats me. Some pretty boy." And on this note, she yanked open the door, holding the pepper spray aloft, just in case.

She was right. The man who stood framed in the door was indeed a pretty boy. Though the word boy perhaps wasn't the best way to describe him, as he was probably in his early twenties, so not exactly a boy anymore. His hair was blond and perfectly coiffed, his eyes were a clear blue, and he reminded me of the last fellow who played James Bond. He had a slightly rough quality that added to his appeal. And when he saw Aunt Aurelie and his face broke into a smile, I added charm to this new arrival's list of attributes.

"Mrs. Marshall!" he cried, as he opened his arms.

"Clovis!" Aunt Aurelie said, and gave the man a heartfelt embrace. "I'm sorry for not letting you know sooner where we were," she said.

"That's all right," said Clovis, as he approached the bed and glanced at the comatose woman. He then pressed a kiss to her temple in the most tender fashion, and shook his head. "What did they do to her?" he lamented.

The four of us stared at this newcomer.

"Who's he?" asked Brutus.

"I have no idea," said Harriet.

"Could be a boyfriend," I ventured.

"Or he could be Ella's brother?" Dooley guessed.

"So who are you?" asked Gran in her direct way.

"Oh, let me introduce you," said Aunt Aurelie. "This is

Clovis, Grace's boyfriend. Clovis, this is Vesta. She's Alec's mom."

"Hi, Miss Vesta," said Clovis, and gave Gran a polite shake of the hand. "Thank you so much for taking care of Ella. When I heard what happened I offered to put her up myself, but Mom didn't think it was safe, since Ella's dad knows where I live."

"You know Ella's dad?" asked Gran, much surprised.

"I met him once," said Clovis, nodding. "I didn't know who he was, obviously. But Ella once introduced me to this guy—a friend of the family, she called him. And then later when I asked her about it, she told me he was her dad."

"You should have told me," said Aunt Aurelie, a slight notion of disapproval in her voice. "If you did this would never have happened."

"I know, and I'm sorry," said Clovis. "But she told me she'd found out who her dad was, and she'd been corresponding with him since he lived out of state."

"If you can call a Mexican prison out of state," Aunt Aurelie scoffed.

"When was this?" asked Gran. "When did you meet him? And where?"

"Um… Must be two weeks ago now?" said Clovis. "We met at the mall. Bruno bought us all ice creams and we just walked around and talked about this and that. But then I had to leave, since I had to work, and she and Bruno were going to see a movie."

"And you didn't think it strange that she would go to the movies with a man twice her age?" asked Aunt Aurelie.

Clovis shrugged. "I just figured he was like an uncle or something. He seemed nice, so I didn't see the harm."

"Bruno always had a way about him," said Aunt Aurelie. "He could be charming if he wanted to be, and cruel and manipulative the next minute."

"Correct me if I'm wrong," said Gran, "but I thought the night that Ella met her dad was the first time they had arranged to meet?"

"Actually it was the second time," said Aunt Aurelie. "And all the while they kept me in the dark. I only found out about it when I went through her diaries and their correspondence. But by then it was already too late. He had already put her in this coma." She glanced over to her daughter and tears filled her eyes.

"She'll be fine," Clovis assured her, rubbing her back. "She's young and healthy and she'll wake up again."

"I'm not so sure," said Aunt Aurelie. "The doctor said that even if she wakes up she might have suffered brain damage, and she might never be the same again."

"You know what doctors are like," said Clovis. "Doomsayers, every last one of them. We have to think positive, Mrs. Marshall. We owe it to Ella to try and stay upbeat."

"I know," said Aunt Aurelie, wiping her eyes. "But seeing her like this just breaks my heart."

"Yeah, same here," said Clovis as he regarded his girlfriend affectionately. He then whirled on Gran. "Has your son arrested Bruno yet? Made the man pay for what he's done?"

"Not yet," said Gran. "But we're going to catch the bastard." She held up the can of pepper spray. "I'm armed to the teeth, and so is the rest of my watch. If that man shows his face around here again, he's going down!"

"I'm sorry," said Clovis with a frown of confusion. "What's this watch?"

"The neighborhood watch," said Gran. "Of which I'm the proud leader. We're watching the house twenty-four-seven and we've sworn a solemn oath that we'll catch the guy. And then there's the cats, of course."

Clovis's frown deepened. "The cats?"

"My cats," said Gran, gesturing to the four of us. "Make no mistake, cats are the best guard dogs you can imagine. They're silent, they're lethal, and they never miss a trick! Have you ever seen those Ninja Turtles on television?"

"Um…"

"My cats are exactly like that—only better!"

"Oh, boy," said Brutus. "No pressure, you guys."

He was right. Gran was clearly expecting a lot from us. And so the moment she had finished her little speech, we decided to show her what we were made of and spread out. Dooley and I were going to watch the front of the house, while Harriet and Brutus would watch the back. Between the four of us, Bruno Watts didn't stand a chance.

CHAPTER 33

*D*ooley and I had decided to hide in the bushes located across the street from our house. The bushes line the front yard of our neighbor, and once upon a time a dog had been known to roam these premises. Lucky for us, though, the dog seemed to have vacated the premises, or at any rate wasn't interested in stepping out at that time. We did find one desiccated old piece of dog poo, and took great pains to put some distance between ourselves and the piece of poo.

And so we hunkered down and commenced our vigil. The sun had lowered itself across the sky, and night had fallen, so if ever there was a time for Bruno to put in an appearance, that time was now. Unfortunately it's hard to rely on a criminal to adhere to a strict schedule. And so it was that three hours later we were still in that same spot, getting a little desperate.

"This stakeout business is boring, Max," Dooley intimated.

"I know. It's excruciatingly boring," I said.

"So maybe I can take a nap now? And then you can take a

nap? Cause if we're going to be here all night we're going to get tired. And we have to remain alert in case Bruno shows up."

"We do have to be alert," I agreed. And so I said I liked his idea about alternating naps. I would take the first shift, and Dooley the second one, and so on and so forth, until Ella's dad finally decided to put in an appearance.

Soft snores soon emanated from my friend's side of the bushes, and meanwhile I tried to keep my eyes peeled. It's hard to stay awake when you're listening to the soothing sound of a snoring friend, though. Not unlike when a person yawns in one's vicinity, listening to a fellow stakeout professional snoring away to his heart's content exudes a powerful soporific effect. And so it wasn't long before I was sound asleep myself.

I was awakened by the sound of a twig snapping, though it could have been a branch, of course. When I looked up, I saw Bruno standing right next to me, big as life!

And so I nudged Dooley, who was instantly awake.

"What's going on!" he cried. And when I gestured wordlessly to the tall man standing next to us, he gulped audibly. "It's him, Max! It's the escaped convict!"

"We have to warn Gran," I said. I glanced over to the house, then to the car located further down the street, where Gran had told us she would be. And so moments later Dooley and I were hurrying in the direction of the car. Only when we got there, we found that the car was empty!

"Where is Gran!" Dooley cried.

"No idea," I confessed. "Looks like she abandoned her post."

"But she can't abandon her post! Nobody can abandon their post! Lives depend on it!"

"Let's go," I said, after having scanned the street and

found no sign of either Gran or any other member of her neighborhood watch.

"Where are we going?" asked Dooley.

"To save Ella!"

We hurried back to the house, and I hoped we wouldn't be too late. Bruno looked big and burly, and if I wasn't mistaken he might be out for revenge. He might even murder his ex-wife to get at his daughter, and so we had to make sure he never got anywhere near his former family.

We hurried around the back, then in through the pet flap and into the living room. And as we got there, a strange scene met our eyes: Bruno was wrestling with Clovis over Ella's bed, and consequently they started exchanging punches!

"Ouch!" said Dooley when Bruno landed a firm left hook on Clovis's jaw.

"Oooh!" I said when Clovis gave Bruno an uppercut that sounded particularly painful.

In a corner of the room, Aunt Aurelie looked on, paralyzed with fear. She had pressed her knitting work to her chest, and looked determined to save at least the fruit of her labor from this brute.

The ruckus must have awakened Odelia and Chase, for moments later they came stomping down the stairs. And through the pet flap Brutus and Harriet streaked in. Even Gran finally decided to put in an appearance, and came barging in through the kitchen door, pepper spray in hand.

"What's going on here?" she demanded. She looked sleepy, which told me she hadn't been staking out the house as she had promised, but had simply turned in for the night instead.

"They're fighting," Dooley explained.

"I can see that, but who's winning?" asked Gran.

It was hard to determine, since neither Dooley nor I have

ever attended a boxing match, so we don't know the rules of the game. And since there was no referee present, there was probably a lot of foul play going on.

"I'd say they're about evenly matched," said Brutus.

Chase, who had moved forward to break up the fight, was now being pulled back by Odelia, who presumably didn't want her husband getting punched in the snoot.

And so the fight would have to play itself out. Inevitably at some point it would end, as these boxing bouts invariably do. The two sluggers slugged it out for another ten minutes or so, taking advantage of the situation to crash into walls, the furniture, and send several vases filled with fragrant flowers smashing to the floor. But finally it looked as if they had depleted their energy, and instead of slugging, they simply stood there hugging each other.

"Aw, look at that," said Dooley. "They're ready to kiss and make up."

"I think they're simply too tired to keep on fighting," I said.

"Yeah, they're both finished," said Brutus. "Only they don't know it yet."

"It's a vile sport, this boxing sport," said Harriet with distaste. "Look at all of that blood. Is that nice? Is that kind?"

"It's not supposed to be nice or kind," Brutus said. "It's not figure skating, cuppy cake, it's boxing and this is how it goes."

"Well, I don't like it," said Harriet. "There should be a law against it."

Odelia had released her husband, probably figuring it was safe now to intervene, and as Chase approached the two exhausted sluggers, suddenly Ella opened her eyes and uttered a slight cry.

Immediately her mom came to her side. "Ella!" she said. "Ella, it's Mom!"

Ella eyed her mother without a sign of recognition, and then swallowed with difficulty.

"Water!" said Aunt Aurelie. "Give her a glass of water!"

Odelia immediately headed into the kitchen to adhere to her uncle's sister-in-law's request.

As everyone's attention was riveted on Ella, for a moment we lost sight of the fact that we were still in the presence of two boxers who might be honoring an unspoken agreement to take a breather, but who were by no means about to declare defeat. And as Bruno glanced over to his daughter, and started staggering in her direction, Clovis took advantage of the man's lowered defenses to deliver a resounding right hook.

This time Bruno went down for the count, and didn't come up again.

"Well done!" said Gran, grabbing the young man's arm and holding it up. "The winner is Clovis!"

"Better arrest him," said Odelia, referring to Bruno. "Or maybe call an ambulance first," she added after she had taken a closer look at the fallen man and had put her finger against his neck to see if he still had a pulse.

"All this violence," said Harriet, shaking her head. "Am I glad I'm not a male. Women would never resort to this type of barbaric display of savagery. We're too refined and too civilized."

Ella had taken a few sips of the water Odelia had provided her with, and was slowly returning to the land of the living. "What happened?" she asked in a croaky voice. "Where am I? Mom? What's going on?"

Clovis had joined her on the bed, looking a little bruised but otherwise more or less fine, and took his girlfriend's hand in his. "Don't you remember what happened?" he asked.

She furrowed her brow in a powerful attempt to recollect the events that had put her in that coma, but finally had to declare defeat. "I don't," she said, shaking her head. "It's all a blur."

"It'll come back to you," said her mother.

"Maybe it's better that it doesn't," said Clovis. "It must have been a pretty traumatic event if she doesn't remember."

"The important thing is that you're awake," said Aunt Aurelie. "How are you feeling?"

"Dizzy," said Ella with a grimace. "And my head hurts."

"Just lie down and relax," was her mother's advice. "And I'll get you something for that headache."

"Oh, darling," said Clovis. "You really scared us."

"How long have I been out?" asked Ella as she swallowed the painkiller her mom offered her.

"No need to get into all of that," said her mom, shooting Clovis a warning look. 'Let's not talk about anything that might upset her,' that look said, and Clovis nodded that he understood. "Let's just get you back to the hospital."

Now that Bruno had finally been caught, there was no need to keep her at our home any longer. And the doctors might have to run tests to determine whether she would suffer any lasting damage or not.

And so in due course an ambulance was called, and the same burly paramedics who had installed Ella in our home arrived to take her away again. With Aunt Aurelie and Clovis by her side, she was wheeled out of the house, and half an hour later the operation was concluded and the ambulance was on its way back to the hospital.

An odd silence hung in the living room, as Odelia and Chase started cleaning up the mess Bruno and Clovis had made.

"I'm going to miss her," said Harriet. "I mean, was I happy that she took over our home? No, I wasn't. But I'm still going to miss her."

"Me too," said Brutus, though he didn't look it.

"I'm not going to miss her," said Dooley. "But I hope she's fine, and I hope she will pay us a visit once she's out of the hospital and feeling like her old self again."

"Same here," I said. "I'm glad she woke up, and I'm glad they caught the man that put her in that coma."

"Good thing Clovis was here," said Brutus. "I can only imagine what that man was going to do to her."

"Probably finish the job he set out to do," said Harriet, and shivered as she thought of what could have been if Clovis hadn't intervened.

"Do you think she will ever remember what happened, Max?" asked Dooley.

"I don't, know, Dooley," I said. "The brain is a fickle thing. She might remember, or she might not. We'll just have to wait and see."

"It's true," said Odelia. "Sometimes memories never return, and sometimes they do, but it takes time."

"How much time?" Dooley wanted to know.

"Oh, could be days, or weeks, or even months."

"Poor Ella," said Dooley.

"Gran, where were you?" I asked. "We looked for you in your car but you weren't there."

Gran gave me a shamefaced look. "I know. I fell asleep. But it's not my fault. Scarlett was supposed to pick up Wilbur and Francis, and then join me here at the house. And while I was waiting I decided to close my eyes for a minute, which is why I wasn't at my post as promised."

"So what happened to Scarlett?" asked Dooley.

"I don't know, but I'll find out," she said, and took out her phone. Moments later she was calling her friend. "Voicemail," she said, a look of concern on her face. "I hope nothing happened to her." Then she called Father Reilly, but couldn't reach him either. And when she tried Wilbur she got the same result, which is to say none.

"She probably fell asleep," said Odelia. "Just like you. It is the middle of the night."

"I know, but it's not like Scarlett not to show up for an important mission," said Gran. "Or Wilbur or Francis." She thought for a moment, then made a decision. "I'm going over there to see what's going on. Anyone wants to come?"

Dooley and I shared a look, then raised our paws. Brutus and Harriet yawned and said they were going to sit this one out, and Odelia and Chase obviously weren't going to drive across town to see if Gran's friend was awake or not either. They had stuff to clean up, and Grace to take care of. The little girl had slept through the whole thing, which was probably for the best. All of that violence wasn't fit for one as young as she was.

And so moments later we were in Gran's car, racing along empty streets on our way to Scarlett's place. When we arrived there, and Gran rang the bell, nothing stirred, which was Dooley and my cue to climb a nearby tree and enter the apartment through the pet flap.

We found Clarice on the couch looking wide awake. At first I only saw a pair of eyes glowing in the dark, but soon I saw the whole cat and she didn't look happy.

"What have you done with Scarlett?" she demanded. "She said she was going out, and she hasn't come back."

"She was supposed to watch our home," I told her. "But she didn't show up. So we figured she must have fallen asleep."

"She hasn't," said Clarice in icy tones. "She left and didn't even deign to suggest to take me along with her. I swear, humans can be so inconsiderate. Did she think for one moment that I might get worried when she didn't come home? Of course she didn't. Inconsiderate, like all humans."

I smiled, and said, "Sounds like you're starting to become

domesticated, Clarice. You're even missing your human, and worrying about her."

"And so what if I am?" she said defiantly. "Humans can't take care of themselves, that's a proven fact. They need us to keep an eye on them. So if they take off without letting us know where they're going, how are we supposed to fulfill our task? Huh? Tell me that, clever guy!"

"I'm sure she didn't mean to leave you behind," I said. "She probably figured you wouldn't like to be cooped up in a car with the four members of the watch."

"Are you kidding me! I would love nothing more!"

"If you like you can come with us," Dooley suggested. "Gran is trying to track down Scarlett."

"I thought you'd never ask," said Clarice, and immediately dropped down from her perch.

Moments later we were filing back into Gran's car, and when we told her that Scarlett had left and hadn't returned, Gran's concern multiplied by a factor of about a thousand.

"Where can she be!" Gran cried as she pounded her steering wheel. "And why isn't she picking up her phone!"

"Let's think this through logically," I suggested. "We know she left the apartment intending to join the stakeout, but she never arrived. So maybe she was sidetracked somehow?"

"Of course she was sidetracked! But where! And how!"

Now that was a hard question to answer, mainly because I'm not a psychic, and neither are my two friends. But since we were facing a life-or-death situation, or at least an old lady going a little berserk with worry, it behooved us to put our best paw forward and try to figure this out.

And as I gave myself up to thought, I thought I saw a familiar figure wandering by across the street. So I asked Gran to let me out of the car pronto, and hurried to catch up with the nocturnal wanderer.

I thought I had recognized him as Boris, the dog

belonging to Bruno, and whose acquaintance Harriet had made. The dog didn't recognize me, of course, since we had never met. But when I introduced myself, and asked him what he was doing there, he gave me a sad look.

"I lost track of my human, Max. One moment he was there, and the next he was gone. And now I don't know what to do!"

"He's in the hospital," I said. "There was a big fight, and Clovis, that's his daughter's boyfriend, beat him up pretty bad so they took him to the hospital. When he wakes up he'll be arrested, though, since he broke into our home to harass his daughter."

"Oh, dear," said Boris, who was big but looked like a good sort. Dooley and Clarice had also joined us, and gave me a searching look.

After I had made the necessary introductions, Clarice said, "I thought dogs could sniff out their human simply by putting their nose to the ground?"

"Not me," said Boris, giving her a shamefaced look. "I don't know why, but I've never been able to sniff out anything. I just can't do it. My dad wasn't happy about it. He said I was bringing shame on the whole family, but I just can't help it. It's the way I am."

"There's nothing to be ashamed about, Boris," I said. "I'm not all that big on sniffing things out either."

"Yeah, but you're a cat," said Boris. "Cats aren't the same as dogs. We're supposed to be good at this stuff. It's our raison d'être. It's what we do."

"You're a loyal, loving dog," I pointed out. "That's your raison d'être, and that's all that matters."

He looked slightly relieved at that and asked, "So what are you guys doing here?"

"We're looking for Gran's friend," I said. "She lives across the street and she seems to have gone missing."

"What does she look like?" And after I'd described Scarlett to him, he said, "I'll help you find her."

"I thought you couldn't track down a human?" said Clarice.

"I can't. But I've been wandering these streets for hours, and I saw a lady leave in a cab a while ago. And she looked exactly like the lady you just described."

CHAPTER 34

*B*oris might not be good at tracking down people, but he had a good visual memory and so he could tell us the logo of the cab company. Before long Gran was on the phone with the company, trying to track down her friend. Turns out that the cab had taken Scarlett to the park, of all places. Which is the reason we soon found ourselves entering the park, accompanied by Boris, who wanted to see this thing through. The promise from Gran that she would take him to the hospital later on to be reunited with his human didn't hurt, of course.

"We could still make it in time for cat choir," said Dooley.

"It's more important that we find Scarlett," I told him.

"Yes, Dooley," said Clarice. "What's more important to you: finding my human or meeting your friends?"

This was a tough one for Dooley, and it took him some little time to come up with an answer. "Um… I guess… finding Scarlett?" he finally ventured.

"It's not a difficult question, Dooley!" Clarice growled. "So I really don't understand why it took you so long to answer it! Clearly you've got your priorities all mixed up!"

"I'm sorry, Clarice," he said. "It's just that you're such a formidable presence I find it hard to think when you're around." He said it in such a disarming, honest way that we all had to laugh.

"Oh, Dooley," said Clarice. "I'm sorry if I come on a little strong from time to time. I'm still trying to find my footing. But just so you know, I think you're one of the best."

"The best of what?" asked Dooley.

"The best of friends."

In response to this, Dooley blushed under his fur. Or at least I thought he did.

"So where do we begin?" asked Gran. "This place is pretty big."

"Where did the cab company say they dropped off Scarlett?" I asked.

"At the entrance."

"Then that's where we'll start," I said. "You've got three cats and one dog at your disposal, Gran. Between the four of us we should be able to find Scarlett."

"I just hope she didn't get herself into a lot of trouble," said Gran. "I mean, she does like men, you know, and I know she likes this online dating business, even though she assures me she's through with all of that. And you never know what kind of guy she might run into. The world is full of weirdos, unfortunately."

Her words spurred us on to ever greater urgency, and soon we were searching the park for any sign of Scarlett—dead or alive!

We searched high and we searched low, but of Scarlett there was no trace. Which is when I got the idea to involve the rest of cat choir. There's strength in numbers, after all, and a couple of dozen cats is better than three. So I went in search of our friends, and I found the remnants of cat choir still hanging out at the playground. Rehearsals were over, as evidenced by the presence of plenty of shoes on the ground where the neighbors of the park had thrown them in their usual nightly ritual. When I told Shanille about what happened, she immediately rallied her choir, and moments later we were out in force, covering every square inch of the park.

"Found her!" suddenly a voice rang out. But when we hurried over, it turned out that Buster had discovered a discarded mannequin in the bushes.

"We're looking for a human, Buster," Shanille pointed out. "Now is this a human?"

"She looks like a human," the hairdresser's cat insisted.

"Well, for your information she's not," said Shanille. And as she turned away, I heard her murmur, "I hope for his sake that his own human can tell the difference."

"As a hairdresser it's important to tell the difference between a real person and a mannequin," I explained to Dooley as he gave me a questioning look.

"Oh, I see," he said. "Because mannequins don't have money to pay the bill?"

"Something like that," I agreed with a smile.

And so the search went on. And I'd just traversed a small bridge that spanned the little stream that passes through the park when a glint caught my eye. It was the light of a nearby lamppost that reflected on an object. And as I neared, I saw that it was a shoe. A shiny red lacquered shoe of the kind that Scarlett likes to wear!

It didn't take me long to reach her, and as I approached, I saw that her legs were sticking out of the undergrowth, but that her head and torso were stuck deep into the weeds. By the time I reached her head, my breathing was labored, not from the exertion but from the fear of what I was about to discover! Luckily she was still alive, but barely so.

"Over here!" I yelled. "I found her!"

"This better not be another mannequin!" Gran yelled back from somewhere in the vicinity. But when she followed my voice and came upon the scene, she choked up for a moment, then cried in a strangled voice, "Scarlett!"

She was upon her friend in seconds, and then she was checking her pulse. "She's alive, but her pulse is very weak," she said.

There were marks around Scarlett's neck, and it was obvious that someone had tried to strangle her.

"Isn't this where Ella was found?" I asked.

Gran stared at me. "If Clovis hadn't knocked Bruno's block off, I would!" she cried, and took out her phone to call an ambulance. As we waited for help to arrive, she sat next to her friend, and gently stroked her hair. And for the first time in my life, I actually saw Gran cry.

It didn't take long before the ambulance arrived, even though it felt like hours. All around, members of cat choir sat looking awed by the scene that we had encountered, and when the paramedics finally made their way to our location, they were surprised to find the victim being guarded by dozens and dozens of cats—and one dog.

Scarlett was soon put on a stretcher and wheeled away, and as Gran decided to follow the ambulance to the hospital, we tried to figure out what had happened to her, exactly.

"Okay, so one of you guys must have seen something," I said. "So please think back and try to recollect."

Unfortunately the business of cat choir had apparently taken prevalence over anything else, and no one had seen anything out of the ordinary. So I turned to Boris. "It's likely that your human did this," I told him. "But even so, do you want to help us figure out what happened?"

He nodded sternly. "Of course. Though I can tell you right now that Bruno would never do such a thing. He may come across as gruff, and I know he's done some stuff he shouldn't have, but he's never laid a hand in anger on any woman in his life."

"Okay, so we know that's not true," I said. "Because he tried to strangle his own daughter."

"But he didn't! I told you he was never even near her. We waited and waited and waited, but she never showed."

An old lady had shown up, walking her dog, even though it was the middle of the night, and I nudged Boris. "Go over there and talk to that dog."

"Okay, Max," he said dutifully, and hurried over to the old lady. In a reflex action she took out a can of pepper spray and held it up. But when she saw that Boris was by himself, she put it away again.

Boris and the doggie conducted a whispered conversation, and then he came traipsing back to where the rest of us were seated.

"I think we just caught a break, you guys. That dog over there suffers from an overactive bladder, and her human from insomnia, so they're out here all the time, day and night. She says she thinks she saw Scarlett. Or at least she saw a woman who answered Scarlett's description walking in that direction. And soon after she had disappeared, a man appeared, who seemed to have been waiting for her, and followed her from a distance."

"What did this man look like?" I asked.

Boris smiled. "I can tell you that he didn't look like Bruno." And then he described the man in great detail.

I studied the dog. It was entirely possible that he was lying to us, trying to protect his human. But somehow I didn't think he was. And as I tried to puzzle everything together, I quickly saw the whole picture. And it wasn't pretty!

CHAPTER 35

*E*zra and Sylvie had gone out to dinner, celebrating their newfound union. Sylvie hadn't expected it, but now that she'd started getting to know her husband a little better, he turned out to be a sensitive, gentle soul. Underneath his slacker appearance, he was a kind man. Intelligent, too. After their vigorous acrobatic activities, she had taken a nap, and when she woke up she had found him sitting next to the bed and gazing at her in the obscurity of the room. When she asked him what time it was, he checked his watch and said it was probably time to have a bite to eat, which is when they decided to go out to dinner, since Sarah hadn't arrived home yet from her date with her boss.

Turned out that not only had Ezra bathed Julie and changed her diaper, he had also found the time to make a couple of drawings of Sylvie. When she found them on the nightstand she was surprised by how good they were. The guy had talent—and plenty of it, too.

During dinner they talked for what felt like the first time since they met, and agreed that it seemed as if they were doing everything backward: usually a couple met through a mutual friend, started dating and eventually, if they felt a spark, dated some more before falling in love and getting married. Babies were usually the end result of their union. In this case it was the other way around: Sylvie already had the baby, and they got married before they started dating, which seemed to be what they were doing now.

"So this is actually our first date?" asked Ezra.

"I guess it is," said Sylvie.

He smiled, and she decided he had a pretty great smile. "So what's next for us? More dating? And then maybe I can go down on one knee and propose?"

"You never did propose," she said. "Unless you consider that contract you made me sign a proposal."

"I can go down on one knee now," he suggested. "But I have to warn you that my knees are pretty bad, and if I go down I might never get up again."

"Please don't go down on one knee," she said, laughing. "Let's just skip all that and get back to the apartment before my sister arrives home."

He got a mischievous glint in his eyes at this point, and asked, "So does that mean you like me?"

"The jury is still out," she said. "It's like buying a bicycle, you see. First you ride it, then you ride it some more, before you decide if you want to buy it."

"So I'm your bicycle now, am I?"

"You're *a* bicycle. And I'm trying to decide if you're *the* bicycle."

"Let's go," he said, and threw down some bills.

When they arrived home and went into the apartment, kissing and such as new couples will do, suddenly Ezra whispered, "I think there's someone here!"

"Darn it!" said Sylvie. "I'd hoped Sarah wouldn't be back so soon!"

"I hear voices."

"Must be Barnaby. They were probably hoping *we* wouldn't be back so soon!"

They both giggled, but then must have woken up Julie, for she started yammering in her baby carriage. Instantly the whisperings stopped, and Sylvie could have sworn it came from their own bedroom!

"They're using our bed!" she said.

"No way!" said Ezra, and pushed through to the bedroom and swung open the door.

The sight that met their eyes was something to behold: the two detectives who'd been stalking them all this time were seated on the bed. One was taking samples from the bedsheets with a pair of tweezers, while the other was actually sniffing Ezra's pillow!

Both Ezra and Sylvie were too stunned to speak, and merely stared at this gross invasion of their privacy. The detectives didn't hang around, though, and were quick off the mark. They jumped from the bed, and moments later were practically flying through the window. And when Ezra and Sylvie crossed the room, they saw that the detectives were in their car, brazenly staring out at them from across the street as if nothing had happened!

"I'm calling the police," said Sylvie. "How dare they!"

"Don't," said Ezra, staying her hand. He gave her a pained look. "The inheritance."

"For crying out loud, Ezra! They were sniffing the pillows!"

"And that's a good sign!" said her husband. "At least now they know we're not faking it. We're sleeping in the same bed. We're an actual couple, not just pretending so I can rake in that money my Aunt Emily left."

Sylvie stared at him. He had a point, of course, but how far were these people prepared to go? Would they put cameras in the bathroom? Take samples from the toilet bowl? It was all starting to look pretty outrageous to her.

When she had finally calmed down, though, and saw Ezra's wide smile, she couldn't help grinning. Moments later they were both laughing so hard her sides hurt and tears came to her eyes. And when all was said and done, they tumbled back into bed and made love once again. And they didn't even close the curtains.

* * *

When Sarah and Barnaby arrived home later that night, they were careful not to make too much noise. They would have gone back to Barnaby's place, but unfortunately he still lived with his mom. Though it was actually more accurate to say that his mom lived with him. And since the last thing Sarah wanted was to wake up in the morning and bump into Barnaby's mom in the bathroom, they decided to go to her place instead. Her sister wouldn't mind, and neither would Ezra.

When they arrived, they took great pains to be as quiet as possible. At some point during their date Barnaby had professed his undying love for her, and Sarah had to admit that she had fallen for the flower shop owner as well. It was hard to imagine, but it was true. She loved Barnaby Blossom, and possibly had since the moment she had walked into his store. It had taken her until the end of the evening before she had made the confession that she had never actually answered any ad in any paper. She had simply been desperate to find a job—any job—and so she had walked into the store and lied her little heart out. She had tried the same technique in a dozen other stores before arriving at Barnaby's Blossoms, and all of them had turned her down flat. So it came as something of a surprise when Barnaby had hired her on the spot.

He had taken her confession in stride, and said he had a confession of his own to make. Which is when he told her he'd fallen in love with her the moment she walked into his store and would have said yes to anything she asked.

It was at this point that they decided to skip dessert and started discussing ways and means of ending the evening on a more intimate note—preferably without the overbearing presence of Barnaby's mother.

Strange noises had protruded from Sylvie and Ezra's room, and when Sarah had put her head to the door, and so had Barnaby, it didn't take them long to realize that Sarah's sister and her husband were engaged in the exact same physical activity the two of them had been envisioning ever since their mutually shared confessions.

And so it was a giggling pair who finally entered Sarah's bedroom to consummate their newfound affection.

All in all not a bad way to start their new life together.

CHAPTER 36

Clovis was seated next to the hospital bed where his girlfriend was lying. Even though she had insisted she was feeling fine, the doctors wouldn't allow her to go home just yet. They wanted to run some more tests now that she was fully awake to determine any consequences she might have suffered after the ordeal she had gone through.

"But I feel fine," she told her boyfriend. "Can't these people tell that I'm fine?"

"It's only natural that they would want to take some precautions," he told her as he gave her hand a tiny squeeze. "You were in a coma, honey. And you never know what that did to your brain."

"Oh, my brain is feeling just great," she assured him. "Though it's true that I still have a headache."

They had given her some painkillers for the headache, but it was still worrying that she would experience the pain. Which told him she wasn't ready to go home just yet.

Aurelie walked into the room, carrying a cup of tea for the patient, a steaming Styrofoam cup of coffee for Clovis and also one for herself.

They were both determined to stay by Ella's side, even though frankly speaking Clovis was beat. It had been a long night for him, with plenty of action. He'd been in that fight with Bruno, and even though he had finally bested the guy, Ella's old man had given of his best and had dealt him a couple of vicious blows that he felt in his ribs and chest. But when Aurelie told him to have those checked out, he wouldn't hear of it. After all, he wasn't the patient, Ella was.

He directed a loving smile at his girlfriend. She looked so beautiful, he thought. So sweet and pretty, in spite of what she had gone through.

"I hope they ship that man's ass back to Mexico," Aurelie was saying. "And put him in jail and throw away the key this time."

"So I went out to meet him and he assaulted me?" asked Ella. "Is that what happened? It's hard to imagine, after the kind words he wrote in his letters."

"Oh, you remember those, do you?" asked Aurelie, an edge to her voice.

"Now is not the time, Mrs. Marshall," Clovis said warningly.

"I'm sorry I didn't tell you, Mom," said Ella. "I just figured you'd be upset when I said I wanted to meet my dad."

"You bet I would have been upset. I know that man a lot better than you do, honey. And I know he's as bad as they come."

"He didn't strike me as bad when we met at the mall," said Ella as she took a sip from her tea, then coughed.

"Oh, he can be charming when he wants to be," said Aurelie. "How do you think I ended up marrying him? But it didn't take long before the cops showed up at our door and hauled him off to prison. The first time I was shocked. It was the last thing I expected for my husband to be accused of being a burglar and a thief. When he got out he promised me that part of his life was over, and he was a better man thanks to me and thanks to our little girl. But six weeks later the police were back, and this time he went away for a year. Which is when I told him we were through."

"I know Bruno was a bad husband, Mom," said Ella. "And a bad father. But you shouldn't have told me he was dead."

"To me he was," said her mom stubbornly. "All I wanted was to make sure he never entered our lives ever again. And I told him. I told him to stay away from us and he promised me he would."

"You shouldn't blame him," said Ella. "I was the one who found him, and I was the one who got in touch with him."

Aurelie was shaking her head. "And see what happened."

"I know," said Ella, much sobered. "You were right."

Aurelie patted her arm. "You couldn't have known," she said. "And that's entirely my fault. I should have told you about him as soon as you were old enough. Warned you about him. Now you probably thought he was some kind of prince charming and I was the bad witch who had driven him away."

"It wasn't like that," said Ella. "He only had good things to say about you, Mom. He even defended you when I said you lied to me. He said you did it to protect me, and you were probably right."

Aurelie frowned. "He said that?"

"He did. He also said he's changed."

"Yeah, right. That's probably why he was in jail."

"And why he attacked you in that park," said Clovis.

Ella grimaced and touched her hands to her temples.

"Pain?" asked her mom.

Ella nodded. "Every time I try to remember what happened that night, it's like a shooting pain cuts through my head. As if it doesn't want me to remember."

"Just rest," said Clovis. "It will come back to you."

"I hope so," said Ella, laying her head against the pillow. "It's horrible not knowing what happened to me."

Hours later, Aurelie had fallen asleep in the armchair in the corner of the room, a blanket covering herself. Ella was also asleep, after the nurse had given her a sedative that would help her battle that headache and give her some rest. The only one still awake was Clovis, and he eyed the IV stand next to his girlfriend, where the drip-drip-drip of the liquid sedative distracted him. He'd been eyeing that IV for a while now, and wondered how it worked, exactly. He glanced to the entrance to the room, and listened intently for any noise. Nothing. The ward was quiet, the patients asleep and the staff relaxing at the nurse's station.

So when he took the syringe out of his pocket that he had filched from a medical trolley earlier and removed the safety cap, he was convinced that he was going to get away with this.

He liked Ella, he really did, but allowing her to live was simply too risky. The moment she remembered that it was in fact him who had attacked her in the park, his life was over. He'd go to prison and they might even connect him to the other women he'd attacked over the years.

He knew he should probably get help for this compulsion that compelled him to assault women, but if he did he might jeopardize his safe existence. These shrinks all claimed to be all about patient-doctor privilege but he knew they would probably blab to the nearest cop the first chance they got. And besides, he enjoyed the hunt. In fact he loved it. The thrill of the chase was what he lived for.

He tenderly stroked Ella's cheek with his finger and whispered, "Goodbye, Ella. I love you."

But as he was about to plunge that needle into the IV, to add a little spice that would end his girlfriend's life, suddenly the door of the room swung open and Vesta

Muffin came charging in. She was accompanied by three cats and a dog!

And as he watched her with non-comprehending eyes, she blasted him with a steady stream of some noxious substance!

"There," she said in a triumphant voice. "That's for attacking my friend Scarlett!" And as he wailed in agony and clawed at his eyes, he dropped the syringe to the floor. Which is when there was a loud hissing sound and suddenly a small object was propelled against his back. Moments later claws dug in, and he knew he was being attacked by one of those cats.

As he tried to fend off the hairy little monster, the old lady must have picked up the syringe, for he heard her say, "And what do we have here?"

Which is when he knew that the game was up.

CHAPTER 37

"So what was that all about?" asked Harriet.

"What was what all about?" asked Brutus.

"Exactly! Stuff happens and nobody even bothers to tell me about it. It's not fair."

"I'm not following. What stuff? When did what happen?"

"Last night an arrest was made," I explained. "The man who was responsible for what happened to Ella, and also for what happened to Scarlett."

"What happened to Scarlett?" asked Brutus.

"Oh, Brutus," said Harriet. "You're even more in the dark than I am."

"Okay, so where do I begin?" I asked, looking from Harriet to Brutus.

We were seated on the porch swing, located in Marge and Tex's backyard, the whole family gathered to partake in a nice meal provided by the doctor himself. And since this was a special occasion, the usual suspects had been joined by no less than two couples: Sarah Mitchell and her fiancé Barnaby Blossom, and Sarah's sister Sylvie and her husband Ezra.

Present were also Sylvie's daughter Julie, who was the subject of much attention by Odelia and Chase's daughter Grace.

And since the band would not be complete without Aunt Aurelie and her daughter Ella, Marge had decided to invite them to the party as well. All in all a full house!

"Just tell us the whole story in your own words," Brutus suggested. "And leave out no detail, however small. How does that sound?"

"That sounds great," I said. And so I told our friends in a few words about the events that had transpired the night before. I even included the parts about the role cat choir played in saving Scarlett's life. Which reminded me of something I'd been wondering. "When all this was happening, where were you guys?"

Harriet and Brutus shared a coy look. "We renewed our vows," Brutus finally admitted.

"What did you renew?" asked Dooley.

"Our vows."

"What vows?"

"Well, *the* vows, of course," said Harriet, starting to get a little snappish. "You know—our vows."

Dooley continued to look thoroughly puzzled, and since no one seemed eager to explain to him what vows were, it finally came down to Footsie to step in.

"Vows are the promises a newlywed couple makes about the life they're going to share. You know, how they're going to love each other and take care of each other and all of that stuff." The pet rat rolled his eyes. "And I can tell you right now it's something of a big deal. Sarah is getting married, and she's been working on her vows non-stop. Trust me when I tell you it's exhausting having to listen to her repeating them over and over again to her sister—and the rest of her captive audience. And in this case you can take the word 'captive' literally, you guys."

"Okay, so methinks the rat doth protest too much," said Clarice, who was also present at our little gathering. "Vows are great stuff, Footsie! It means your human is about to embark on a new course. That she found the man she loves above all others and she's going to start a family."

"She already has a family," Footsie grumbled. "Me!"

"Well, there's always room for more," said Clarice. "At least your human wasn't attacked by another human, like mine was. So you should count yourself lucky."

"I guess you're right," said Footsie. "How is Scarlett, by the way?"

"She's over there, tucking into some great nosh, so all things considered she's doing really well."

We all looked over to Scarlett, who was indeed nibbling from her plate of goodies with relish, and looked pretty great. She had already thanked us profusely for the role we had played in her rescue, and had even bought us all little coats to wear when the nights got cold. Not that we would ever wear them, of course, but it's the thought that counts.

"What I don't understand is what she was doing at the park in the first place," said Harriet. "Wasn't she supposed to go on a stakeout with Gran?"

"She was, but for some reason they got their wires crossed," I said. "Scarlett thought they were supposed to meet up at the park, which is how she happened to run into Clovis instead, who was on the lookout for another victim."

"A regular predator," said Clarice, sheathing and unsheathing her claws. When we had walked in on Clovis at the hospital, about to murder Ella, Clarice hadn't been able to restrain herself and had thrown herself across the room like some kind of ninja fighter, complete with claws extended and the appropriate screeching noises. It had taken the concerted effort of Gran and a couple of nurses to wrest her away from the man, who had suffered some serious claw marks on his person as a consequence. This on top of the pepper spray Gran had used.

"I should have gone for his eyes," she now said with a touch of regret. "Oh, well, there's always a next time."

"Let's hope not," said Footsie with a shiver. "Imagine that your boyfriend tries to kill you. Twice!"

"Okay, let's back up for a second," Brutus suggested. "I'm still a little fuzzy on the details. Who tried to kill whom, exactly?"

"Okay, so as we discovered last night, Ella's boyfriend Clovis turned out to be a psychopath of the first order," I said. "As Uncle Alec dug a little deeper into his background, he's now being linked to at least half a dozen murders in different parts of the county. His latest victim was Scarlett, and the one before that his own girlfriend."

"But they both survived," Harriet pointed out.

"In Scarlett's case he was interrupted while he was strangling her—probably by someone walking their dog," I said. "And in Ella's case he was stopped by Bruno, Ella's dad. Which is why Bruno was so adamant about finding Ella so he could keep an eye on her. He knew nobody would believe him when he told them about Clovis, who seemed to be the perfect boyfriend, but he knew what the guy was capable of, and he was determined to protect his daughter."

"But didn't you say Bruno never came anywhere near Ella?" asked Harriet. She directed this question at Boris, who had temporarily been adopted by Aunt Aurelie and Ella, while Bruno served out his prison sentence.

"I have to confess I didn't always keep an eye on the man," said Boris with a touch of embarrassment. "Bruno is one of those humans who doesn't believe in keeping their dogs on a leash. So the moment we set paw in the park he unleashed me, which is how I missed that whole business with Ella and Clovis."

"You should have told us, Boris," said Harriet sternly. "You lied to the police and you perverted the course of justice."

"I don't think Boris did it on purpose," I said. "He just didn't want to get his human into any more trouble than he already was. Isn't that right, Boris?"

Boris nodded. "There's a big sign at the entrance to the park that says that dogs must be on a leash at all times. Mention is also being made about certain fines that are applicable. So I guess I didn't want to compound Bruno's troubles with the law, especially since you guys are police cats, so I just figured I'd neglect to give you the full picture." He gave me a shamefaced look. "I'm sorry, Max."

"That's all right, Boris," I said. "It's totally understandable. You did what you thought was best for your human, which is actually commendable."

"You're a good dog, Boris," said Footsie.

Boris smiled at this. "You think so?"

"Absolutely. Though next time try telling the truth, even if you think it might get your human into trouble."

"Oh, I will," said Boris gratefully. "And at least Bruno won't have to serve out his sentence in Mexico, so I will still get to see him."

And so would Ella, who could visit her dad whenever she liked. And since Bruno's role in saving his daughter's life had been officially established it would probably lead to the man's sentence being reduced.

"So… why did Clovis try to kill his girlfriend a second time?" asked Brutus. "That part isn't really clear to me yet."

"Because he knew that when her memory returned, she would remember that he was actually her attacker, and not her dad," I explained. "He knew it was only a matter of time before she remembered, and then it was the end for him. So he decided to kill her before that happened."

"Good thing we got there in time," said Clarice.

"Yeah, we were lucky," I agreed.

"Luck had nothing to do with it," said Clarice. "You figured it out, Max. The same way you always do."

"I didn't figure it out," I said. "There was a witness to the attack on Scarlett, and he gave a very detailed description of the attacker, which fit Clovis to a T."

"I still think you did a pretty great job," said Clarice, patting me on the back while she eyed a nice piece of steak Tex had dropped in front of us.

"We all did a great job," I said. "All of cat choir, in fact."

"I'm sorry we weren't there to help you out," said Harriet.

"That's all right, Harriet," said Dooley. "Renovating your bowels is very important."

"Renewing our vows, Dooley," Harriet corrected him. "Though I wouldn't mind having my bowels renovated, too." She grimaced as she spoke these words.

"We had dinner at the Hungry Pipe," Brutus explained. "And I had the impression it was a little spicy for our taste."

"It was way too spicy," said Harriet, grimacing once more. "I'm sorry, guys, but I have to run," she announced. And without awaiting our response, she jumped down from the swing and hurried into the house.

"Where is she going?" asked Dooley.

"Renovating her bowels," said Clarice dryly.

This had us all in stitches, except Brutus, who was also looking a little pale around the nostrils. "Gotta go!" he finally croaked, and hurried after his mate.

"Spicy food isn't good for you, is it, Max?" asked Dooley.

"I guess it depends on the food, and the state of your bowels," I said.

In the backyard, Charlene was discussing the upcoming wedding of Barnaby and Sarah, giving them some pointers about the ceremony. It's always convenient to have a mayor in the family. Scanning further down the line, I saw that Ezra was showing his latest artwork to Tex, who was admiring it greatly, before showing Ezra some of his own stuff. Ezra studied the painting of Gran Tex had produced and I could tell he wasn't all that impressed, but still nodded politely and told him how good it was. To be honest her face looked like a big potato with watercress around it, which wasn't surprising, since Tex loves to paint fruits and veggies.

Rumor had it that the marriage between Ezra and Sylvie had started out as one of those marriages of convenience, which had somehow turned into an actual marriage, which was convenient for both parties involved. Ezra had even changed his hair color, which wasn't blue anymore but blond, and he also got rid of the pink goatee, which was probably easier on the eyes for his beloved wife. These are the little sacrifices one makes when hooking one's little wagon to that of another person and deciding to travel through life together. The only person who didn't seem particularly pleased with the upcoming wedding was Barnaby's mother.

Dooley had noticed the same thing, for he said, "She doesn't look happy, does she, Max?"

"No, she most definitely does not."

"She'll get used to it," said Footsie. "And if she doesn't, I'll bite her."

"You shouldn't go around biting people all the time, Footsie," I said.

"It's all right," said Footsie. "Sarah gave me permission."

"She did? When did that happen?"

"When she turned to me and said, 'I give you permission to bite Barnaby's mom when she's being nasty again.' So I said, 'Fine. I'll just do that little thing for you.'"

Clarice seemed to like what Footsie was saying, for she was grinning widely. "You're a rat after my own heart, Footsie. I think we'll get along great."

"Great minds think alike," Dooley agreed.

I wasn't so sure about that. Biting mothers-in-law simply because they don't like their daughters-in-law sets a bad precedent for cats and rats everywhere.

But Dooley had more wisdom to share. "You can please some of the mothers-in-law all of the time," he said, "and you can please all of the mothers-in-law some of the time, but you can't please all of the mothers-in-law all of the time."

And that summed the thing up pretty well indeed.

THE END

Thanks for reading! If you want to know when a new Nic Saint book comes out, sign up for Nic's mailing list: nicsaint.com/news

ABOUT NIC

Nic has a background in political science and before being struck by the writing bug worked odd jobs around the world (including but not limited to massage therapist in Mexico, gardener in Italy, restaurant manager in India, and Berlitz teacher in Belgium).

When he's not writing he enjoys curling up with a good (comic) book, watching British crime dramas, French comedies or Nancy Meyers movies, sampling pastry (apple cake!), pasta and chocolate (preferably the dark variety), twisting himself into a pretzel doing morning yoga, going for a run, and spoiling his big red tomcat Tommy.

He lives with his wife (and aforementioned cat) in a small village smack dab in the middle of absolutely nowhere and is probably writing his next 'Mysteries of Max' book right now.

www.nicsaint.com

ALSO BY NIC SAINT

The Mysteries of Max

Purrfect Murder
Purrfectly Deadly
Purrfect Revenge
Purrfect Heat
Purrfect Crime
Purrfect Rivalry
Purrfect Peril
Purrfect Secret
Purrfect Alibi
Purrfect Obsession
Purrfect Betrayal
Purrfectly Clueless
Purrfectly Royal
Purrfect Cut
Purrfect Trap
Purrfectly Hidden
Purrfect Kill
Purrfect Boy Toy
Purrfectly Dogged
Purrfectly Dead
Purrfect Saint
Purrfect Advice
Purrfect Passion

A Purrfect Gnomeful

Purrfect Cover

Purrfect Patsy

Purrfect Son

Purrfect Fool

Purrfect Fitness

Purrfect Setup

Purrfect Sidekick

Purrfect Deceit

Purrfect Ruse

Purrfect Swing

Purrfect Cruise

Purrfect Harmony

Purrfect Sparkle

Purrfect Cure

Purrfect Cheat

Purrfect Catch

Purrfect Design

Purrfect Life

Purrfect Thief

Purrfect Crust

Purrfect Bachelor

Purrfect Double

Purrfect Date

Purrfect Hit

Purrfect Baby

Purrfect Mess

Purrfect Paris

Purrfect Model

Purrfect Slug

Purrfect Match

Purrfect Game

Purrfect Bouquet

Purrfect Home

Purrfectly Slim

Purrfect Nap

Purrfect Yacht

Purrfect Scam

Purrfect Fury

Purrfect Christmas

Purrfect Gems

The Mysteries of Max Collections

Collection 1 (Books 1-3)

Collection 2 (Books 4-6)

Collection 3 (Books 7-9)

Collection 4 (Books 10-12)

Collection 5 (Books 13-15)

Collection 6 (Books 16-18)

Collection 7 (Books 19-21)

Collection 8 (Books 22-24)

Collection 9 (Books 25-27)

Collection 10 (Books 28-30)

Collection 11 (Books 31-33)

Collection 12 (Books 34-36)

Collection 13 (Books 37-39)

Collection 14 (Books 40-42)

Collection 15 (Books 43-45)
Collection 16 (Books 46-48)
Collection 17 (Books 49-51)
Collection 18 (Books 52-54)
Collection 19 (Books 55-57)
Collection 20 (Books 58-60)

The Mysteries of Max Big Collections
Big Collection 1 (Books 1-10)
Big Collection 2 (Books 11-20)

The Mysteries of Max Short Stories
Collection 1 (Stories 1-3)
Collection 2 (Stories 4-7)

Nora Steel
Murder Retreat

The Kellys
Murder Motel
Death in Suburbia

Emily Stone
Murder at the Art Class

Washington & Jefferson
First Shot

Alice Whitehouse
Spooky Times
Spooky Trills

Spooky End

Spooky Spells

Ghosts of London

Between a Ghost and a Spooky Place

Public Ghost Number One

Ghost Save the Queen

Box Set 1 (Books 1-3)

A Tale of Two Harrys

Ghost of Girlband Past

Ghostlier Things

Charleneland

Deadly Ride

Final Ride

Neighborhood Witch Committee

Witchy Start

Witchy Worries

Witchy Wishes

Saffron Diffley

Crime and Retribution

Vice and Verdict

Felonies and Penalties (Saffron Diffley Short 1)

The B-Team

Once Upon a Spy

Tate-à-Tate

Enemy of the Tates

Ghosts vs. Spies

The Ghost Who Came in from the Cold

Witchy Fingers

Witchy Trouble

Witchy Hexations

Witchy Possessions

Witchy Riches

Box Set 1 (Books 1-4)

The Mysteries of Bell & Whitehouse

One Spoonful of Trouble

Two Scoops of Murder

Three Shots of Disaster

Box Set 1 (Books 1-3)

A Twist of Wraith

A Touch of Ghost

A Clash of Spooks

Box Set 2 (Books 4-6)

The Stuffing of Nightmares

A Breath of Dead Air

An Act of Hodd

Box Set 3 (Books 7-9)

A Game of Dons

Standalone Novels

When in Bruges

The Whiskered Spy

ThrillFix

Homejacking

The Eighth Billionaire

The Wrong Woman

Printed in Great Britain
by Amazon